Born the heir of a mast defined by guilds and matrilineal inheritance, nonbinary Sorin can't quite seem to find their place. At seventeen, an opportunity to attend an alchemical guild fair and secure an apprenticeship with the queen's alchemist is just within reach. But on the day of the fair, Sorin's mother goes missing, along with the Queen and hundreds of guild masters, forcing Sorin into a woodcutting inheritance they never wanted.

With guild legacy at stake, Sorin puts apprentice dreams on hold to embark on a journey with the royal daughter to find their mothers and stop the hemorrhaging of guild masters. Princess Magda, an estranged childhood friend, tests Sorin's patience—and boundaries. But it's not just a princess that stands between Sorin and their goals. To save the country of Sorpsi, Sorin must define their place between magic and alchemy or risk losing Sorpsi to rising industrialization and a dark magic that will destroy Sorin's chance to choose their own future.

FOXFIRE IN THE SNOW

SNOW

J.S. Fields

A NineStar Press Publication

www.ninestarpress.com

Foxfire in the Snow

Printed in the USA

ISBN: 978-1-64890-341-0

First Edition, July, 2021

Also available in eBook, ISBN: 978-1-64890-340-3

WARNING:
This book contains sexually explicit content, which is only suitable for mature readers. Warnings for misgendering by side characters, and unintentional misgendering by a main character; warning for the deaths of family members, gore, fantasy violence, body dysphoria.

For Marilyn, and all the other nonbinary lesbians out there. You are seen, and you are valid.

Guilds of the Three Countries

The Carpenter's Guild, held by Sorpsi, encompasses functional woodcraft. Symbol: handplane tattoo.

The Cooper's Guild, held by Puget, encompasses woodcraft used solely for alcohol. Symbol: barrel tattoo.

The Glass Guild, held by Sorpsi, encompasses all glasswork. Symbol: stemmed cup tattoo.

The Masons, held by Eastgate, encompasses all stoneworkers. Symbol: three vertically stacked bricks.

The Music Guild, held by Eastgate, is the home to all professional musicians. Symbol: bass clef tattoo.

The River Guild, held by Eastgate, encompasses fishers, boatspeople, and those who work with the waterways. Symbol: black fish tattoo.

The Shepherd's Guild, held by Eastgate, encompasses ranchers and other livestock owners. Symbol: picket gate tattoo.

The Smith's Guild, held by Sorpsi, encompasses all metal work. Symbol: two crossed hammers.

The Textile Guild, held by Puget, is the home to weavers, dyers, spinners, and knitters. Symbol: cotton boll tattoo.

The Trapper's and Trader's Guild, held by Puget, houses those who work with pelts, skin, and other animal-derived materials. Symbol: beaver tattoo.

The Woodcutter's Guild, held by Sorpsi, encompasses artistic woodcraft. Symbol: leafed branch tattoo.

The Alchemy Guild is one of two unbound guilds and, as such, does not have a primary guildhall in any of the three countries, nor do they have a grandmaster. They are symbolized by a black cauldron tattoo with a beaker suspended above it.

The Witch Guild is one of two unbound guilds and, as such, does not have a primary guildhall in any of the three countries, nor do they have a grandmaster. They are symbolized by a black cauldron tattoo with a daisy growing from the middle.

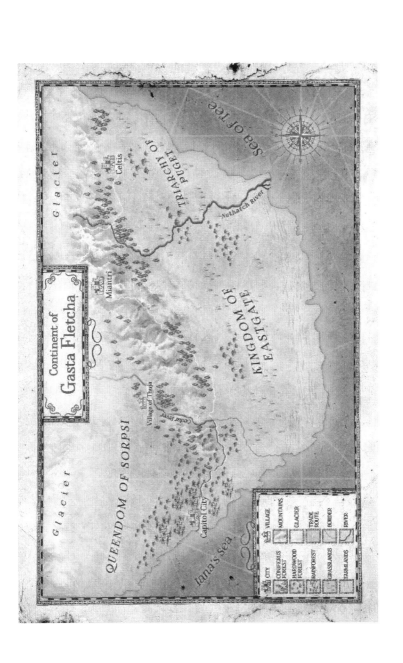

Continent of
Gasta Fletcha

One: Fire

Steam twirled from the bones in my cauldron. The heavy smell of their marrow sagged in the air. Gods, I hated the smell of the solvent, but it would be worth it once the bone oil evaporated, taking that horrible dead fish smell with it and leaving behind the final, extracted compound. I'd never get the smell out of the woodwork, but at this point, I didn't care. Mother was weeks late returning home. Again. She could yell at me when I returned. If I returned.

I coughed into the steam as it curled through my lungs. I needed fresh air, and soon, or I'd end up facedown on the hemlock floor I'd hewn and laid myself in my thirteenth year. A knot curled inside me, and I swallowed bile and frustration. Fine. I'd be done with distillation for the day, but I still needed to perform a fungal extraction with the solvent to impress Master Rahad at the fair tomorrow. I'd been aiming to attend the alchemical guild fair since I turned twelve—the year I should have declared a guild and begun my apprenticeship. I'd never made it. Each year, Mother found another marquetry to work, another finish to make, another tool to sharpen. This year, I was seventeen. I'd barely left this forest, this house, in five years. This year, the queen's master alchemist had a position open and wanted someone with fungal expertise.

Someone like me.

This year, I was going.

I removed the thin olive branch from my collection basket that would earn me my apprenticeship, despite my older age and guild lineage. The branch shone mottled blue green, almost a lime color in patches, with a blue as dark as evening sky in others. Along a four-centimeter band sprouted cup-shaped fungal fruiting forms, tiny enough to be overlooked by untrained eyes. With a pair of tweezers, I plucked the blue-green cups from the branch and dropped them into a second pot of the very combustible bone oil distillate. The smell of dead fish rose up and stung my eyes, but I couldn't look away.

As each cup sank, the color seeped from them into the solvent and expanded outward in concentric rings. The pigment slowly dropped down until the liquid looked like the deep blue of Thuja's lake. I held my breath as the fruits bubbled back to the surface. The first turned white, the second turned white, and the third and fourth—white as well. I waited, still hardly daring to breathe. One minute, then two. *Please...*

The solution's color remained stable.

I dropped my head back and exhaled at the ceiling. The trickiest part was over, and if the solution set well, it would be ready by morning. Success! I carried the extract to the windowsill, opened the pane, and began the evaporation process. Tomorrow...tomorrow would be a wonderful day. A defining day. Tomorrow, I would leave the woodcutting guild and finally, *finally*, get to be an alchemist! A *guilded* alchemist! I would not spend the rest of my life bound to this wooden house, with its wooden tools, stuck within this simplistic, wooden trade any longer.

Three loud raps sounded on the front door. Visitors? At this hour? They were in for a rude surprise, the idiots. If they were here for me, it was because the villagers had a clear misunderstanding of what alchemy entailed. I had no potions to offer them. Cauldrons and a stinking house didn't put me in the witch guild, despite the villagers' insistence to the contrary, and even if I had been a witch, I still would not have been party to their foolish fascination with magic.

However, if the visitors were here for Mother and her marquetry business, they'd leave disappointed. She had neglected to finish several large commissions before her abrupt departure. Contracts were coming due that I would not fulfill, and her clients didn't tolerated delays well. Mother took these walkabouts yearly, but she usually returned before the fair. This time, she was overdue.

I pulled at the door handle and lifted, and the thick wood glided open. A breeze came in first and blew mist right in my face. Behind the damp stood two men, squinting at me from the doorstep. They were Queensguard, both of them, dressed in the signature fitted red cloaks, though the waterproofing layers had worn off some hours ago. Both were mud-covered and had sodden pants and boots. They were sloppy, for Queensguard, and they were overdue. Mother had finished the queen's commissioned piece just before she left, and it had yet to be collected.

The taller guard moved to step into the house, flipping a layer of long, wet hair over his shoulder with a *splat*. The smell must have hit him right then, as he stepped back into his partner and kept going for three steps. The shorter guard stumbled into Mother's blackberry bush and had to rip himself free of the thorns. The taller sneezed, then spat, and then sneezed again.

For Queensguard, I was decidedly unimpressed.

"What sort of witchery is that!?" he demanded, coming no closer. "Where's the woodcutter?"

I frowned and crossed my arms, careful not to crush any of the pouches of fungal pigment that dangled from my leather bandolier.

"No witchery," I responded coolly. "I made bone oil. I discovered it. It's a type of alchemy. I'm not guilded yet, but I have a trader's permit." Which I did, in the back room, but I'd be hard-pressed to find it under all of Mother's unsharpened tools.

The tall one glared and rubbed at his nose.

The short guard stepped to the doorframe, bit back a grimace, and tried to restart the conversation. "Apologies for the hour. We're looking for—"

"She's not here." I cut him off, hoping to forestall awkward questions I couldn't answer. "She left under the last full moon, for professional obligations. It is unknown when she will return. I apologize."

"Are you her daughter then?" the short one asked.

My stomach twisted. I was no one's daughter, and that word would stick in my chest for days. It would squirm there, under bindings and layers of clothes, and make me second-guess myself at the fair with every introduction and every awkward stare at my body. In that moment, I hated them, these two men, so sure of their position despite the mud and the hour. *Daughter*. No. I had never been one and had no intention of starting now.

"Sorin the..."

"The *alchemist*," I finished for him.

"I am her *heir*," I said through gritted teeth when neither responded. "I have the queen's last commission. Will you be taking it tonight?"

The men exchanged a glance, but neither answered. The second man sneezed, sending a spray of water across the threshold. I rubbed my palm on my forehead. If they were going to get the house dirty just by being outside, it made no sense for them to stay there. Bones were one thing; mud was just unprofessional. I stepped back and gestured to the small brown oak dining table—the one with the white streak down it where I'd first discovered what the refined, clear parts of bone oil could do to fungal pigments—and grabbed my cloak from the wall.

"Sit," I said as I fastened the oblong buttons at the neck of the cloak. The men moved in with heavy steps, which grew increasingly hesitant as the fish smell concentrated. They sat and stared at me with disgusted, pained expressions as mud dripped from their boots onto that stupid handmade floor. I'd have to refinish it now.

I didn't bother speaking again.

Daughter.

Let them sit in the bone oil stink, pooled in their own mud. I turned and left the house, heading to Mother's woodshop. My feet crunched along the woodchip path, the ground cover damp but still springy. I tried to let the smells of the forest—especially the earthen smell of fungal decay—take my mind away from the word I so hated.

The men had parked their cart, and their ox, near the door to the longhouse Mother used for her shop, but I could still maneuver around it. The sun had already set, but moonlight streaked through the needled canopy of conifers and across my path. Ten short steps brought me to the double doors made from cedar plank. I stripped the padlock from the right door, the one that had been fastened since Mother's departure, and entered.

I'd not been inside the shop for a month, and the smell of cedar and wood rot reminded me why. Here were my mother's heart and legacy, as her father's before her, and her grandmother's before that. The whole place felt tattered and used and smelled worse than the bone oil.

In the back, near an old leather chair, was where her mother had been born some eighty years ago. To my right, just in front of a treadle lathe, was where my grandfather had died.

Mother had birthed her children here too—myself and the son she gave to another guild for an apprenticeship, and taken none of their children in return.

The whole building was familiar, like an old wool blanket, but scratchy just the same. This was a legacy of guild woodcutting, and the queen's mandate of matrilineal inheritance, and I didn't belong here. A woodcutter was not who I was, a daughter was not who I was, and while the former hurt less than the latter, both made me want to pull at my skin and scream.

Mercifully, the commissioned panel was right where I had last seen it. It was complete, save for a finish. An oilcloth lay on the floor near the door, already coated with paraffin. I picked it up and draped it over the panel, taking one last look at the cut veneer so expertly placed and dyed in the shape of a parrot on a branch.

The parrot's feathers and the leaves of the branch were blue green. That was my contribution. There were no pigments, natural or otherwise, that could make that color save the elf's cup fungus. The queen's order had specified a parrot, in real colors.

She'd asked the impossible of my mother: we had delivered. *I* had delivered. Pigmenting fungi and their use in woodcraft was a trade secret of the woodcutter's guild, but the ability to take those pigments from the wood and use them for other purposes—the solvent that entailed— that was mine alone.

With the cloth wrapped around the panel, I hauled the piece back to the house and propped it against the door. The Queensguard had tried to close it, but it had snagged halfway when the bottom of the door caught the ground below. The wood had swelled, as in any wet season, a common problem in the temperate rainforests of Thuja as well as the tropical ones of Sorpsi's capital. Yet, they'd not even reasoned through simply lifting the door up as they pulled it closed. What was wrong with these men? Queensguard should have been much better educated than this. They should have known about the door, and the forest, and how to address me. Trekking from the village of Thuja to Mother's house, at night, in the forest mist could addle anyone's mind, but these two... I wiped mist from my nose and frowned. They weren't quite right, and I didn't care for that feeling in my own home, with no one else about. Giving them the panel was the quickest way to get them to leave.

I pushed the door back open, lifting as I did so, and propped the panel against it so it couldn't swing shut again. The cool, damp air would help fumigate the house and would keep the bone oil from combusting as it dried.

"It's here and ready." I pulled enough of the cloth off so the two guards could see the detailed work underneath. It was best to get them on their way, whomever they were. Mother could chase the panel down later if needed. I was done with babysitting her business and hiding away in her house—hiding from the Thujan villagers, hiding from the capital city, hiding from my life.

The Queensguard, however, no longer seemed interested in the panel or me. The idiots had reached into the extract and removed my bones. They'd pieced parts of a skeleton back together—a primate, of course. Two small hands, a foot, and half the skull were laid out across the floor as if alive. The smaller guard, hunched over his bone puzzle with his comrade, had shoved his hands into the bone oil and now had the puffed cheeks and grayness of one about to vomit.

"That's none of your business," I grumbled. "And I'd appreciate it if you didn't mess my floor."

Gods, why did people have to be so nosy?

"Smells of fish, but these are no fish bones," the shorter guard said. He held up a piece of a hand and bobbed on his haunches as he turned to look at me. "Explain."

"It's a monkey," I said flatly.

"Which you used for your witchcraft?" said the other as he, too, turned around. "Expansive knowledge here, of magic. This dwelling isn't licensed for that type of activity, and you don't bear the witch guild mark." His tone was more curious than accusatory, but I didn't care.

"I'm currently a trade alchemist," I repeated again, as if talking to a particularly stupid villager. "Which we are licensed for because, otherwise, we couldn't protect any of the wood. How do you think wood finishes are made?" When the guards continued with their stares, I looked to the ceiling and grunted. "Just take the panel. Go. Don't get it too wet, and make sure the court carpenter lets it sit for a few weeks before coating it. If you really want paperwork, I can have a copy of the permit for trade work delivered to the Queensguard hall tomorrow."

"I don't think so." The guards stood and kicked at the bone pile. Neither one had looked at the panel yet. The hair on my arms rose. That was a fourteen-hundred-stone commission, lying against the door, open to the elements! That was more than the entire town of Thuja made in one year.

They hadn't come from the palace; that was now abundantly clear.

I took a step toward the door, making sure to keep my growing unease from showing on my face. *Knife in the boot*, I reminded myself, for I'd been out foraging this morning and had not yet removed it. *People aren't so different than monkeys.* Of course, I had never killed any of the animals I used for bone oil, but then again, none of them had ever called me a daughter either.

"What guild did you say you belonged to?" the tall one asked as he eyed my throat. I brought my hands up to cover the unadorned skin and flushed with embarrassment. I didn't need a reminder of my failure to declare to my Mother's guild, or any other, for that matter.

"I'm unguilded," I muttered, unable to meet the man's eyes. Anyone could be a trader, but to join a guild you had to first be an apprentice, and I had no formal education. "Since you're not Queensguard, why are you here?" *And why pretend, especially if you're not going to steal the panel?*

The man snorted. "The grandmaster of witchcraft asked to meet with the master woodcutter. I don't want to return empty-handed, so our girl alchemist might make a reasonable substitute, guilded or not."

I dropped my hands to my sides and raked my fingernails over my pants. There shouldn't have been a grandmaster of witchcraft because the unbound guilds— witches and alchemists—weren't beholden to any of the three countries and therefore couldn't set up a guildhall. But that didn't matter right now because my skin was too tight, all of a sudden. I gripped fistfuls of cloth to steady myself, to keep my hands busy so they wouldn't find the skin of my arms. I snarled at the men, though tears collected in my eyes. *Girl. Daughter.* They burned as deeply as the smell of the bone oil. As interesting as the grandmaster of witchcraft might be, I didn't care anymore about anything these men had to say.

"Get out," I hissed. I marched to the door; I would throw them out if I had to. But the shorter guard grabbed me by the wrist before I reached the threshold.

"No!" I pulled back, turning to slap him, and just as I spun around, he let go.

Laughter chased after me as I stumbled and caught my ankle on the doorjamb. My equilibrium was off from the bone oil fumes, and I hit the ground, elbow first. Now I too was slicked with mud and wet wood shavings, which kept my feet from finding purchase as I tried to stand and face the demeaning laughter. The tears I was determined not to shed burned my eyes.

Before I could get my feet under me, thick fingers dug into my arms and I was hauled up and dragged forward. Their hands were wide, and their arms much stronger than my own, and when I pulled, their grips tightened. The mist was thick in my mouth as I sucked in gasps of air, trying to kick or somehow injure the men who held me.

"I'm not worth anything. The only thing of value is that panel!" I yelled.

"A master woodcutter would be worth more than a confused imitation," the taller one said. "We'll work with what we have."

"I am *not* a *woodcutter*!"

We were at the cart now, and when the shorter man reached past my head to grab a rope that hung over the side, I bit his hand, separating flesh. The not-guard screamed and dropped my right arm. Blood splattered across my front as he flailed. The tall one tried to grab my wrist, but I fell to my knees, grabbed him between the legs, twisted, and pulled.

He collapsed, howling, and I skittered back toward the house.

"Leave!" I screamed at them. These things weren't supposed to happen at Mother's house. Wasn't that why I was always here—to avoid this? What was the point of giving up apprenticeships, friendships, if I was going to be accosted in my own home?

The tall one gasped and grabbed me by the front of my shirt just before I cleared the cart. I wrapped my fingers around his and tried to pull free, but he slapped me across the face and, for a moment, I couldn't see. I babbled instead.

"I have money," I said. "In the house. I have wood species from across the world worth double their weight in stones." *I have solvents I could melt you with if you'd just come back inside.*

"We will have Amada the master woodcutter," the short one said with a gap-toothed grin. "She'll come for you, if nothing else, seeing as how well she's kept you to herself all these years." He grabbed my legs and, with the taller one, dumped me into the cart. The taller man secured my ankles to iron weights anchored to the cart bed, punched me in the stomach, and left me to lie, staring dumbly at the canopy overhead as he went to assist his partner. Mother would come for me, certainly, but it was the other part of the man's words that clouded my thoughts.

The cart began to move, jostling over the uneven forest floor. As I tried to regain my breath, my mind jumped, irrationally, back to the house.

"You forgot the panel!" I wheezed over the noise of the grunting ox and snapping branches. To leave it seemed like a stupid waste, even if they had no interest in it themselves. It'd taken us two years to make that thing, Mother and I. Someone should have it, even if just ignorant kidnappers. It was worth more than my life, certainly. I had no guild mark, no formal apprenticeship, no friends to come looking for me, and an undocumented journey-woodcutter was worth only as much as their master was willing to pay. They were going to be very disgruntled when Mother did not appear. And if they found her...gods, if they found her... What did witches want with a woodcutter?

I had my breath back, so I sat up and leaned over the side of the cart. Even with the moonlight, it was too dark to see more than outlines, but I could just make out the taller one breaking away and moving back toward Mother's house.

Panic gave way to puzzlement as he entered. Had they changed their minds about the panel? I squinted into the night. Was he moving the panel then, or going past it? I'd not yet lit any oil lamps for fear of combustion during the extraction, and so the spark from the guard's flint burned my eyes. Something caught in the guard's hand—perhaps a ribbon of paper or a sheet of Mother's veneer. Whatever it was, the man tossed it inside the house.

"No!"

I screamed it, I think. My throat hurt, either way. The guard jogged back to the cart, and I screamed again, nonsensically. The idiot. The absolute uneducated toadstool. If he didn't quicken his pace, if *we* didn't—

Mother's house exploded.

Two: Earth

Bits of roof and wood slats rained onto the cart. The ox bellowed and ran, as much as oxen do, and one of the men screamed. I screamed. I couldn't tell one from the other as I stared at the burning house, my ears filled with the peppered explosions of bone oil and wood finishes. I had sought to leave Mother's legacy behind, not burn it to the ground. If I got away from these men, what was I going to *do*?

Another smaller explosion followed, and the screams of the man abruptly cut off. I sank as low as I could into the cart, curled in on myself, and tried to understand the ache in my chest as shingles and their fat, handmade nails slapped across my body. The cart hit a root, and the left side jumped into the air. My torso slammed into the right wall, my legs still held by the chains. *The house...the shop...my extracts...all of Mother's work...*

The home that was my prison. Gone.

I refused to be killed by idiocy. When the cart bumped again and I was flung to the back, close to the inserts of my manacles, I grabbed the wooden frame with one hand. I used the other to untie the first pouch from my sash. Using two fingers on the outside of the bag, I cinched a clump of the red granules to the top and undid the tie, being careful to let none of it touch my skin. Blocking the breeze with my shoulder and trying desperately to not let the rocking of the cart spill the contents, I rubbed the top of the pouch around the edges of both ankle manacles.

There was a cracking noise, hopefully too low for the remaining man to hear as we crashed along the path. I couldn't see the reaction, but I didn't need to. Instead, I counted as I tied the pouch back to my sash with shaking hands and, at twenty, brought my ankles sharply together. There was no clang. Instead, the two sides of the manacles collided into a spray of metal filings and grainy red crystals. I'd already turned my head, but metal fragments still beat into my left cheek. I cringed and brought my hand, the one that had been holding the frame, to my face. It came back wet. Well, I was already covered in blood. A bit of my own wasn't going to make much difference. I scooted to the end of the cart and peered over the edge.

When had we stopped moving?

"Get back, girl." The man came around from the side, his voice low. He had a dagger in his hand that remained pointed at me as he climbed into the cart. I pushed back. It wasn't the knife I was afraid of. He said "girl" the way the villagers said "witch," with a swish at the end, and used enough disdain to curl the word into illegitimacy. When people spoke with their lips sneered up and their eyes narrowed, it didn't matter what they said. The effect was always the same, and this time, it felt sharper with the screams of the burning man in my memory.

"I'm not a girl." I'd meant to enunciate each word and sound brazen, but it came out in a squeaky jumble. I had to get away before his words eroded my confidence and I became unable to think. It happened, sometimes, though not in recent memory, mostly because I'd not risked venturing even into Thuja, the village that bordered our land, for the past three years.

The man snorted, the dagger tracking dangerously close to my face. I ripped the third pouch from my belt, pulled open the strings, pinched the bottom of the leather, and with a flick of my wrist, threw the entire contents in his face.

He coughed first, as I leapt over the side of the cart and backed well away, then rubbed his eyes with fisted hands. In the moonlight, I could see the yellow granules clinging to his skin and clothes like pollen, When, furiously blinking, he tried to wipe himself clean, the yellow stuck to his palms and fingers.

"What is it!?" he yelled through gritted teeth. "Your trick won't work!"

"Alchemy isn't a trick," I muttered, though I doubted he heard me. He brought a hand up to his face and scratched the skin around his cheekbones. A yellow film had formed there, and it pulled his skin tightly together. He scratched harder. The strokes of his nails became feverish and caught the edge of the film. It peeled off, taking his skin with it. It was horrific to watch, and yet, yet...a part of me couldn't help but be proud. Those were my extracts. My alchemy. I might not be good with a sword, but I could definitely defend myself.

"You useless piece of chattel!" His face bled, and still the extract continued to form sheets on his skin. It covered the right side of his face and down his neck. I took another four steps back. The novelty had worn off, and I wanted to run—gods how I wanted run and not watch the obscenity that was taking place. Unfortunately, he could still catch me if he wanted to, and if that pigment got on me as well... It was best for him to think I was too afraid to bolt, and let the pigment run its course well away from my own skin.

As if he had just remembered his legs, the man jumped from the cart and grabbed for me—foolishly, for I was well out of his range—but his hand pulled back, and instead, he raked his nails over his other hand, now coated in yellow. I shuddered and swallowed bile. The man screamed—a horrible, dying hare scream—and I couldn't force myself to look away as he fell to his knees and cursed me, his partner, and a host of men and women whose names were not familiar. He...he looked like he was melting, although he wasn't, not really. More like binding to himself as his skin sloughed off... I looked away. He'd forced my hand. He had. He'd tried to kidnap me.

The screams turned to a whimper as he fell to his side. He curled up like a bug, moaning and clawing. His noises became throaty as he gagged on his coated tongue. I took a step back, then another. He didn't even look my way. I had thought my heart might stop pounding once the man was down, but it still rammed about in my chest, reminding me I'd been dragged from my home, chained to a cart, and all of this had been meant for Mother, my mother, who was missing.

Missing, with witches looking for her. With a *grandmaster* witch looking for her.

She was a *woodcutter*. What business could the grandmaster witch have with her that warranted thugs and kidnapping? And when had the witches erected a guildhall? Did the alchemists have one now too? I'd been cut off from the world for half a decade, but guilds were consistent. Unchanging. Maybe some of the rules had slacked, but they did *not* kidnap people.

My hands still shook, so I shoved them into my pants pockets. My chin still trembled, so I clamped my jaw. The logical thing to do was to go back home and see if I could salvage anything, though I did have jars of bone oil stored throughout the various outbuildings, and everything was still burning. I might end up combusting along with the house.

Still...

No.

I didn't want to go back there. Hadn't I been trying to get *away* from those suffocating buildings for the past five years? Hadn't I put my life on hold long enough? Who knew what memories, what guilt, was waiting for me there, ready to bind me again to my mother's house like I'd bound the man with the fungal pigment? This was Mother's mess, and I wasn't going to clean it up for her. Not this time.

I was going to the capital.

I was going to the alchemical fair.

I tore myself away from the tree and the wet stench of blood and ran into the forest, my bandolier of fungal pigments slapping against my chest. I ran past redwoods and tan oaks, maples and hemlocks, stumbling toward the Thujan lake, the smell of Mother's burning house behind me.

I would *not* be a woodcutter's unguilded apprentice for the rest of my life.

It was time to be an alchemist.

Three: Water

It poured rain the entire boat ride to the capital. I spent the hour near the prow, watching smoke slip across the forest canopy of Thuja—thinking about Mother. She had been proud of her profession. I was proud of her profession. I was proud of her, just not proud to *follow* her, but really, none of that mattered because her woodcutting legacy was smoking to charcoal.

By the time I disembarked from the long-tailed canoe, well after the rest of the passengers, I looked more like a sodden wharf rat than a guilder. The rain had washed off most of the dirt and blood but left me chilled. I had no cloak to protect my clothes, for I'd lost it amongst the cart's many jolts through the woods, and the garments stuck to my skin like shellac. I ran flat palms down my front, trying to smooth the wrinkles and prevent bunching, but the cotton clung to my binder and accentuated my breasts.

I scowled, then wrapped my arms around my chest and stepped from the boat onto the soft sand of the west dock, taking long, calculated breaths that weren't slowing my heart at all. I cursed the water and the cotton binding. It was looser, now that it was wet, and I could breathe easier, but I'd have to walk through the city like this, to get to the square where the other potential apprentices were being interviewed. I didn't care about the stink or the dried, caked blood, or looking like a waif, but I wasn't sure how long I'd make it, looking like a girl.

I tried to ignore the gathered fabric and the shivering that was from more than the cold. Ahead of me, the access road swarmed with fishmongers and fruit peddlers, all with their wooden pushcarts. The smell of Sorpsi's river and lake ports was distinct, each of them, but this one was by far the most fragrant. I'd played here often as a child, while mother delivered marquetries or had meetings I was not allowed to attend. Today, it looked...busier?

I squinted into the distance, down to the next row of pilings where three more long-tailed canoes floated, tethered and heavy with passengers. No, not just any passengers—guild passengers, although there were a fair few dock workers and sailors as well. But there was at least one guild family on that boat, and while I couldn't make out the guild tattoos on the necks of the adults, I could see enough of a dark smudge to know they were there.

A group of four people dressed all in leather boarded the first boat. The person in front scoured necks and forced each passenger to look at them in turn, but ignored the scruffier hands—the dock workers, the tattered children, the beggars.

I took a few steps forward, then stopped when the family was led from the boat, surrounded by the leather-clad people, and marched in a line toward the palace.

"What?" I said to myself but apparently loud enough to attract the attention of an old woman standing next to me.

"For-hires," she said. "They're rounding up guilders, though all that are around anymore are apprentices. Did you want some pineapple? I have some leatherwork, too, in the bottom of the cart if you're interested. Get it now before the price goes up."

None of that made any sense. "Before the price—why?" I asked. "What are you talking about?"

The woman sniffed and crossed her arms.

It took me a moment to realize what she was waiting for. Wasting her time answering my questions would cost her sales. I fished in my pocket and took out the first stone I had, not even looking at its value.

The woman eyed the stone, and me, then waved dismissively. "Just keep it. I'm talking about relocating. Insurance. The woodcutters just lost their grandmaster. Dead. The same thing happened to the River Guild, but their grandmaster just straight up quit, I heard, 'cause of the steamboats moving in from the west. The other guilds of Sorpsi probably aren't far behind, and it *is* a census year, after all. Where have you been, especially looking like this?" She frowned. "You *do* look kind of like the master woodcutter, from Thuja. Anyone ever tell you that?"

"*What?*"

"Yeah." She made a circling motion with her finger around my face. "Same curly black hair, same funny little dimples. Same body shape. You got that curled bow lip thing my husband thinks is beyond attractive." She snorted.

Guild problems seemed really far away, all of a sudden. I looked down at myself, dripping muddy water, my clothes torn, my brown skin scratched and welted from the wood cart. The binding under my shirt was only sodden, not unraveling, but with my shirt clinging so close, I looked unquestionably female. I'd pass easily enough for a dockworker, but I couldn't be seen like this. I could *not*. They would know, the fishmongers and the fruit vendors and the tailors with their treadle machines. They wouldn't see the *woodcutter's* daughter, for I was too covered in grime, but they would see a woman—a girl—and that was wrong.

I'd be a witch before I'd be a woman.

But I couldn't go to the alchemy fair looking like this, or I'd spend the whole time huddled in a corner, trying to mash my chest down. I needed clothes, and I had a few stones in my pocket—enough to buy the high-quality cotton that had the correct tautness of fabric. I knew where to go—I'd always enjoyed the capital's textile district back when Mother had let me travel. It was still morning, and the masters wouldn't leave until sunset. That was plenty of time. I could do this.

With my arms still crossed high—for I would crush my damn breasts if I had to—I thanked the fruit vendor and walked as confidently as I could onto the access road. She called after me with more things to buy, but I forced myself to keep walking. I had to, or I'd spin to shavings. I passed yet more vendors. Some were stationary, and these I could weave around and ignore the calls to purchase, but the ones with pushcarts dogged my heels despite my appearance.

"Fresh pineapple!"

"That shirt! Let me repair it for you! Ten minutes! I'm the finest trade tailor in Sorpsi!"

"Apples and blood oranges and limes! A bounty to bring home to your family!"

There were too many voices. Too many people looking at me and making assumptions. I broke into a run as their words chased after me and battered my ears. They weren't being specific. It didn't matter.

"We have the best price here! No need to go down the road! We can even beat guild prices!"

"Your family will love the mangosteen! We guarantee it!"

It was hard to swallow. My throat burned as I dodged arms and elbows on the crowded street. Women in bright hats and dresses turned their exasperated eyes on me, tsking my haste. Men stepped from my path and looked past me, trying to discern the manner of the disturbance. I pushed children away with my hips and nearly collapsed onto an insect cart coming into the access road as I turned left, off the main street.

Here, it was quieter. Shoppers still milled about, of course, and several meters away, another cart vendor, this one selling smoked meat on sticks, didn't even look up from his cart as I pressed myself into the side of a brick building and tried to breathe.

I dug my fingernails into my palms and forced myself to look at the overcast sky, then to the plaza a few streets away. I had to get a new binding before attending the fair, so melting into a puddle of tears and scratched skin was not an option. I pushed from the wall and wrapped my arms back against my chest. This time, I positioned them high enough that the front of my shirt flattened. That looked better. It looked *right*, or, at least, right enough to get me through town.

When my heart still pounded and my breathing made me feel dizzy, I shut my eyes and remembered the last time I'd been in the plaza. I'd been eight or nine at the most. Magda and I had been playing on the old limestone statue of Sorpsi's last king that sat in the center of the plaza—the one of him abdicating his throne to the peasant woman who had defeated him. Magda and I had been fighting with bamboo swords, wearing identical white linen dresses, her long black curls braided with ribbons, and me with the dress's blue sash tied around my face so I looked like a bandit. Or something.

I remembered how uncomfortable the dress made me. Not because I didn't like it, but because of how everyone looked at me in it. How their eyes became soft and mushed. And then I remembered how much Magda hated the dress, too, because she hated frills and constricting fabric, and how there was the perfect puddle at the base of the statue, filled with thick mud, that was so satisfying to jump in.

I remembered the mud, and the laughter, and the mischief in Magda's eyes and took a deep breath. I smiled at the memory, and it was enough to center me. I started walking again, through the narrow streets that widened as the spires of the castle became visible. Three blocks later, the city centered bloomed—a stonework plaza peppered with fountains and the old king's statue. It wasn't nearly as crowded as I'd expected, which was puzzling, but it was the second day of the festival.

Closer to the plaza, the road was cobblestone, with wood footpaths raised a good handspan from the surface. I passed two stores, one selling silk bolts and the other tailored suits, before I stopped. The Tailor's Wench, while not the most attractive of names, should have been bustling this time of day. I often shopped here with Mother as it had the best quality cotton for binders, but it was closed and the door locked.

I frowned and rubbed my arms. It wasn't a holiday. Guilders and traders alike had to make a living. The queen gave neither handouts nor sponsorships. Why would they be closed?

"Out of business. They couldn't keep up with the water frame that's being tested a few countries over. I heard it can spin more than one hundred threads at a time. For cotton, they just couldn't compete."

I turned to the short gentleman behind me. His gaze flicked only briefly over my personage, and then he gave me a friendly nod. I relaxed, but my arms stayed high. The drape of his shirt was caught, only slightly, near the top of his chest where a binder would have started. We weren't exactly the same, he and I, but his presence was a comfort nonetheless.

I pulled my shirt away from my body. "I don't know where else to go." I smiled halfheartedly.

He stroked his chin, which was smooth and free of stubble. "You weren't going to walk around the city like that, were you?"

He wasn't referring to my clothes, although with the damp leather smell mixed with the blood and wet, he had every right to do so. Instead, his eyes grazed my bandolier and the three pouches that hung there.

My brow furrowed. "The alchemist fair?" I asked, stuttering on the words. "Isn't everyone wearing them?" Although now that he mentioned it, I hadn't seen anyone during my walk from the pier with a bandolier, or the long alchemical coats some wore. This close to the main plaza, we should have been swarmed by both guild masters and apprentices. Where was everyone?

"The fair?" He clasped his hands and rocked back on his heels. "It's been cancelled, order of the royal daughter. You'll run into Queensguard, soon enough, who will ask you to take your bandolier off as well. There's just too much suspicion. Too many people are on edge." He pointed back toward the docks. "Guessing you came from that way? Surely you saw the for-hires?"

My shoulders sagged. My mouth gaped. Something dropped, too, deep in my stomach, and tears stung my eyes. "Cancelled? But...but *why*?"

The man picked a piece of lint from his jacket. "Because the queen's gone missing, country mouse. Three weeks now. And when things like this happen, you know it's always the unbound guilds that get blamed. The consort is at his wit's end. The queen has to meet with the Triarchy of Puget and the King of Eastgate in four days to reestablish the border treaty. This is the first time it's come due since Queen Iana took the throne. I'm sure you can infer what no attendance would mean. Her daughter isn't exactly jumping up to help either. But it boils down to not needing a bunch of alchemists about when you're trying to find a missing royal."

"But Mag—" I stopped myself before saying her full name, and the sound died, bitter, in my mouth. He didn't know the royal family like I did. Like Mother did. It was a lot to filter all at once—watching the dream I'd finally decided to chase summarily squashed right in front of me, while I dripped fetid water onto the shoes of possibly the only person in town I wasn't embarrassed to be around.

Cancelled. The fair was cancelled.

I wanted to yell. I wanted to scream. I wanted to take one of my pouches and toss it onto the roof of The Tailor's Wench just to watch the straw explode in a shower of red crystal flowers.

"Cotton for binding?" My eyes went down to the stone, down to my sodden boots. My hand went to my pocket and pulled out the stones—the largest stamped with the parrot of the queen's crest, the other three with aspen leaves to denote their low value—and held them flat on my palm. "I can't do anything without a new one, whether the fair is happening or not."

"Nowhere around here. Not anymore. Has to be imported from factories outside the three countries, and the quality is low. The three countries are the only ones left on the continent with guilds now, what few remain. Everyone else has traded quality for quantity. I can give you my cloak if you like?"

Everything was too tight, from the wet clothing to my binding to my bandolier. I took the cloak—thin brown wool with a deep hood—and offered my stones.

"Keep them," he said, his tone soft and apologetic.

I couldn't respond. My throat and eyes burned. Instead, I bowed and turned sharply back toward the plaza. I'd always been stellar at running away from things.

So I ran to the only place in the capital I knew would be empty of people. To the last place I had ever been able to just be *me*.

I ran through the streets, around the king's statue. I ran past the guildhalls I knew too well, past pubs I recognized from Mother's stories. I ran past the palace courtyard, the spires of the building looking like they might pierce the sky, the clouds, and spill yet more rain onto my pathetic form.

I ran past the palace itself, and behind it, stables where people called to me to stop, to wait, that I wasn't allowed. I had attached the cloak around my neck but would not take off the bandolier. Without my extracts, what was I? Without alchemy, without an apprenticeship...I would not remove the last part of my dream, and damn everything for taking this from me!

I didn't pause as dirt and stone gave way to trees and sedge. When the humid air of Sorpsi's tropical rainforest hit my face and further curled my hair, I took deeper breaths, daring the air to choke me. As the ferns grew wider and scaled the trees, as the sounds of insects and the rustling of foragers overpowered the crashing of my feet, I kept running. I stopped only when I could no longer see the castle's spires, and when the trees grew so densely together that I could see the pale-blue glow of foxfire fungi at my feet. I stopped when I could no longer hear the voices of the people calling after me. All around me, only insect hums. Bird calls. The digging and rustling of some unseen rodent.

Here, on the prone trunk of a massive cedar tree, I knelt and dug my hands into the decay, a patch of green-glowing foxfire pressed around the edge of my boot.

I sobbed—for who was around to hear? Did it matter? I sobbed and coughed and nearly vomited on feelings too long buried. I'd have to go back to the capital before dark. I knew where Mother was at least. The death of the grandmaster woodcutter meant she was likely at his guildhall, now hers, for she was next in line. I would have to tell her about our house. We'd have to go back and rebuild, and really, there was no reason for me not to go back. I had nothing here, not with the alchemical fair cancelled.

So much for finally breaking away.

I pushed my fingers into the rotten wood and tore off a chunk, letting bits crumble down my hand. Stupid. This whole thing had been stupid! I tossed the wood as hard as I could at a funny-looking stump in the distance, hoping to hear the satisfying explosion of brown, brittle wood on a hard surface.

"Ahhhhhhh!"

The stump expanded into a very short, graying man in a brown cloak. He swung his head in my direction, looking, no doubt, for the source of the wood missile, and in doing so, slipped on the wet sedge. The plants he'd picked flew from his hand. He landed on his back in a thick blanket of fog. The sedge engulfed him, and through the patches of gray and green I could only make out the brown of his cloak.

"Sorry!" I called out, trying to keep the frustration from my voice. The queen's forest was no place to come alone. What was he—

I saw movement in the mist. I hopped the log and moved to the edge of a small clearing. The sedge grew knee-high here, and the ferns arched over my head. Sunlight flitted down but pierced the mist only in fragments. The man sat up, muddy and scowling, but there was movement behind him that I was more concerned with.

A slender form emerged from the fog.

I stumbled. My heart pounded.

Nothing human moved like that.

The fog fell away and revealed a spindly trunk and a thick halo of wide leaves. The magic *thing* pulled itself across the ground with flapping, piercing roots toward the man *still* just sitting on his backside! A collection basket lay upended to his left, with bits of herbs and mushrooms spilled across the sedge.

I took another step forward before I could stop myself. My boot crunched down on some unseen twig, and it was only then that the man turned toward me, his lips bunched tightly together and his brows furrowed into rebuke.

His face snapped into my memory, and I choked back a yell.

Master Rahad.

The queen's royal alchemist.

Four: Earth

He didn't stand but, instead, waved me back, pulling a machete strapped awkwardly at his side as he did so. Roots wove toward his limbs drunkenly, blindly. I wanted to comply with his unspoken request but...that was a *palm tree*, coming toward him, and it was *not* alchemy that animated the thing.

There was no law against magic, of course, the same as there was none against alchemy, but I'd never *seen* magic before. I shivered, though it wasn't cold. Someone had enchanted the tree, or there was an amulet nearby. The stupid things were artifacts left by the old king, used to store magic and spells, and were so old they leaked. He'd had them buried everywhere, and our first queen, the one who had defeated him, had never managed to find them all after she took his crown. They still popped up every once in a while, spilling their poison. They were the reason for the abrupt climate changes across the three countries, too, or at least that's what Mother had told me. That was how powerful magic was. Master Rahad, alchemist or not, couldn't fight it, surely. And I couldn't just leave him to die since his fall and the enraged monocot were entirely my fault.

And the palm... I tilted my head. Its fronds were enormous strips of green so high up I couldn't have reached them if I jumped. I was only a few bounds from Master Rahad, but the palm was only a meter or two away. Hovering.

I held my breath. The wind stilled.

Master Rahad sneezed.

The palm whirled into motion. A black, speckled root no thicker than my pinkie finger shot from the trunk and slithered up Master Rahad's leg. He scooted back as quickly as he could, but the root pulled, halting his movement, and then slid him back across the wet sedge. He batted it with the side of his machete, spanking it like a wayward child instead of cutting the damn thing off. The fronds quaked, but instead of moving, the palm sent another root swaying toward his head.

"Master Rahad," I whispered, edging closer. "I could tackle it maybe—"

He made a hissing sound and again waved me away. The second root slithered across his chin, and this time, he did try to sever it, but the root slipped past his machete and wound around his neck.

"*Hey!*" I yelled at it, hoping to get the palm's attention, although I had no idea what I'd do once I got it. Still, Master Rahad couldn't do anything if he couldn't breathe.

Another root rose from the palm trunk, as thin as a porcupine quill, and jerked toward me, the tip bobbing up and down and dripping a clear fluid into the sedge. Gods, the thing had walked right out of a nightmare into reality, thanks to *magic*.

"Get away!" Master Rahad yelled at me.

"Master Rahad, I can help!" Or at least I could die in the general proximity of my dream.

"You're an idiot! Just back away slowly and get out of here before it—"

The root that had been pointing at me gave a final jerk, then embedded itself in Master Rahad's leg.

He screamed. Only a few drops of blood oozed out, so thin was the root, but I closed the short distance between us anyway, my mouth filling with the wet taste of decaying plant matter. Another root, thicker this time but only just, struck Master Rahad through his other shin, pinning him to the ground.

"I said keep away!" Master Rahad yelled again as he whacked the machete against the rigid spine-roots. Pinpricks of blood welled from his wounds and stained the sedge a diluted crimson. The thing's attention was now entirely on Master Rahad and his clanging machete as he tried to sever the roots.

New fog blew in and swirled at my ankles, lapped at my hips. The air stank, and sweat dripped over my eyebrows and into my eyes. It was really hard to ignore his orders. I wanted to run, but another root smacked the machete from Master Rahad's hand as the blade nearly cleaved the first one apart. The root around his neck tightened and pulled him down flat, crushing the sedge. The palm bent, *bent* over, and its fronds pointed like knives at the alchemist-shaped indent in the sedge.

I had to cover my mouth to dampen my scream. This was no mild, vestigial magic. Well, I'd wanted to impress him, hadn't I? What better time than during our impending deaths? I took a deep breath of the fetid air, for the fog was past my eyes now, and grabbed for my pouches with a shaking hand. I was out of the yellow, and the blue green, from elf's cup, would do no good; I doubted I could poison a palm. The red—the one that made the crystals—might work, but the palm was too close to Master Rahad to just fling pigments around.

"The amulet!"

I heard the choked cry as the palm began to shake. I hadn't seen one, but I hadn't really looked, and logic said it had to be there, somewhere. I shifted my attention to the trunk that was more a mass of teeming roots than a central stem. I had a vague idea of the shape since Mother had a small collection of magic books in her woodshop that she used to prop up one leg of the treadle lathe. Over the years, I'd skimmed most of them out of sheer boredom. In the middle of the roots lay a mahogany-colored, oval amulet leaking clear fluid onto the palm.

The palm gave a final shudder, and its fronds fell like spears down on Master Rahad. He gurgled as I took my foraging knife from my belt, waved it briefly in the air to collect a bit of fog, opened the top of the red pouch, and stuck the blade in. I yanked it back out, hoping the fog would give me enough of a water barrier that the metal would not explode in my face, then threw the knife at the center of the palm.

The blade embedded in the bark. My aim was terrible, but I hadn't been aiming for the amulet, and the stem was wide enough it didn't matter. The palm straightened, half its fronds still attached. It pulled all its roots back, though, including the ones in and around Master Rahad, and sent them to the handle of the knife to bat at it ineffectually.

"You missed!" Rahad groaned.

I balled my fists in frustration and bit my lip hard enough I tasted copper. It was the wetness. It had to be. The pigments didn't solubilize in water. The fog and the water inside the palm were preventing the pigments from binding and reacting, and we were both going to die out here, and it was entirely my fault.

"Master!" I cried out, fog and failure thick in my throat.

The wind changed direction. It blew from the north, from the mountains of Puget and the glacier just above, and brought a chill to the air. The fog thinned as the air cooled and droplets of water formed on the leaves and sedge. I shivered at the beading moisture on my exposed skin, and the palm...the palm stopped moving.

Its roots dropped away as the moisture fell from the cooling air. My knife handle quivered in the bark though it was no longer under attack. Suddenly, it shot back out at me. I ducked, barely missing the wood handle, and it smashed into a cedar some twenty feet away with a loud *thunk*. I caught my breath. From the open wound in the trunk, red crystals flowered. They didn't explode, but as the air continued to cool, more and more of the red pigment bound together. I ran to Master Rahad and pulled him back, his wet clothes sliding easily across ferns and sedge, until we were beyond the bounds of the clearing.

The monocot thrashed. Roots batted the forming crystals, but for every one it dislodged, three more took its place. It was a chain reaction because alchemy had rules and didn't try to kill you in the forest, unlike magic.

Fissures spread across the bark in a jagged circle, and the bark sloughed like old skin, dropping red and brown shards in a wide circumference. I stared the tree in detached, horrified fasciation. It was like watching wood decay, kind of, as the bark and stem disintegrated into red petals of crystal. The palm screamed, I think, as two roots intertwined and rubbed against each other, producing a screeching sound. The wind shifted again. The temperature rose. The fog slid up past the fronds and consumed the palm and the clearing.

The screeching faded. The fog stayed, but through it, red and orange glinted—proof that my alchemy was worth *something*. Plus, we were both alive.

I turned to Master Rahad and knelt at his side. With the high fog, darkness shrouded us. If he was bleeding heavily, I had no way of knowing. I offered him a hand, and he sat up, groaning, and clung to my arms.

"Gods, are you all right?" I skimmed my hands over his wounds. Would pressure help? A tourniquet? My mind skipped like a stone. If I had the yellow pigment, I could have bound his wounds enough to get him back to the castle! Was I strong enough to carry him? Surely two palm pinpricks wouldn't be fatal, but there were the leaf slashes, too, and who knew how deep those were.

"I'll live, likely." Rahad coughed, but mercifully it was a dry cough. "They pierced muscle but no artery. The leaf cuts are minor. Still, I'll need help getting out of the forest. I don't think my legs will take my weight."

"I can try to carry you. It's not too far to the palace, right?" I cinched the red pouch closed and pushed an arm under his knees and another around his torso, preparing to stand. I'd hauled logs from the forest for years for

Mother, on sleds and with straps. Master Rahad couldn't possibly weigh more than a tan oak.

Master Rahad's voice cracked as he responded. "Ten minutes of brisk walking. Twenty with me in your arms, if you can manage."

I did manage, and we were only a few steps down the path I'd made during my flight from the plaza when Master Rahad shook his head and really looked at me.

"Sorin?" he asked, his voice slurred, though with pain or confusion I didn't know. "Master Amada's heir? Care to tell me what you flung around? How did you become an alchemist?"

His words warmed me, though it was plenty warm in the forest already, especially from carrying my literal dreams in my arms as they slowly bled out. My stomach fluttered as I tilted my head back, showing him my unadorned neck.

"Not a guild alchemist, only a hopeful apprentice. I've worked under a trade permit for years, but I'm done with that. I wanted to see you today at the fair. To beg, really, because I've tried to come year after year to get an apprenticeship and..." The ground sloped uphill briefly, and I had to stop talking to catch my breath. That my throat felt tight was irrelevant.

"The powders?"

"I made a new solvent from bone oil. Smells awful, but it pulls color from wood fungi—these funny pigments I've never been able to extract before. Mother used to send me mushroom hunting, and I stumbled upon them in our wood lot." I bit my lower lip and looked him in the eyes. Hope pushed a smile to my face that I was desperate to squash. I didn't need to look too eager. "I mostly use the elf's cup, golden mango, and flaming dragon fungi. Their pigments are the most...active, but it works on many other fungi too. But these main fungi, they grow in your forest as well. I wouldn't mind collecting some later, assuming you get patched up okay. I could show them to you, too, if you'd like. Show you the bone oil. I made it myself."

Damn, I'd already said that last part, hadn't I?

Master Rahad chortled. I was on the wrong side of him to see his guild mark, but on his bare arms the thumbnail-sized elemental symbols ran in a spiral down his forearms. I did smile then. I'd known of the master for years, even met him once or twice as a child when Magda and I had snuck into his laboratory to pilfer some small treasure. When I was seven, I made wild fantasy stories about his tattoos and their meaning, but now I knew them all. Every single one. Now, I wasn't a little kid in a lace dress and my hair tied with ribbons. I was competent, and I'd saved his life, and gods, if he still had that apprentice position open...

The fog and the green of the forest faded as the lights of the palace appeared. As the trees turned spindly and the red cloaks of the Queensguard became distinct, Master Rahad tried speaking again.

"I've not had an apprentice in years, you know."

I nodded. "I had heard. I also heard you were looking."

He coughed. "A solvent from boiling bones. It never would have occurred to me. You've turned out different, haven't you, than what Master Amada expected. An intriguing dichotomy."

"I'm just me."

Queensguard rushed to us as we lurched onto the palace lawn. They took Master Rahad from my arms and laid him on the short grass. One ran to the palace, likely to get a doctor.

"You're sure it's not magic you're interested in?" Rahad still had a grip on my cloak, so I knelt to the ground next to him and took his hand. "The guilds are precious things because they are our history and our culture, but even as they give way to the factories, we'll never truly be rid of magic. Alchemy and magic are unbound guilds for a reason as I'm sure you know—not beholden to any of the three countries. Few people practice magic anymore, but fewer still practice alchemy."

"I've no interest in magic. Mother was forever warning me about witches and amulets, although I questioned whether amulets really existed until today. Witches were one of the reasons she kept me in Thuja." One of the reasons, but not the primary one.

Master Rahad sniffed as one of the Queensguard pulled a tight bandage around his left leg. "Your mother was no fool. The old king's artifacts are everywhere. Not just the one amulet in the glacier, you know, from that silly fairy story everyone tells their children. Our first queen, Iana, dug that up almost a century ago. No, the amulets are everywhere as you've just seen with that blasted palm. But there's good money, and good magic, to be had in the witch guild. Alchemy is a hard life. Our solvents are caustic, and most of us don't live well past thirty."

I shook my head, determined to not foul up the opportunity I was certain Master Rahad was about to offer. A short life was better than no life at all. "I'd much rather work with solvents, and make observations, and work with the natural world."

"I specialize in chrysopoeia and other forms of transmutation. Is that what you want? If you're only interested in playing with solvents, you don't need a guild. There's a cult of chemists running wild somewhere you could join up with. They've got no mind for real work." He almost snarled when he said "chemists."

I pursed my lips. "I *want* to apprentice with you. I think I've earned that."

Master Rahad barked a laugh when the doctor came running from the palace, slid on the wet grass, and landed in a heap next to the master alchemist's bloody legs. As the doctor recovered and rummaged in her bags for medicines, Master Rahad coughed again, and then a smile broke over his face.

"Caused, but yes, then earned. Well, young Sorin. With your mother's permission—as I've no power to steal the firstborn heir from another guild—you may start in my laboratory immediately."

What should have been joy transmuted into dread. No, not dread. That word was too heavy, too leaden. Melancholy, maybe, or frustration. Or maybe it was the weight of our history together, Mother's and mine, falling back on my shoulders.

Amada. Amada, now grandmaster woodcutter, whose heir sat with a master alchemist, dripped in his blood, trying desperately to leave what should have been a cherished birthright.

I closed my eyes and sat back on the grass. I pulled my cloak around my shoulders, brought my knees up, and rested my forehead upon them.

"Sorin?" Master Rahad prodded.

"Tomorrow," I said through the wool. "I'll start tomorrow, right after I talk to Mother."

Five: Salt

Master Rahad was bandaged quickly and taken inside the palace before we had a chance to speak further. There wasn't anything to say, anyway, until I found Mother and she released me from the woodcutters, which sounded so unlikely as to be ridiculous. I would convince her though. I had to. I wasn't going back to that house, but I would go to the grandmaster's guildhall, one final time, to find her.

The guildhalls—both the large ones held by Sorpsi and the smaller outpost ones held for the guilds housed in Puget and Eastgate—were only a few roads from the palace, separated by the plaza. I wound around the king's statue, turned left onto the brick, and again had to weave around people. They were primarily apprentices. No matter where I looked, I couldn't spot a master, which was weird, because the Queendom of Sorpsi held four guilds, and all of those grandmaster halls were here in this plaza. I didn't have time to debate the whys of that just now though. Instead, I pushed forward to the woodcutting hall where the grandmaster lived. The building was set back behind the main row, nestled between the master halls for the guild of glass and the carpenter's guild. The smell of sweetbread floated in the air from the dinner meals, and it was a nice relief from my own odor.

When I made the sharp turn between the two halls, the small woodcutting guild house came into view, dwarfed by the others in both size and stature. Mother was clearly here as her signature need for perfection was stamped on every surface. The ceramic tiling on the roof was perfectly laid. It had been moss-covered and cracking the last time I'd been here. The wood shingles on the walls were new and not yet gray from the sun. A rough lumber delivery was stacked in the covered bay to the right of the house, sorted by grade and still beading moisture from the end grain. Even the saw oil marks on the lumber looked fresh, and the lumber was quartersawn, something Mother always insisted upon.

I took a calming breath as I reached the wood door. Its paint was fresh and bright without a hint of algal growth, and here I was, damp and blood-soaked, shivering, my hair slicked against my head. The palace staff had offered me clothing, but I didn't want to deal with their questions, and I didn't want to dawdle either. Still, looking like this, I'd be lucky if Mother let me inside at all. Maybe we could say everything we needed to from the doorway. Maybe she wouldn't care because now she had dozens of apprentices she could pick from—masters, too, if she wanted, even the grandmaster's own firstborn daughter. Maybe everything would be all right.

I knocked.

It sounded too loud, set in from the main square as I was. When I looked around, however, there was no one on the street to notice.

No sounds came from inside, so I knocked again. This time, the door swung ajar. I walked in, daylight spilling across the threshold, and stopped just inside.

"Mother?" I called out.

My voice echoed, and the sound chilled me further. The room was bare. Where lathes and saws had once crowded, there were only shadows of sun-damaged wood flooring. The room had been an eating area where the master's first daughter and his thirteen fosters had shared a meal with Mother and me during our last visit. I'd sorted wood shavings by color, there, with the first daughter as we chatted about our parents and our inevitable inheritance under Sorpsi's matrilineal inheritance laws. She'd shown me her new carving knife, and we'd doodled our names into the lacquer finish on the bottom of the table. It, too, was gone. The walls were stripped bare of their marquetries and the paneling underneath sanded down and smooth to the touch.

My breath stuttered as I ventured past the threshold. Every room was the same. The three bedrooms were bare and smelled of rough-hewn wood. The outbuilding was scrubbed clean with a hint of lemon. The outdoor workspace didn't have a single scrap on the floor, not even curls of dust. Woodshops were never this clean.

Mother wasn't here. And if Mother wasn't here, if no one was in the grandmaster guildhall, then there *wasn't* a grandmaster. Residency was a requirement. Sorpsi held the woodcutter's guild. Without a grandmaster, and a guildhall, that meant...there wasn't a guild. We'd lost control, and there'd have to be a census, and the country with the most woodcutters in residence would win the guild, but... I forced myself to take a deep breath. Calm. I needed to work on being calm. They might have just... moved? The guildhall might not have been to Mother's liking, even after all her improvements. If I could find her before the queen found out and before the treaty talks...

I slapped the wall and cringed. The treaty talks! The census would come around any day now if it hadn't already passed. If they saw the empty guildhall, the woodcutting guild would be lost to Sorpsi, and the guild secrets along with it. We'd be stuck with...with *trade craft*.

Where was Mother?!

I moved to the courtyard and slumped to the dirt floor of the outdoor workspace. A thick layer of woodchips had covered it the last time I was here. It had smelled like burnt mahogany. The floor had been streaked with teak oil. It smelled sterile now, and new, and foreign.

Had other guilds suffered the same fate as the woodcutters? The textile guild, perhaps, with the cotton machine that the man had spoken about. That guild was housed in Puget, but still, what about it? Had the woodcutting guildhall closed down, the same as the clothing shop? What manner of machinery would cause *that*? Would it be machinery, to make a guildhall this clean? This...this suggested magic, and witches, and *gods*, why did it have to be witches? I'd had enough magic today to last a lifetime.

I gave in to the weight of my eyelids and the dizziness in my head and curled onto my side on the dirt, too tired to go back inside. My mind drifted away from the guildhall, away from the queen's forest, back to my own bed, somehow intact, and the thick blankets, the warmth of the fire. I could hear ghostly sounds, too, of saws on wood, of hammers, of laughter...

"Sorin? Sorin, what are you doing here?"

I sluggishly pulled from sleep and opened my eyes to a blur of blue and red. The imaginary sounds of saws and gouges faded into the shuffle of boots and the chatter of voices.

I rubbed at my eyes, failing to clear the blurriness away. A woman stood before me, my height, with long black hair braided against her scalp, in fine leathers. She wasn't wearing her circlet, but she didn't need to.

Her silhouette was enough.

In my sleep-fogged mind, I had expected to see the apprentices back and working with their handsaws, the treadle lathe spinning, and perhaps even a master expectantly standing over me, a sheet of fine veneer in their hand. Or maybe not a master, but at the very least my mother, annoyed and bemused, covered in wood shavings and leather and demanding to know why I had left Thuja.

Magda wasn't any of those things. She was the Royal Daughter of Sorpsi, heir to the throne, and she was staring at me as if I were a drunken smith in a shepherd's guildhall. I caught swirls of red from behind her— Queensguard, no doubt, further in the house—but the yard around me was as empty as when I'd fallen asleep, and the scent of lemon still hung in the air.

"Sorin," Magda demanded this time, her voice so much deeper than I remembered and laced with authority. I shivered at the formality. It cut deeper than it should have, especially since I was still having a hard time seeing her as anything other than the mischievous child I'd known.

She offered me a hand up, and I took it, my still-damp, bloody clothes clinging to my skin and the cloak wrinkled around me.

"Hello, Royal Daughter," I managed, swallowing, then squaring my shoulders. "It's been a long time."

Magda snorted and put her hands on her hips. "Yes, one could say that. You didn't think to say hello, apparently, after bringing Master Rahad back to the castle?" She continued to stare expectantly at me, and I pursed my lips, wondering how best to explain. That stare of hers could melt steel if you let it.

How long had it been since we'd stood together like this? Five years? Six, maybe, since Mother had forbidden me seeing her again and stopped our visits. Too long to pretend I still knew Magda. I didn't know how to act. I didn't know what to say. The royal daughter was strong, and well dressed, and...regal. I was, what? Damp, and I smelled like blood, and was sleeping on a dirt floor of an abandoned guildhall. And she was right. I had avoided her because it was hard to think of anything outside of getting Mother's consent and beginning my life with the alchemists.

I put a hand over my pouches, more to comfort myself than hide them.

Magda's eyes flicked down. "Alchemy?" she asked, incredulous, the irritation dripping from her voice. "One of the unbound guilds? That's new. What are you doing here, Sorin, if you're not a woodcutter?"

"Looking for Mother. I didn't do this." I gestured to the empty yard, then berated myself for acting so defensively. I had nothing to hide, but this encounter felt more like an interrogation than a reunion.

Magda raised an eyebrow and straightened her vest. "I know. Calm down. The guildhall has been closed for almost three weeks. Even before the grandmaster died, the journeys and masters were drifting away. Demand isn't what it used to be for any of the guild wares, and somewhere outside the three countries, they've got new saws and a way to cut nails with machines. We're still doing it by hand over in the smith guild." She tossed her hands up in frustration. "Hand-cut nails hold so much better, but people don't care. We can't compete with the price and speed of machined nails, and the woodcutters and carpenters can't keep up with the new saws." Her brow wrinkled. "Surely you know about this."

"I still... The grandmaster is dead? Really?"

"I just said that. Have you not left that Thujan house for five years?"

I looked away. I had, for the most part, been either in the Thujan woods or in Mother's house. It sounded terrible, thinking on it, but there'd been so much work to be done, and going into the town proper, or even venturing to the capital, all too often came with stares and comments I didn't want. "No, of course not."

Magda folded her arms across her chest. She tilted her head, but there was no playfulness in her expression— only irritation, or what looked like irritation. "Uh-huh. Where *have* you been, Sorin? Why aren't you a woodcutter?"

Her voice had that same authoritative tone I remembered from childhood, but I couldn't seem to meet it with the same brashness I'd once possessed. Magda's confidence, it seemed, had only grown in the intervening years. The same could not be said of mine.

Magda sighed and uncrossed her arms. "Never mind. It isn't important. I'm here because I want to turn the hall into the new Queensguard office. The one in the palace smells like woodsmoke from the queen's last visitors. Imagine my surprise to see Amada's daughter sleeping on the floor. Were you going to lay claim to the building through matrilineal inheritance? That's fine if you are. Just say the word, and I'll take a look at the abandoned textile hall instead."

I ignored the tone. I ignored the question. The word "daughter" hit like a slap, but I didn't correct her. I'd still used that word, back when we'd played together, and the royal daughter certainly didn't keep up to date on the evolution of guild children, no matter how familiar.

"No. No, I don't want the hall. I'm not a woodcutter. I lay no claim to it. Mother can," I started, but Magda cut me off with a sharp wave of her hand.

"Let's talk about Amada. Where is she? Why isn't she with you? I've never seen you not glued to her side or hopping at her every command." Magda's eyes were sharp with accusation, which I didn't understand.

I swallowed a lump in my throat and scratched the inside of my palms with my fingernails. My chest felt tight, and it wasn't because of my binding. "She was supposed to be here. She should have taken over for the grandmaster. That's why I'm here." I sounded meek. I hated that.

"Missing? That seems convenient. She'd *never* let you out into town alone. Where is she, Sorin?"

I blinked at the steeled words. My hands shook. "I really don't know!"

Magda growled and balled one of her fists. "Of course you don't. My only decent lead. Well, you should know, then, that the master woodcutter is under suspicion for kidnapping. She took a meeting with the queen at the palace, and neither came back out. Vanished. In a room with only one exit, no windows, and well guarded, and— damn it, Sorin, are you trembling? I'm not going to eat you!"

"Huh?" I looked down at my shaking hands and clasped them. They were sticky as well. I'd torn skin. "No. Of course not. I've just...I've had a rough night. I'm tired, that's all. I don't think Mother would kidnap the queen. They were friends, weren't they? Like us?" That last part felt wrong to say—like I was pleading for her to remember some fondness for me so she'd stop yelling. To prevent myself from derailing into babble, I asked, "Am I under arrest?"

Magda's eyes opened in startlement, and the tension dropped from her shoulders. She laughed then, a full, throaty sound that sounded much more like the Magda I remembered. The corners of her eyes crinkled. They were eyes I remembered, dark and intelligent. They were so familiar that if I hadn't been damp and cold, I could have easily imagined us standing on the palace lawn, the queen sipping tea and smiling, while we chatted about the curious topics of adolescence.

"Arrest? Don't be silly. You're being silly. Just, we should talk, you and I." Again, she looked at my clothing, and when she spoke, there was a trace of confusion in her voice. "I could get you some new clothes? Maybe something to eat? We could catch up."

My clothes. An uncomfortable reminder that my cloak didn't cover as much as I would have liked, and my sagging binding was, in fact, noticeable. Gods, I couldn't go back out into public like this. I couldn't make eye contact anymore. I pushed my arms into my sides as if I could make my chest somehow smaller.

"Hey, we'll sort it out." Magda laid a strong hand on my shoulder. The odd familiarity came again at her touch, along with the scents of flowers, the tang of metal, and an echo of childhood laughter. I looked at her muscled arm and wide shoulders, and memory crossed my mind. She'd joined a guild, hadn't she? Blacksmith maybe? I vaguely remembered Mother telling me about Magda completing her journey. That meant she was a master now, a master smith. I was...I was nothing. Not even an apprentice.

"Yeah," I said, my voice scratchy and hollow. I quickly corrected my informal words. "Yes, Your Highness."

Magda made a noise somewhere between a cough and a grunt. "We should get you dry, at least. The royal daughter can't be seen with a vagabond, right? No matter how well she'd grown up."

I understood the attempt at levity, but my emotions seemed to eat it, crushing it beneath the pain in my body, the wrong pronouns, and the events of the past day. Magda offered me her hand, calloused and ink-stained, but I declined. She shrugged, then lead me from the hall and onto the road. There, she pointed west to a string of shops with deep alleys along a brick lane. The second one, with a thatched roof and cedar plank siding, had a swinging sign with a glass wine decanter on it.

"I've set up an operations table at the pub there. It's closer to the Queensguard building than the palace, and I manage a lot more paperwork without servants nagging me. We'll go there. Pour you something warm to drink, and see if we can't get a runner for new clothes." She cocked her head to the side as she studied me, this time, her eyes lingering on the lumpiness of my chest. "This is a different look for you."

I didn't know how to respond, so I didn't. Magda looked so similar to her child self—the same neatly braided black curls, her skin a deep umber-brown, although more scarred now than it had been as a child. Her chin was more pointed than I remembered, her brow more furrowed, but she was still Magda. And I was still me, just a little different.

"Sorin?"

"I'm not a she," I mumbled.

She paused, eyes still questioning as they went down to my hips, then back to my chest, and finally, my face. "Okay," she said, nodding. "I can work with that. Come on. We'll get you dry, get you fed, and then maybe you can explain...well, explain Sorin the Alchemist. Explain why Master Rahad talked to me for two hours last night about fungal powders and some funny oil, and an enchanted palm, and Sorin, his next apprentice."

I nodded, still not speaking, and followed her from the guildhall into the main road, my arms wrapped high around my chest. Eyes followed us, but mostly, they were on Magda as they had always been in our youth. It was surreal to walk with her now, tracing cracked bricks around the old king's statue, tripping over the same clumps of weeds we'd tangled up in during our youth. We fell into the same old walking rhythm. If Mother wasn't at the guildhall, and she wasn't at the palace, then I had no idea where to look. I'd tried. Surely that would be enough for Master Rahad. If not, well, the royal daughter could release me from a guild bond too. Maybe if we chatted for a bit, I'd get up the courage to ask.

I stumbled on a chipped brick as I continued to follow her but managed to stay on my feet. Magda turned immediately around.

"You all right?" Magda's eyes flicked down to my crossed arms, and she frowned. "You'll lose your balance walking like that."

"I'm fine, and I'm used to it." I pulled my arms tighter because it was a lie, and she knew me well enough to know it. I expected her to laugh or shake her head, but Magda set her jaw in a manner I couldn't quite interpret, then reached out and lightly touched her fingers to the back of my left hand.

"No one will say anything, Sorin. Not with me around."

I smiled tightly. People didn't have to say anything. Sometimes their stares were plenty.

"It's really nice to see you again. I'm sorry if I didn't make that clear earlier."

I nodded, knowing my smile couldn't look anything but forced.

"I missed you."

I bit my lower lip and looked down at the red brick of the street. Something deep in my belly twittered. "I missed you too. Mother said—"

"It shouldn't have taken both our mothers going missing for me to see you." The bite returned to her tone, and when I looked up, her eyes were stormy again.

"I'm sorry." I didn't know how to explain, not in the middle of the capital, and not with so many eyes upon us, but neither could I look away. Magda snorted, and though she started walking again, her arm went around my shoulders and drew me to her, close enough that our shoulders and hips touched. She was warm, and I wanted to lean into her, but my shoulders stayed rigid, and my back refused to bend.

"You can explain at the pub, and it had better be detailed and sufficient. You're a terrible liar."

I shivered at the sting in her words. "Royal Daughter, we need to talk about the guilds. Also, in Thuja, people came, and..."

Magda directed me through the door to the pub, then pointed to a narrow staircase. She stepped away, leaving a gap of cool air between us. Her voice calmed and warmed, and when she spoke again, it was with a gentleness I never would have believed she possessed.

"It's all right, Sorin." A smile ghosted across her face, and I shut my mouth. I hadn't known what to say anyway. "Get clean, get warm, and then we can talk about the woodcutters, and the alchemists, and any other dead guild that will never return to Sorpsi. Then maybe, if we have time, we can talk about us."

Six: Mercury

Dry clothes, still warm from the sun, pressed against my skin. I finished wrapping my new binding and slid a long gray tunic over my head. It lay smoothly, but I ran my hands down the front anyway, clearing where the fabrics caught together. I pulled on soft cotton trousers that were loose on my legs and stuffed the ends into leather boots so new they squeezed my feet. On the belt, I hung my three pouches, dry now save for the very bottoms. My foraging knife, I'd already sheathed and attached.

My sash and old clothes had disappeared—taken while I was in the pub's upstairs bath. I wasn't sure if they'd come back, but I didn't need to see them again. It felt...cleansing to be in new clothes. As if the stains from the forests had been scrubbed from the textiles as well as my memory. I felt like an alchemist, no thick woodcutting leathers left to remind me of my past, only the pouches, snuggly tied to my belt, upon which to base my identity.

I left the bathing room and went down the stairs to the main floor of the pub. Magda waved me over to a small table covered in paper. In this lighting, she looked tired. Half-moons of darkness shaded under eyes, and her shoulders sagged almost imperceptibly. Only someone who had steadfastly measured height against hers for years, back-to-back and ramrod straight, would have likely noticed.

"Better?" she asked.

"Warmer," I replied as I ran a hand through my damp hair, trying to push it into some semblance of order. Without a fire to stand over, the waves would turn to curls, so I pulled the strands as I combed, straightening them.

Magda's body seemed to soften as she watched me grapple with a tangle. It was nice to know I could still amuse her, though I wondered what she thought of the much shorter cut. I'd had long hair when we'd last played together—hadn't cut it, in fact, until perhaps a week after we'd seen each other our final time. Sometimes I missed the length, and the way Magda or my mother would weave flowers and ribbons between my curls. But short hair brushed easier, and didn't get in your eyes, and didn't confuse people when you had a flat chest.

"We had to toss your clothes. The pub owner didn't think the stains would lift." Magda held her hand out, her palm cradling the small amount of money I'd had in my pockets. "Salvaged these. Is this all you're carrying?"

"I...yes. And the clothes can burn. That's fine." They could burn and take as much of Mother's legacy as possible with them. I took the money, put it back in my pocket, and turned my eyes to our table. It was bloodwood, by the color, and had only one chair at it.

"They're bringing food. Come sit, and we can talk."

Magda brought around another chair. I sat, but not before running my hands over the turned spindles that made up the back support. They were poorly done, with the beads and coves not aligning properly. If I turned it over, I suspected I would not find a carpenter's guild mark. The owner likely hadn't wanted to pay guild prices and had hired an amateur woodturner with a rudimentary understanding of guild skill. That was shoddy, and illegal, by guild law if not by country law. Mother would have demanded a refund and left the establishment. I wanted to toss the entire thing into the fireplace and strike the flint myself.

Instead, I sat on the wobbly thing as Magda gathered the paperwork to one side of the table and attempted to stack it. Wax seals hung from edges. I caught sentence snippets in passing as sheets slid from the tabletop and onto the floor. Treaty talks. King of Eastgate and his son. The Triarchy of Puget. Amada.

I wasn't going to be pulled into Mother's vortex again. "Royal Daughter, could I talk to you about Master Rahad? I need some help with guild semantics and—"

Magda cursed. "Could you help me with these papers first, Sorin?"

I let out a long breath and moved to my knees. The first sheet I lifted had Mother's name across the top, followed by the masters from three other guilds. The unique marks of all thirteen guilds that spanned the three countries of Sorpsi, Puget, and Eastgate covered the rest of the page.

I held the paper tightly between two hands, letting Magda gather the rest. Amada, master woodcutter. Ervin, master of glass. Walerian, master witch. Badria, master of textiles. All names I knew. People who had been to our home or us to theirs. Ervin had taught me color theory, back before I could even read. Badria had made me special clothes after menarche. Walerian...I hadn't known as well, but his name had been on Mother's lips often enough, and he was...a witch, apparently? I'd met a witch?

My hands shook. The paper rustled, threatening to tear. Were they *all* missing? Had anyone found...bodies? Mother out gallivanting was one thing. Mother dead was...well, very different.

Magda took the sheet from my hand, firmly, for I had it in a death grip and had to let go so as to not tear the edges. She stacked it in the middle of the others. "They're just daily reports. I don't know how much you need to... I mean, you know how it is. You saw the paperwork the queen used to do when we were little. It was what she used to make those folded paper animals you loved so much." Magda rubbed at her forehead with her palm, leaving a red mark. "Now it's my job, I guess, until she comes back." She forced a smile. "It's been a long time, Sorin. I've missed you. You're...different. Although I am, too, I'm sure." I caught a hint of melancholy in her voice. "Guess you had a good reason for disappearing. Don't suppose I could interest you in a puzzle?"

"A puzzle? Probably not, unless we can solve it tonight. I'm starting my apprenticeship with Master Rahad in the morning, which is why I wanted to speak with you. He wants Mother's permission, but with her gone, yours would work just as well."

If Magda caught the unmistakable eagerness in my voice, she didn't show it. Instead, she released a heavy sigh as the proprietor, a short woman with a plunging neckline, placed mugs of hot cider on the table. Another woman followed with bowls of wild rice and hot tea. The proprietor winked at Magda as she placed the second bowl and brought her arms together, pushing her chest forward.

I blinked several times and tried not to stare. It had to be...interesting, having that level of confidence in your appearance. I sipped at my drink, Magda's paperwork puzzle momentarily forgotten. The tea had a bitterness I was not expecting, and my cheeks puckered.

Magda laughed, her eyes on the intended target. "Thank you, Iroume. That will be all for now." The woman gave a short bow and left the room. Magda's eyes followed.

I coughed.

"Thoughts, Sorin?" Magda turned to smile impishly at me, as if half a decade, and a forest, weren't between us. She pinched a small amount of rice into a ball, then popped it into her mouth.

"She's very nice," I returned dryly. She did have very nice breasts, which I was sure Magda was driving at, but I didn't see the need to remark on them, especially not to the royal daughter. Besides, it wasn't as if I couldn't appreciate them on others. I just...wasn't keen on displaying my own.

"Not a fan?" Magda asked with her mouth still full. Her eyes went to my flattened chest, and suddenly she straightened, like I was a puzzle she'd just realized was put together differently. "Are you a man then? Your breasts did come in eventually. I remember. You never wanted to compare or talk about them when we were kids. You were so embarrassed."

That brought my mood crashing back down and I froze, unable to speak. Years ago, I'd have corrected her, or thrown something at her, or giggled and told her to shove off. We were too old to forgo our stations now, despite my reading of the paper earlier, and she was too old to be asking such forward questions.

Magda finally noticed my rigid posture and waved her hand about, managing to include my entire upper torso in her explanation. "I don't mean in reaction to the barmaid. This is just...new. Should I be thinking of you as the sister I never had, or the brother?"

"Royal Daughter, I am not a man." I managed to pull the words from my mouth. There were several more subtle ways she could have asked that question. She had chosen none of them. It was hard to stay mad at her, however, since her tired eyes were filled with sincerity. I took a large mouthful of tea, letting the heat scald my mouth, ensuring I'd have time to think before answering her inevitable follow-ups.

Magda surprised me by snorting and banging on the table. "At a formal function, that title is fine. Otherwise, I'm Magda, especially to you." She took a sip from her cup and winked at me.

My face became entirely too warm. "Fine. Magda. Would you please release me from the woodcutter's guild so I can begin my apprenticeship tomorrow?"

Magda's brow creased, and she pointed to the stack of papers. "I was actually hoping we could talk about Master Amada—"

"I don't care."

"Sorin—"

"No, listen." I took a deep drink of my cider and set the cup down on the table, more loudly than I'd intended.

"Mother is three weeks late returning. I was going to the alchemy fair to see Master Rahad but—" My voice wavered. Had Magda caught it? From the slight raise of her eyebrow, it seemed so. I continued in a rush, hoping to get the words out before emotion tangled them. If I was going to turn down this mysterious offer, I had to do so with confidence, or she'd just keep asking.

"Men came to the house and took me from it. I don't know who they were. Not guild. Not Queensguard, though they were dressed like it. They said they were sent by the grandmaster witch for Mother. A *grandmaster* witch, Magda! If Mother is in trouble, then it's her business, not mine. I've had enough."

What joviality remained bled from Magda's face. She pushed her bowl away and rested her head in her hands. "I'm sorry, Sorin." She rubbed her fingertips at her temples and didn't raise her head. The quietness of the inn was suddenly too much, and I pushed my chair back across the wood floor just to hear something.

Magda peered at me between two fingers. "You're not hurt, though, right? I mean, aside from the obvious." She looked at my forehead where I'd grated it across a tree during my forest escape. It had scabbed over but was still exceedingly sore.

Hurt. Did people's words count? Not likely. I was too old to let such things bother me, or rather, I should have been. Physical hurt was likely what she was asking about. I took another sip of cider and considered how best to answer. I didn't have a home, or family, currently. My small laboratory could be rebuilt, but Mother's shop, that would take years. While *I* didn't mind its destruction, Mother would.

So the answer was no, then. I was bruised but not hurt.

"I just need rest," I said. The next words came before I realized I was saying them. "I killed one of them."

Magda's eyebrows raised. "You did?" She looked me over incredulously. "How? You don't know how to use a sword. Unless Amada relented on that education? I know the queen let you sneak a few lessons with me, but that hardly counts."

I patted the belt in what I hoped was confidence, although my stomach knotted. "Alchemy. Trade level, but still. I've discovered a new use for some of the Thujan fungi. That's what Master Rahad was talking about. He's offered me a guild apprenticeship, but I can't take it without Mother's permission, or yours." I pursed my lips and stared at her, hoping she might actually respond this time.

Magda sat back and wrinkled her nose. The feet of her chair skipped a few millimeters across the floor, and I winced at the sound. She'd definitely scuffed the finish. "I don't know, Sorin. Woodcutting is much safer, I'd think. I can't imagine Amada wanting you to mess around with the unbound guilds. There's too much bad history there."

Damn it. "Yes, well, I'm done with woodcutting. I'm an alchemist now," I reminded her.

Magda turned to the window. It was early evening, and the sun beat through the glass. "I'd prefer you weren't in any guild if we're being honest," Magda said as she relaxed into her chair. "There's been a distinct hemorrhage of grandmasters as of late. They're fleeing by the boatload. To where, we don't know. Maybe outside the three countries to work in the new trade factories. Maybe to somewhere the factories can't touch. Either way, Sorpsi is effectively crippled without them. We've lost the woodcutters and the glass workers. We've all but lost the smiths, too, even though I'm still here. One smith does not a guild make." She paused and frowned. "I'm glad you weren't caught up in it. I'd worried, knowing how much you worked with Amada."

I grunted and sat back in my chair. "I *was* caught up in it, though I'm no master. I'm not even a journey. I refused all of Mother's offers."

"You are in woodcutting," Magda countered evenly. She swirled her fingers in her rice. "Master level, I'd guess, even without the journey to prove it. You couldn't have lived with Amada this long and not absorbed that level of skill. You've been a woodcutter since birth."

If she was going to jab, I could counter. "I don't want to talk about woodcraft. Tell me what you want, or why Mother's name is all over those documents, or release me from my guild and let me go back to the castle."

Magda tilted her head and frowned. Apparently, stations did matter then, if not names. I turned from the table, toward the bar. It was a darker wood than the furniture, but with the glossy finish, I couldn't make out species. This finish was oil of some sort, that much I could tell, though not a well-made one. More cut corners, it seemed.

"There isn't a single master or grandmaster left in Sorpsi, other than you, myself, and Master Rahad." She tapped the stack of papers. "These are leads, some of which directly concern the queen and Master Amada." Magda put her elbows on the table, rested her chin on her hands, and stared pointedly at me. "I know you want that apprenticeship, but...you need to come with me. Whatever trouble our mothers are in, chances are they are in it together. I suspect this is more than just guilders looking for greener pastures free of the threats of industrialization."

Magda stood, grinning, and offered me a hand. My heart sank. "What do you say? Want to go an adventure? A real one, this time?"

I spun in the chair to face her, a deep frown on my face. "I am not going anywhere, except to bed. In the morning, I am going to Master Rahad's alchemical laboratory and starting my apprenticeship. *Please*, Magda. Mother can take care of herself!"

"But can you?"

Seriously? I'd foiled a kidnapping attempt and fended off a sentient tree, and she was worried about me leaving the capital? I stood, refusing to look up at her like the tradesperson I was. My chair fell back and hit the floor, cracking along the top rail. No point in feeling bad over a heretical chair. I kicked the thing to the side, and it hit the table leg with a hollow *thunk*.

Magda put her left hand on the pommel of her sheathed sword, although what message she hoped to send by doing that I couldn't imagine. Would she run me through if I declined? That'd be a fitting end to my day.

"I'm not giving you a choice, Sorin." Her tone held the formality of the courts. "I was trying to make it sound less like a command. You need to come with me. Whether you do it out of familial loyalty or because you're being forced doesn't much matter. You need protection, and as fond as I am of Master Rahad, in his current state, he is in no position to offer you any." She sighed. "Please don't look at me like that."

I suppressed the urge to growl. "And who is protecting you?"

She folded her arms to match mine. "I don't need protection. I know how to use a sword."

Her patronizing tone rankled. "I'm not exactly defenseless, you know." I kicked at the fallen chair again, which stubbornly refused to break further. "Where are you even going?"

"Tomorrow I leave for the mountains, then over to Puget for the treaty talks." Magda tempered her tone, although her posture stayed rigid. "Someone has to negotiate for Sorpsi so our borders aren't redrawn. After that, I'm traveling beyond Puget to see the source of these mechanization rumors for myself."

"But the queen?" I asked, cutting in. "Isn't someone going to look for her?"

Magda nodded. "I am."

"Don't you have...people for that?"

Magda's gaze remained level. "Not that I trust. I'm taking the forest route to our side of the mountains, at least at first. There is a village of interest on the border, right on the trade route. It's not far from where Iana's Lake is rumored to be, as a matter of fact. A few of the missing masters were sighted in the border town of Miantri. It's the best lead we have, and it is on the way to Puget." She gestured toward the stack of sheets. "I have some...lists. Not as specific as you might think. It's a lot of conjecture, but Sorpsi is crippled like this. If I can find a few grandmasters, or even masters, before the talks, and convince them to come back, I might save some of our borders. There is a very real possibility of losing our country, Sorin. I'm taking this seriously, despite what your tone implies."

Had the royal crest been on the sheet I'd seen, along with the guild marks? I couldn't remember. "The queen?" I asked again. "Has she been seen, or are the sightings just of Mother?"

Magda's head rolled back as she exhaled. "Gods, Sorin, those papers weren't for you to read. I'll find the queen, but it might not be before the treaty talks. I have to find the guild masters first. I can rule in the queen's stead, but without the guild masters, I'll have no country to rule over once the treaty talks commence. Without guilds, by Iana's law, we have no right to our borders. Our land will be divided between Puget and Eastgate. No guilds, no country. That's just how it's written."

I let out a long breath and rubbed my nose. "Magda, I don't want to go with you." It sounded too coarse since a sizable part of me *did* want to go with her and perhaps find the friend I'd lost. But a bigger part of me, the louder part, wanted that apprenticeship.

"Not even to help find Amada? Your mother is in danger, Sorin. I'm sure of it."

"Magda—"

"She could be injured! Injured, or trapped, or kidnapped, along with my mother. We have so many reports and—" She pointed to the stack of papers as her voice became more insistent. "—she's the grandmaster of woodcutting. You know her better than anyone, and where she might be. And if she's dead, Sorin, if she's dead, you're all we have... I can't lose you too."

Magda met my eyes in a stare that felt like it might stop my heart. I opened my mouth, unsure what would come out, but Magda spoke first.

"Sorpsi can't lose the woodcutters."

I rolled my eyes. The woodcutters. Of course.

"There's really no one else? No apprentices? Journeys?"

She shook her head, the ends of her braids bobbing across her back. "You're all that's left."

"Damn it, Magda." I scuffed the toe of my boot on the floor. I could deal with Mother's disappointment, but I couldn't shoulder the responsibility of destroying an entire guild—especially not the one I'd been raised in, and I certainly didn't want the fate of the woodcutters on my shoulders. *Damn it*! Mother's house had blown up, and I could feel the rough cedar walls closing in on me. Suffocating me. Crushing me.

"Master Rahad will wait for you," she said, her voice soft. "I'll ask him to. It's just a little delay."

"A delay during which I follow you around the mountains like a lost kitten," I retorted. "Instead of starting the life I've wanted, that's always been just out of reach."

Magda bit her lower lip thoughtfully, then walked to the door, opened it, and gestured for two Queensguard to come inside. They were men, one of whom yawned into the fading light.

"Take Sorin to the palace."

I looked at the royal daughter, dumbfounded. The guards nodded and came toward me, sluggishly, as if they'd been asleep at their posts. With Magda being, well,

Magda, I suspected this particular job did not see a lot of action. I backed away, skirting my fallen chair and, stupidly, ended up with my back against the wall.

"How would you deal with them, Sorin, if they were bandits on the road? Show me you can defend yourself if I leave you with Rahad."

"Uh." I fingered the pouch of red pigment. "This isn't really the best setting to be using my powders."

Magda rubbed her temples again and sighed.

One of the guards grabbed my left arm. "Come on now. As she says."

I stomped my foot and jerked my arm away. Gods take this whole situation, this whole damn day! I was tired of being dragged around, whether by kidnappers or Queensguard, and knowing my mother, whatever mess she was in, was half her own doing. If she was in that mountain town by choice, no royal daughter was going to convince her to leave. I didn't want to go on this trip, but I couldn't just let the woodcutting guild die either. If I was going to be forced to follow Magda, it was going to be on my terms.

"Sorin—"

"*No.*" I unfastened the pouch of red pigment and eased open its strings. As both guards made to grab for me, I flicked my wrist to the right, sending a few granules onto a nearby chair.

The chair exploded in a shower of red flowering crystals.

I ducked instinctively, but the guards did not. They grunted and tripped over one another as wood and crystal pelted them. Several pieces hit my tunic, small enough that they wouldn't even bruise. I hadn't used enough to start a chain reaction, so the crystals were stable and wouldn't get any bigger, but it had definitely been enough to get Magda's attention.

"I don't need protection," I said calmly as splintered wood crackled at my feet and hooks began to form on the edges of the "flowers." I stood and kicked the debris away. "If I come, it's as your equal. Not in stature, obviously, but in skill. And I'm not your ward, and whether or not we find Mother, you *will* release me from my guild when this is all done, right?"

Magda looked incredulous. The guards stepped back—way back—and watched me. "I...Sorin, this isn't a game of bandits where we go down to the lake and throw stones at the water while trying to get as muddy as possible. We have to go to outlying villages. We have to travel over a glacier since that's the only path that connects the three countries to one another and the rest of the world. Granted, your display was impressive, but you can't fight, and you can't strategize; you don't know the first thing about snow and ice, and you know virtually nothing about the political landscape." She looked back at the remains of the chair and the palm-sized red crystals that had sprouted from the wood fragments. "Can you really control those things? Wouldn't it be safer to be my extra set of eyes? My insight into Master Amada's haunts?"

I walked up to her, arms wrapped across my chest, and stated, as firmly as I could, the only thing I could think of to make her to take my powders seriously.

"I have poisons. I can do things no other alchemist can do. I don't work in transmutation. I work in solvents and reactions."

The guards shuffled to the other side of the bar, making no attempt to hide their haste. I snorted. I hadn't said I was going to poison *them*.

"Magda?" I prodded, refusing to look away from her.

Magda closed her eyes and groaned. "Poisons are an intimate weapon. Not very good against bandits."

I bit my lip in frustration, unhooked my belt, and tossed it onto the table with our food. "Not just poison," I said through gritted teeth. "These extracts, they're something we've never seen before. At least let me show you what they can do. More than scaring two guards and shattering a chair anyway."

Magda stared at me. Her eyes didn't wander, but I couldn't help blinking at the intensity. We'd had staring contests when we were younger, but this was wholly different. Here, I was being assessed by my monarch, tried and stretched and imagined based upon childhood familiarity and one short bar conversation. It was ridiculous. I felt ridiculous. I *was* competent. Well, maybe not to ride a horse, but I could take care of myself, and I could do it without a sword.

Finally, Magda nodded. "One test. But this doesn't negate the danger of the trail, or the glacier. Powders or not, you are not to even *attempt* leaving the trail without supervision. I'm heading high into the mountains. The terrain will be jagged, and I don't know who will be out looking for stray guilders without an obvious means to protect themselves. Afterwards, once we find the queen and if Amada is... I'll release you, I promise, but you have to stay alive long enough for me to do that, which means you have to listen. Okay?"

With anyone else, the jab would have hurt. With Magda, I brushed it off and nodded as I pushed past her, anticipation leaping inside me. I hadn't won many of our arguments when we were young. This felt like a greater victory than it probably was.

"No wandering. I agree." I gathered my belt from the table and motioned for her to follow as I headed to the center of the room.

While I walked, I fingered the contents of each pouch. I had plenty of the elf's cup and red dragon extract for a jaw-dropping display. The mango, the yellow I'd emptied on my kidnapper, was mostly gone, but likely there were a few granules left in the pouch. It would be enough to convince, of that I was sure. If she wasn't leaving until tomorrow, there was even a chance I might be able to make more, assuming Master Rahad let me use his laboratory and the fungi of the royal forest. He had all the other supplies I needed on hand, and I could show him how to make the bone oil too. That would definitely ensure my apprenticeship.

I stopped at the center table and set all three pouches on the top. Magda stood next to me, her broad shoulders touching mine as she squinted at the three lumps of leather. I smiled. I couldn't help it.

"How much money do you have on you?" I asked as I eased open the pouch with the red pigment. Inside, iridescent flakes gleamed back at me.

Magda raised an eyebrow. "Why?" she asked, drawing out the end of the word.

I smiled sweetly at her. "I just want to know how much of the pub I can destroy."

Seven: Air

"Wait, I'm riding this?"

"Will it be a problem?" Magda asked, coming over to me.

She handed me the reins to a horse that was twice my height. Maybe. Maybe it just looked that way because I had no idea what to do with the thing. I had forgotten we'd be riding. I should have remembered, but I'd been too focused on collection and extraction last night, and walking Master Rahad through the steps to make bone oil. I'd barely slept for two nights in a row. Now, rabbit fur lined the collar and hood of my new wool cloak. Now, I had a new foraging knife in my boot and felt like a competent human again.

Except now, I had to get on a horse and stay on it. That wasn't going to end well.

"The pub's west wall fell in this morning. When the table broke apart, or maybe after you dissolved the bar, it must have sent some of your fungus stuff into the air. We'll need to be mindful of that in the future." Magda paused and brushed a leaf from my shoulder while she attached a long, royal-blue cloak with a white ermine hood around her shoulders. It wasn't that early, but there were no servants about, nor guards. It seemed strange, but then again, what did I know about royal protocol? Definitely less than I knew about horses since all I could do was stare at the thing with my mouth hanging open.

"I don't think I've ever seen you quite so...animated."

"That's me," I said absently. I couldn't stop looking, wide-eyed, at the horse. With its chestnut-colored, silky coat, it looked expensive, or well-bred, assuming one valued horses by their size. Hopefully, my ineptitude wouldn't break it.

Magda must have caught my hesitation. "You know how to ride, right? Or is that another thing Amada wouldn't tolerate?"

I laughed awkwardly and toyed with the pouches on my belt. "I can figure it out. I'm just..." I searched for deflection. "I'm just warm in the cloak. I'm not used to such heavy materials. It's never very cold in the forests of Thuja."

Magda's forehead wrinkled, and she pursed her lips. "The temperature will drop fast as we climb. Keep it on. About the horse—" She patted the thing's forehead. Possibly its nose. I wasn't very familiar with horse anatomy. "If you have problems, call up to me. We can ride double for a while until you get the hang of it."

Something—nervousness probably—fluttered in my stomach. "Wouldn't that be hard on the horse?" I asked. My own horse butted my cheek with its nose, and I stumbled backward. "Is it supposed to do that?"

Magda laughed and nudged me back to the horse's side. "Put your foot here. No, the other one. Good. Now grab this." She put my hands on the pommel. "Pull up and swing. There!"

I clung to the saddle. The ground was a dizzying distance below me. I forced my head up.

"They're a lot sturdier than you think, horses," she said as she tapped the reins. "Yours is male, and called Peanut." She grinned when I started to protest the absurdity of the name. "It's a joke, Sorin. Calm down. It's just a horse. You didn't used to be this serious."

I stopped talking, but I did not calm down. My gods, if I fell from the saddle, I'd crack my head open. Then I'd be trampled by the horse and my skull crushed. Hopefully, some alchemist would be around to use *my* bones to make oil because, otherwise, that was a terribly wasteful way to go.

"Head out!" Magda called from the front. The palace gates opened, and she disappeared beyond them. Peanut stayed.

"Go!" I hissed into the horse's ear. "You're supposed to walk now."

Peanut's ear flicked at me, and he turned his head, his eyes unconcerned.

"Go!" I jostled my hips in the saddle. The horse snorted. I tried again, more forcefully this time, bringing my legs into the movement. When my heels connected with the horse's side, Peanut whinnied and finally moved forward. I gripped the pommel, reins wound around my wrists, and prayed to whatever gods there were that I stayed upright, especially if Magda was watching.

*

I fell off just as the sun hit midday position.

It wasn't Peanut's fault, despite his size and refusal to follow the most basic of verbal commands. We'd been on the main road for almost four hours, heading steadily upward, and my thighs were done. The capital expanded throughout the foothills, and the elevation increased almost the moment we left the city walls. Thick conifer forests bordered the road and pass. I was glad of the cloak well before the first hour passed.

Now, the wind stung my fingers. I'd wrapped my hands in the ends of my cloak, but that made it hard to hold on to the saddle. I'd tried to shift, to get a better grip, while at the same time, Peanut had sidestepped a large rock. My thighs should have gripped, but they didn't. I slid right off the saddle. I didn't hit the ground as hard as I could have, however, since my wrists were still caught up in the reins. That left me dangling from a horse with biting tension on my wrists.

"Whoa!" Magda must have heard me fall.

I hadn't called out, hoping I could sort it before she saw and save myself the embarrassment, but my legs refused to support my weight. Magda rode back, dismounted, and, once my wrists were free, helped me to stand. I kept my head down. I didn't want her to see my embarrassment, nor the way I set my jaw against the pain in my legs. My thighs felt rubbed raw, and even my spine tingled from the tortured hunching I'd regressed to halfway through our ride.

"Are you all right?" she asked in far too serious a tone.

"I'll figure it out." With her help, clutching at her sleeves, I stood. "See? Fine."

Magda looked dubious, and I scowled when I realized she was suppressing a smile. "You have any magic potions to help your legs adjust?" she joked as I wobbled.

"I'm an alchemist," I corrected as I collapsed at her feet on the frozen road. I again tried to push up against rebelling thigh muscles. When my legs once again gave out, Magda lowered me to the ground.

"So, no magical cures then?"

"Magic and alchemy are completely different things. I'm not interested in defying the rules of the world." I looked up to curse Peanut and saw Magda's amused concern. At least she wasn't laughing. She could have this riding business. Once we finished this ridiculous quest of hers, I was never getting on a horse again. Alchemists didn't need to ride horses. They had solvents, which were much less likely to toss you onto the ground. "If I wanted to be someone's amusement, I could have stayed in Thuja," I said sourly.

Magda sobered and knelt next to me. "We need to make the village by nightfall, which is sooner than you might think at this elevation. Let me help?"

I shrugged. Magda and I had ridden a hobbyhorse together, once upon a time, through the palace gardens. The queen had commissioned it for my sixth birthday. How different could this be? It was embarrassing, sure, especially after my talk in the pub, but at this point, I was so cold I'd take the extra body heat, embarrassment or not.

Magda put an arm under my knees and another under my arms and picked me up from the ground. I was too surprised to object and was immediately swept into the smell of leather and the wintergreen oil Magda used on her hair. The smithy had given her unusual upper-body strength, and she carried me with little effort toward her horse. I kept my eyes on the clasp of her cloak, intent on not looking down toward her breasts or up at a face that had captivated me from my earliest memories. My heart beat wildly from Magda's arms, from our proximity, and from how utterly incompetent I looked. I couldn't walk. Magda was being reasonable, but as I rested my forehead against her shoulder, each step she took was a further reminder of how she thought I needed protection.

"I'll do better tomorrow," I muttered as she set my foot in the stirrup and helped me mount the horse. She tied Peanut's reins to the back of her saddle, then settled in behind me, the reins in one hand and her other arm wrapped around my waist.

"Tomorrow, I don't need a rider." She kicked the horse, and we started climbing again. It was much warmer with her behind me, though I still needed to bring my cloak around my hands. "Tomorrow, I'll need your insight on Amada, and that will likely also involve walking, so try to relax for the rest of the trip."

I turned back to look at her. Her face was bland and stiff, which had always meant mischief. "What?" I asked.

"I could tell you a story to pass the time," she said. The side of her mouth quirked.

"Okayyy," I drawled. "What story?"

Magda's voice turned higher, and she flared her left arm out wide like a bad stage performer. "Iana, my super great-grandmother, came from some glacier town that doesn't exist."

I closed my eyes and groaned. "I told you that story *one* time to get you to sleep because you were trying to dare me out into the royal forest again. The actions made you pay attention."

Magda smirked. "Oh, I know. I remember it well." Her voice went high again. "Because Iana's town, you see, is lost to history." She made a brushing movement with her arms which was probably supposed to represent time passing. I'd have opened my hands up like a book, but it was silly to compare pageantry on horseback.

Magda continued, doing her best to imitate my ridiculous childhood rendition of the forming of the three countries. "It was a town hidden beyond Miantri. The king's army took her to train on the farms. She became a master of the light sabre and small sword instead of being apprenticed. Then at fifteen, the king picked her for transfer because he was *really bad* at fencing and wanted those skills for his own."

She made a stabbing motion and gave a fake groan.

"You're *really bad* at this," I told her.

"Hush. Then she got all mad and escaped, and she went back onto her glacier and found the biggest of the magic amulets, which you swore didn't exist but have now been literally attacked by a palm tree, so I'm guessing you changed your mind on that one. And she broke it because the amulet held magic in the water, which is how the king could do the transfers, to begin with, because it got the spell he needed into everyone's body." Magda paused and whispered into my ear. "It still amazes me how you can have such an eye for detail in woodwork but not in storytelling."

"That story doesn't have any relevant details," I muttered back. "Amulets are amulets. They're just holders for magic, and the king put a big one in a glacial lake that fed every major river and thereby poisoned all of Gasta

Flecha so he could steal people's skills instead of earning them himself. What more do you need to know?"

Instead of responding, Magda went back to her—my—story. "Iana broke the amulet with a sword she'd imbued herself. With herself." Magda said the last part with an involuntary shudder. "Then she killed the king because he was gross and magic, and took his throne. She divided old Gasta Flecha into three separate countries, one of which was Sorpsi, made the guilds, and kept the witches forever separate because of their involvement in the subjugation of Gasta Flecha's women. And because you hate witches and always make them the villains of your stories. The endddddd." She finished the last word with a deep, bellowing voice.

I snorted and rolled my eyes. It was ridiculous how easy we could become ten again.

"You know there's more to the story than that, right?" Magda asked me in her normal voice, suddenly much more serious.

I shrugged and turned back around to face the winding road ahead. There was more to every story. Like how a witch—some friend of the queen's—had come to Mother's house when I was fifteen and offered to magically remove my breasts. Like I needed correcting. Like I was *broken*. I shivered. Those kinds of details just didn't need repeating.

I forced myself to focus on the present. There were mostly spruce trees now, lining the path, and some firs farther back. It wasn't snowing, but the needles were capped in white and the horses' hooves clacked on the frozen ground. I wanted to relax into her and the smells of our shared youth, but I couldn't. My apprenticeship dragged at my mind, pulling me away from Magda and the easy friendship she offered.

"What is the trade in Miantri?" I asked her, for Mother had never seen fit to have us visit the town proper.

"They trade mostly in furs and lumber, although they're right up against the tree line. They're only a few kilometers from our border with Puget. We have one night there. We'll have to leave in the morning to make Celtis, the capital of Puget, in time for the negotiations." Her horse jumped a fallen log that crossed the road, and I fell back against Magda as she tried to keep me upright. Her arms tightened around me. I welcomed the additional warmth.

"The grandmasters?" I prodded, hoping for more information from the sheets than I had managed to get on my own. It'd be great if Mother happened to be at this first village, and I could gather her up and head back to the capital. Then she could go to the guildhall, and I could be done with this whole mess.

Magda pursed her lips. "Sorin... Yes, but this is just between us, all right? We don't need to start a panic."

I looked as serious as I could at the woman who, the last time I'd seen her, had snuck a toad into the cook's breadbox to see if we could hear her scream on the other side of the castle. "I promise not to start a panic."

Magda shook her head, but I caught the edges of a smile on her lips. "The grandmaster of glass was spotted in a pelt shop in Miantri, missing four fingers." Her voice trailed off, and her eyes refocused on the road.

"And?" I prodded.

Magda let out a deep breath. "He had a woman in tow."

I raised my eyebrows.

"Don't jump to conclusions. It's a tradesperson account, and a hurried one at that. It's enough to identify our glass grandmaster because of that mole on his chin, but not the woman. She was too bundled around the face, apparently. They said she was disoriented."

"Why? It can't be that cold, can it? Do you think she had hypothermia?"

"It *is* that cold. Note how your back is welded to my front."

I scowled, hoping that hid any blush that might decide to bleed onto my cheeks.

"Fine. It's not that cold. Maybe he just lost those fingers due to torture. The cooper's guild has never been on speaking terms with the glassblowers, so this might just be standard guild rivalry, noting how close we are to Puget."

Turning in the saddle to look at Magda was making me motion sick. I turned back around, but not before she finally looked at me. There were small crinkles in the far corners of Magda's eyes, and a smile played at her mouth. Mischief. No different now than when she was twelve. I fought a smile.

"You're keeping your hair pretty short these days, Sorin. For the trade, or otherwise?"

My smile fell away. "Stop it, Your Highness. If this was just coopers, we wouldn't be going to Miantri. Is Mother there, or the queen?"

Her body straightened at the title, and she pushed farther back into the saddle. "The grandmaster was the only one who could be tentatively identified. Ignore the woman. She died a few hours after they hit the town. All the other details are vague, and I'm not going to pass them on."

"Uh-huh," I muttered. "We're chasing ghosts in a mountain town for fun then. Right."

"We don't know anything about her, Sorin." Magda's voice was trying to soothe. "All of our grandmasters are missing, as are most of the masters, and over half are women. It could be any of them or just a regular woman. She could be anyone."

"Just a village woman doesn't warrant investigation by the royal daughter," I shot back. "The queen's favorite woodcutter, on the other hand, or the queen herself..."

An arrow ripped the air. Peanut screamed, and I heard flesh hit the ground.

"Down!" Magda cried. She slipped from her horse and pulled me from the saddle, my legs still raw and useless. She slammed us both onto the dusty snow. My head didn't hit, thanks to her arm, but pain still shot up my side.

"What—"

"Stay down!" Magda jumped to her feet and pulled her sword from its tie on her horse. The horse snorted and stomped in disapproval. Magda transferred the sword to a sheath on her belt, then pulled a bow and nocked an arrow.

To our right was Peanut, on his side, with an arrow through his eye. The ground fogged red beneath him as heat from his blood steamed the snow. Arrows shot from the canopy, one hitting Peanut again, and the other just missing Magda's head. She motioned for me to retreat further, and I finally listened. I clawed my hands at the frozen ground, fingers burning in the snow as I pushed back toward the scrubby trees. I wanted to help, could help, but with swords and arrows, I'd never get close enough to anyone to use the extracts. Maybe I could pick them off one by one if any came back out to the road. Maybe film their boots to the ground, or—

From the other side of the road and well into the forest came the clashing of metal. More arrows soared, tearing through Magda's cloak and across her left thigh. She brushed unconcernedly at the wound and started across the road.

"I can't just stay in the open. I need to go in after them."

"I could come from behind, take one of them by surprise," I yelled out to her, pointing to my pouches.

Magda yelled back, from the other side of the road as she ran. "No. Stay."

"I can help!"

She threw down her quiver of arrows. "*Stay.*"

It was an order from the royal daughter. I exhaled and slumped back down against my worn-out legs. No more arrows sang, but the moment Magda disappeared into the thicket of thin trees, the clang of steel increased, along with the snapping of branches.

"Be safe," I murmured. I wrapped my cloak around myself and tried to warm my fingers. As I pulled the material tighter, the fabric caught on the pouches on my belt. I tugged against them in frustration. Magda was probably right. What good were fungal extracts in an actual battle? A sword would always win because it was faster, came out of its sheath easier, and the user didn't have to worry about accidentally killing themselves with it. I needed to be armed with something more than my foraging knife, and I needed to figure out how to use it or I'd be relegated to my backside for every minor skirmish.

"Hello, Sorin."

The voice came from behind me, but no sound accompanied it. No snapping branches, no crunch of snow.

I jumped to my feet and spun. The pain in my legs was immediate, and I fell back down to my knees in a whimper while I stared at the woman in the forest. The voice was so familiar, the notes of jovial dismissiveness so perfect, that it didn't occur to me to be afraid.

In front of me, three trees back, stood my mother.

Eight: Mercury

Mother was whole. Alive. She wore no coat despite the temperature, and her clothes looked freshly pressed. Her hair sat exactly as it had when she'd left Thuja, the black ringlets pinned to cascade down her back, keeping her face clear.

"Mother," I choked as I pulled myself up on a tree. She looked bored, it seemed, standing there in the freezing snow without cloak or cape. How had Magda convinced me she would be otherwise? Mother had managed on her own for years. She had taken these trips since I could remember. She didn't need saving, especially from me.

"What are you doing out here? Aren't you cold?" Snow had started to fall in pinpricks of white that stuck to my cloak and eyelashes. My rational mind continued to misfire. A part of me wanted to run to her, wrap her in my cloak and cry that she was alive, and safe, and unhurt. Another part wanted to scream at her for her wanderings and secrecy. I had delayed my chance with Master Rahad, my last real chance at an apprenticeship, trailing a woman who needed no help at all.

My rising frustration leaked into tears. I batted them with frozen fingers. Mother, instead of commenting, looked at her arms as if she'd only just realized there should be something covering them. When she looked back at me, her face was still smiling and unconcerned. She didn't comment on my tears, or my embarrassment, or that she was standing, unaffected by the swirling snow, in nothing but a cotton tunic and leather vest. The image chilled me. She looked like a dream. A mirage. I blinked and wiped at my eyes.

"I've been felling. Must have worked up a sweat." Her voice had little inflection, and when she took a step toward me, I saw that her boots were thin hide and unlined. Her feet had to be nearly frozen.

"Where?" I sounded accusatory. Mother's expression didn't change. She never tolerated that tone from me.

She looked back over her shoulder. "Just back a ways. I have something for you too. Something I bought in Thuja that I forgot to give to you before I left. I can give it to you on our way back home. You shouldn't be out here, Sorin. It's dangerous. Come." She turned and headed east, farther into the forest of swirling snow, blackberry, and heavy pines.

I followed. It was automatic, to heed her directions, and Mother always had been a bit...off. It was those parts I usually preferred about her—the parts of her that grinned over new saws, or the color of my fungal pigments on a piece of maple veneer. If she wanted to show me something in this forest, it was certain to be exciting. And if she was here, my trip with Magda was done. We could go back to the capital, together, and leave Magda to her negotiations. That was what I wanted, wasn't it?

Crunching steps took me from the edge of the road onto a game trail lined with sorrel of a variety I'd not seen before. I paused. The trees around me were uniformly coniferous, and all had thin stems and some type of shoot damage. There were no hardwoods, not even spindly vine maples. There was no merchantable decorative timber here at all, nor even any of use in marquetry. The berry bushes grew small and stunted, and any fungi in these types of forests were not well suited to the dyes Mother liked.

This was a useless forest for a marquetry woodcutter unless she'd sectioned burls from some unseen redwoods. Did she need help carrying them perhaps? Without a horse, we'd never get them home. Did she have a sled?

I brought my left foot up, momentarily energized by the thought of a burl pile. We'd talked about a marquetry with a swirling lake. A redwood burl, stained with elf's cup, might just...

No. I stopped myself and lowered my foot. Mother became animated with talk of figured woods. We shared the passion. A pile of burls would be an opportunity for celebration, but the woman picking through the forest ahead acted with eerie calmness.

"Mother?" I called out to her, stepping back as I did so. Suddenly the main road seemed much safer than the game trail, even though part of me wanted to see her eyes light up at whatever wooden treasure she'd found, to forget our house, and our history, and just share a moment of happiness.

"What is it, daughter?" She turned her head to look at me, her smile frozen to her face.

Cold stung my widening eyes. My insides prickled and my chest convulsed. I sucked in air, desperate to stay quiet while my mind cried out. I edged backward. One step. Then another.

"Sorin?" She held a hand out—a hand without a glove, without a trace of frostbite despite the wind and snow. I quickened my backward pace, not wanting to take my eyes from her. Step. Slide. Step. Mother matched my pace, keeping the distance between us constant, and while the wind tossed my cloak around my ankles, Mother's hair and clothes continued to hang unmolested.

Another step and a blackberry vine grabbed at my pants. I jerked away, snapping off the branch in the process. I looked down at the offending patch, hoping to avoid further entanglement, and when I looked back up, Mother was there. A handspan away. Smiling.

I froze. I forgot the sting of her words in the wave of heat that rolled across my skin, melting snow from my hair and dripping cool water over my eyes. The heat thickened everything to steam, and it clogged my lungs, stealing my breath. I gasped for air in quick bursts as my heart raced. Who was she? What was she? Gods, was I going to die here, in this useless, coniferous forest?

"Sorin?" she asked, her tone too sweet. She leaned in, her nose centimeters from mine. There was no smell to her breath—only heat that compounded to a near boil. "I've missed you. We need to talk. I have information on the queen. I know you're looking for her too. We should move back, though, from the road. I don't want to be seen."

Sweat and melting snow stung my eyes, but a drop of sense finally filtered through. I grabbed at my pouches, gliding fingers over each in turn. The heat, this blistering, unnatural heat, was certainly from magic. Little in alchemy caused such an intense exothermic reaction. Not a person then, at all, but likely a sending. A conjuring. Something solid enough to run me through if it wanted to. That was the question, however. What *did* the conjuring want? Not to hurt me, it seemed, at least not yet. That wasn't much of a comfort.

I took deeper breaths and tried to slow my gasps. She was finely done, for a conjuring. As she stayed close, awaiting my response, I let my rational mind step to the side to admire the laugh lines, the crow's feet, the left-cheek dimple, all in perfect placement. Mother's guild tattoo, even, was there, although as I tilted my head to study it, I realized something was amiss in this perfection.

The tattoo should have been a branch with a cluster of needles at one end and a broad leaf on the other. Mother's was a rock maple, to mark her residence in Thuja. This tattoo looked different. Its edges bled back into the surrounding flesh. It looked...corrupted. Old. A section of the conjuring poorly done, or well done, and there were limits to magic and guild marks.

I rubbed at my neck where my own guild mark should have been. The guild mark was a sacred thing. To have it so distorted... I shivered.

"What do you want, sending?" I said it loudly—much louder than needed. I wanted to hear myself, to hurt my ears. I needed to define the boundary between reality and dreams.

"Sorinnnnn," the sending breathed into my ear. "Amada's heir. Neither woodcutter nor alchemist. Strong, to abandon Amada. Won't you come with me, back to your home? I can repair your house. I can speak about your mother." The sending's hand raised to trail a finger along my throat. The heat from her burned my skin and raised blisters. I swallowed a scream and backed into a spruce trunk, the dead branches cutting me through my clothes.

"No?" she asked. Her mouth turned, finally, to a frown.

Any control I had over my breathing was lost. What would work against such a creature? The blue-green elf's cup? I had no solvent carrier. The red flaming dragon pigment? Maybe, if she was, in fact, solid enough. The yellow then, golden mango fungus. It could coat, maybe bind. The conjuring looked like it had at least partial solidity.

It closed the distance between us again. "Daughter?"

I yanked my third pouch from my belt. Keeping my arms low, I pulled at the ties, making sure to keep the opening pointed away. The wind died. This close to the conjuring, it deflected around the both of us. Even a small flick would work.

"Get away from me," I stuttered at the thing reached out again. I raised the pouch and tilted, ready to empty the contents. "I've no business with—"

"Sorin? I told you stay put." A gloved hand fell on my shoulder. I screamed, dropped my pouch, and pulled left, falling lengthwise into a blackberry bramble. The thorns tore at my face and hands, snagged on my burned neck, and I screamed again as the branches held me like hands. It had me! It had me and it was burning and—

"Sorin!" It was Magda, her hands out, trying to calm my flailing, panicking limbs. "Calm down! Everything is all right. I've taken care of them." Her words settled around me, yet I continued to pull. Seams ripped.

Magda eyed me, stepped back, then reached for my pouch, which lay half open on the sorrel in front of her.

"No! Leave it be! Mother!" I turned as much as I could, hoping Magda would follow my gaze. She had to run. I was caught but she could still get away, and Mother...Mother!

Except...except the conjuring wasn't there anymore. Where she had stood was simply a cluster of vine maples covered in light snow. I settled into the thicket of thorns, sinking deeper. I hadn't imagined it. There were no footprints, but I could still feel the heat on my face and the sound of her words—her voice so perfectly that of Amada the master woodcutter. Fluid ran down the side of my neck, likely from a heat blister. My heart still pounded. It had been real.

Magda pulled her hand back from the pouch and regarded me with raised eyebrows. "Sorin?" she asked hesitantly as she knelt and offered me a hand.

I reached for her in as much as I could. Our hands clasped, but I was too deep in the thicket to be pulled free. With a shake of her head, Magda removed a short knife from her boot and began to cut.

Tears dotted my cheek, stupidly, but I had no way to wipe them away. Magda didn't speak as she unwound me from the brambles, although her occasional glances served only to make me feel more self-conscious.

When she pulled the last branch away, I wiped the shame from my face and knelt next to my pouch, careful to close it properly. I was lucky. I'd only been able to half fill it last night, and nothing had spilled with the fall. Yet my hands still shook as I tied it back to my belt and tried to rake the snow and bits of thorn from my clothes.

"Was that one of the poison ones?"

I finally met Magda's eyes. I saw her concern, but behind it lay fatigue and very clear anger. Though it could have been directed at me, or our attackers, and the look on her face made me want to slink back into the blackberries.

"They're all poison of a kind," I said, wiping my face with my sleeve again. "Best not to touch them at all." I checked the pouches one final time, making sure they were all secure. When my eyes came back to Magda, I finally noticed the blood that coated her face and the tears in her tunic and cloak that were from more than arrows.

"You—" I began.

"You were never one for crying," Magda said, turning the conversation again. "I didn't think you'd be so skittish. Why did you wander off? You could have been hurt. You promised me you wouldn't wander."

I looked down. Her bow and quiver were missing, and her thigh had a long gash in it.

"I'm sorry. I...was thinking and..." I didn't know how to finish. I hadn't realized the ache in my chest came, at least partly, from my mother's disappearance. Still, it felt silly to be so afraid of a sending. The things had no real power. They could burn, to a point, from the magic residuals, but they couldn't lift or throw, and they certainly couldn't wield a knife. Well, they couldn't wield a knife *well*. What were a few boils, compared to an arrow in the chest, or being crushed by one's horse? I'd been useless in the real battle and useless in a pretend one as well. I didn't need to highlight my ineptitude by mentioning the magic. I drove the conversation back. "Did we win?"

Magda chortled. "They're all dead, so I suppose we did. Highway robbers, nothing more. Not even very good ones. Likely just local misfits. They seemed more interested with leading me on a chase than taking our purses. Come on, let's keep going."

She put her arm around my shoulders. I let her lead me from the woods. The sorrel thinned as we reached the gap in the canopy, which made the ground feel too firm under my fur-lined boots. "You didn't answer my question," she murmured when I pressed into her side, suddenly very cold. The smell of wintergreen filled my nose, and the ermine on her cloak tickled my cheek. "Why did you wander from the road? Were there more bandits? Did you see something?"

"It was nothing. A mirage, or probably just fatigue. I'm overtired, and you were right; fighting doesn't suit me." We reached the edge of the road. I paused, pulling myself from Magda's arm. Her horse was there, snorting but still, and Peanut...his blood had already frozen to the ground.

Magda stepped in front of me. Her eyes narrowed. "What did you see, Sorin?"

"What don't we have any guards with us?" I countered, perhaps a bit too childishly. It was easy to fall back into old patterns. "You could have been killed."

Magda looked pointedly at my pigment pouches. "You're saying those aren't enough?" When I didn't rise to the bait, her jaw set. "What did you see? Please, I don't want it to be a command."

I imagined myself sticking my tongue out before I closed my eyes, letting the memory, the word "daughter," swirl behind my eyelids and prick my skin. Mother was many things—loud, obnoxious, ambitious—but not bigoted. I'd never been her daughter, and that word had dropped from our collective vocabularies in my twelfth year. It was problematic, in terms of lineage and inheritance rights in Iana's queendom where daughters were the sole inheritors, but there had never been any discussion of trading me out for a definitively gendered foster. She had no reason to call me daughter now, even in jest. She knew the damage that word caused and how it had kept me shut from the world.

"It was nothing," I said finally. When Magda crossed her arms, I sighed and tried again. "I thought...I thought I saw Mother. But she spoke incorrectly. It was just... magic. Maybe old magic. There's probably another of the king's lost amulets around. He buried hundreds of them, right? Anyways, I'm fine."

Magda looked past me, back into the forest. The sun had gone below the canopy, and I could no longer make out the snow on the trees. "I don't trust the woods this close to the glacier either," she said. "I've seen what those amulets can do, even before I saw the damage from the palm with Master Rahad. Mother had a collection of them." She put her arm back around my shoulder and led me to her horse. I mounted on my own, the adrenaline steadying my aching legs. Magda cursed as she tried to bring her left leg up into the stirrup.

"Magda—" I started.

"No! I'm *fine*, and we need to get to the town." She managed to hook her foot in, but her eyes squinted and her lips curled as she pushed off the ground. "I'm fine," she breathed, more to herself this time. She tried again, and I grabbed for her right arm and pulled her up and into the saddle.

"Thank you," she said as her arm again found its place around my waist and the horse began to move.

I smiled, warm with the proximity. "The bandits?" I prodded loosely.

"Poorly trained," Magda returned, matching my tone.

I sniffed. "You're not going to give me any details, are you?"

Magda leaned in and spoke close to my ear. "I'm not the only one keeping secrets. Tit for tat, alchemist."

She was right, but it still felt unbalanced, and I shouldn't have needed to bargain either. A funny smile crossed her face, and I rolled my eyes. Teasing. Right.

"Can we talk tonight, once we arrive?" After a pause, I added, "Not about hair."

"Maybe. If things are calm." Magda's voice turned serious all of a sudden, and heavy. It might have been fatigue, or the wound in her leg was deeper than it appeared.

I settled back into the saddle and nodded silently. Snow began to drift down as we continued on the gradual uphill trail, and I raised my hood. The white rabbit fur caught the flakes before they hit my face and turned to distorted crystals as the heat from my skin partially melted the snow. As I was bundled against the weather and swaying on the horse, exhaustion pushed my mind to wander ahead to Miantri, and what manner of witch lived there who could conjure with that level of detail, with or without an old amulet.

Not all the masters were missing, it seemed. At least one remained nearby and was very interested in me.

Nine: Sulfur

Everything crackled as the horse walked, from the frozen road to Magda's cloak when she shook snow from the wool. Every crunch reminded me of little bones snapping—of dead men, and Mother's house, and the conjuring in the woods. The temperature continued to drop exponentially as the sun finished setting, and I shivered into Magda and her thick cloak, which she'd wrapped around both of us. To compound the cold, what started as white dust soon mutated to thick, fat flakes of snow that iced with our breath.

I sacrificed the well-earned body heat by sitting forward as we passed through the city wall of Miantri, which was little more than stacked stones. Set in a shallow valley halfway up the mountain range, a river ran along the eastern side, likely fed by a glacial lake somewhere farther north. Miantri was just before the tree line, so the houses were mostly brick with steep clay roofs in curved tiles. Smoke curled from every chimney, although I had to wonder if they were burning cow patties instead of wood. To waste scant trees on fuel seemed ridiculous, especially as the trees this high in elevation were scrubby and barely worth harvesting.

Despite the hour and the temperature, the townspeople were about. There weren't any children that I could see, but grown men and women gathered in the square as we passed on horseback. Everyone stared at a woman, wrapped in thick brown furs, erecting a small structure. A man whose hair curled like mine under his cap stood nearby, tatting what looked like lace curtains.

"Late to be building and decorating," I murmured into the snow.

"For a good reason." Magda whispered the words into my ear, her breath leaving a chill as the heat evaporated. "Look."

I scanned the perimeter of the square, then farther into town. Rooftops glowed yellow. Footpaths, what parts could be seen under the snow, shone a strange silver. We passed green paper lanterns hung on every signpost, house, and business. Green candles marked doorsteps and lined paths that led to the square. Everything flickered and danced in the starlight, and it was easy to let childhood fairytales sweep my mind, to imagine fairies laying foxfire mushrooms in a ritual of their own.

"No music though?" I asked Magda as we edged the square. "Don't festivals have music? Or did the musicians already freeze to death?"

Magda shrugged. "It'll get colder. Besides, guild musicians are expensive to hire as is, much less for a mountain town. Eastgate holds the musicians' guild, so I bet the villagers couldn't afford it." Magda skirted the crowd and led us to a well-lit inn on the east side of the square. It had a stable to the right, bathed in the light of flickering green candles, and we headed in that direction.

"But this isn't an Iana ascension festival, right?" I asked as we entered the stable. "We aren't in the right season."

"Miantri is a border town. They celebrate the festivals of Sorpsi and Puget. We're somewhere in the week of *tii*."

Stable boys came out to greet us and took the reins. Magda's hands slid from my waist and she sat back. I managed to drop from the horse without incident and grinned against the stuttering pain in my legs. I was maybe passably good at riding a horse. That was something. I offered my hand to Magda, but she raised an eyebrow at my unsure stance and eased off the saddle on her own. She bit her lower lip when her left leg took on weight.

My grin vanished. "You're still bleeding. You need to see a doctor." I pointed to the fresh red stains on her pants.

Magda waved her hand. "Let's go inside. No doctor will attend someone during *tii*. I'll come in and put some pressure on it. If need be, I'll stitch it." She limped out of the stable and around to the main inn door. I frowned and, on still-unsteady legs, ran-skipped to catch up with her.

The lingering tightness in my shoulders from the conjuring evaporated upon entering the inn. Inside was warm and inviting, with the green lanterns hung on every available hook and the thick smell of chicken in the air. A man with a long beard and icy eyes brushed past us on his way out. I thought I saw at least part of a tattoo on his neck, but he disappeared into the snow and dark before I could figure out what to say. It had probably been my imagination anyway. With only the candlelight, shadows danced everywhere.

There were four other patrons, besides us, sitting in two pairs on opposite ends of the long room. Both sets looked like travelers as their clothes were too thin for the mountains, which perhaps explained why they all looked so angry too. The inn itself had less wood than I was used to seeing, and decorated, tanned hides covered most of the available wall space, but it felt pleasant enough to be in, especially considering the alternative.

"I've only one private room available," the graying proprietor called to us. "You'd better be able to pay too. I've no more space for itinerants. Beds are available also in the communal men's and women's rooms. Take your pick."

All thoughts of food vanished from my mind. A familiar itching rose up on my arms.

"We'll take the private," Magda said as she shook the snow from her cloak. She paused for a moment, possibly because she'd heard the uncomfortable rustling of my own cloak, and turned to look at me. "Okay? You can share with me or go to one of the communals. Your choice."

The proprietor walked past with a mug of yellow liquid in one hand and a key on a leather strip in the other. She tossed the key to Magda, who caught it.

"Y-Yes," I stuttered as my mind jumped between the three options. My fingers curled into fists.

"I want to eat first." Magda looked to the proprietor. "Clean table?"

The woman bent and brushed crumbs off the nearest slab of glued-up wood, straightened, and gave Magda a look I couldn't quite figure out. I caught more than a glimpse of cleavage pushed up from her green bodice. I was certain my face flushed, but if the woman noticed, she didn't comment. Instead, she righted, wiped her hands on her apron, nodded at me, then went back into the kitchen.

I thought about how Magda had looked at this serving woman, and the one at the pub in the capital. I bit my lip. Was it hypocritical to desire the very attributes I sought to hide? It made me uncomfortable to see Magda staring the way she did, but it didn't seem right to be upset with her for an action I'd just found myself engaging in as well.

Magda flopped into a chair and rolled her head back. "Uggh. I could sleep for a week."

"That'd be the blood loss," I said flatly as I took the other chair—a dense walnut without a single glue joint that I could see, clearly guild-made.

Her head snapped back up. She narrowed her eyes. "Food."

I raised an eyebrow but didn't argue further.

"Here you are then. More will be ready in about an hour when dinner is served." The proprietor had returned with half a loaf of rye bread, cut into thick slices, and a bowl of hardboiled eggs. She set a tin pitcher at the edge of the table, then tipped it toward me to show the clear contents. "That's glacial melt water. It's clean and fine to drink, but sometimes tourists get funny about its source. If you want wine instead, let me know."

"I'm sure it's fine," Magda said, a little too dismissively. She grabbed a slice of bread and slathered butter across it. "Thank you."

The woman turned to leave, then leaned in and whispered into my ear. "Maybe you want to tell the royal daughter that if she's trying to stay disguised, giving orders like she's the queen doesn't help."

I laughed, then grabbed one of the eggs, peeled it, and took a bite. I liked this woman. She wasn't staring, and she hadn't gone announcing to the town that the royal heir was here either. The inn was quiet, my binding tight and flat, and I was almost warm again. Missing mothers and queens and guilders aside, it was really nice to feel relaxed and...free. Free of Mother, free of Thuja, free of assumptions.

"You going to introduce yourself then?" the woman prodded, a smile quirking the corners of her mouth. My shoulders finally relaxed.

"I'm Sorin the...trade alchemist, sort of, and it is a pleasure to meet you."

The woman nodded, but her mouth turned down. "I'm Keegan. My husband and I run this inn, though it's quickly turning into a boardinghouse with these ones." She pointed to the booth in the far corner where a man and a woman sat, toying with the remains of their soup.

"Are boarders not good money?" I asked. They seemed like reasonable people, if not a bit...distanced.

Keegan sat in the chair next to me. "They keep wandering in off the glacier with some type of snow madness. They're fine workers and have good minds, but they've got no real skills. Still, they can scrub dishes and clean laundry, so I suppose it's fine." She put her elbows on the table, then rested her chin on clasped hands.

Magda eyed the other woman with amusement as she downed another piece of bread.

Keegan chuckled, then turned her eyes back to me. "An unguilded alchemist? Should I ask about your business so near the glacier?"

I wanted to talk more about the glacial wanderers, but a chance to talk about alchemy to someone who actually wanted to listen was hard to pass up. "I'm about to start my apprenticeship. I'll be guilded and have my tattoo soon." I grinned as I lightly touched two fingers to the burn on my neck where the tattoo would go.

"Hmm," Keegan said noncommittally. "Those tattoos really worth all that much these days?" She jerked her head at the corner table. "Hasn't done much for them."

Magda's eyebrow raised, and my eyes widened. "They're guilders?" Magda asked.

Keegan shrugged. "By tattoo. Not by skill."

"Excuse me." Magda stood from the table and teetered. Spots of blood peppered the cloth covering of her chair. Keegan stared, and my chest twinged.

As Magda gripped the table to steady herself, I stood and put a hand on her shoulder. "Maybe tomorrow?" I said gently, not wanting a rebuke that would almost certainly come. "They live here. They're not going anywhere."

Magda pursed her lips and looked from me to the guild couple, then back at the food. With an exaggerated sigh, she slumped back to the chair. "Fine," she muttered. "Tomorrow. Pass the eggs."

I stifled a smile, although if Magda could be so easily dissuaded, her leg hurt a lot more than she let on. It was best to eat and get her tended to. I took the last piece of bread and lathered it with butter. Light steam curled from the edges, and I reveled in the warmth. "Do you have a guild alchemist in this town?" I asked, hoping to take Magda's mind off the guilders.

Keegan sniffed and crossed her arms. "We don't have the best history with the unbound guilds up here. Too sordid a history with the three countries. You'll want to watch who you talk to."

Magda coughed, and I heard her mutter "not a good topic" before she took a bite of egg.

I glared at her, then looked back to Keegan. "Unbound guilds are still guilds; they just don't have guildhalls or grandmasters primarily housed in one country. They're not part of the census. They're—they're not like traders, who have a base understanding of the skills and refuse to pay guild dues. Besides, alchemy is nothing like magic at all. Be afraid of witches, sure, but alchemy isn't something to be feared, just understood."

Keegan dabbed at her mouth with the edge of her apron, then looked at me with an incredulous expression. "That's what you think, is it? And you think joining a guild is going to help with this 'misunderstanding'? Really? Also, if you already have the skills, why bother? Tradespeople can get just as much work done."

I tried to interrupt, but Keegan flicked her hand and cut me off. "Why constrain yourself with rules and old methods that can't compete with machines?"

"But machines will never be able to do the fine detail," I argued as heat pushed up my neck and onto my cheeks. Tension had seeped into the conversation, and now the piece of bread in my hand was crushed so completely that parts of it squeezed between my fingers. "If you think the guilds will give up their secret knowledge, you don't know much about guilds. They'd rather let knowledge die than share it. And then what? We lose not only methods passed down over centuries, but we lose craftship. Art. Attention to detail. Quality. *History*!"

Magda stood, nosily grating the feet of her chair across the wood floor. "I'm going to the room. Sorin, come see me before you decide where to sleep? We have to leave after lunch tomorrow for Celtis, so don't be up too late."

"Yes," I said, not bothering to look at her. I heard her sigh as she left the main room.

Keegan tried for a look of patience and failed abysmally. "Such vehemence. Is that you talking, alchemist, or the royal daughter? We understand the importance of history here well enough. We're not so far from Iana's Lake, in theory. She might have even come from this town. But we know, too, that we have to feed our families, and guilds." She made a fist with her hand, then flared her fingers apart. "The machines are here, whether or not our queen wants to see it. That means *poof*—the guilds will disappear and take all those too sandy-headed to look around with them. Besides, in the end, a cup just has to hold water. It doesn't have to look pretty or have a fancy rim. We don't *need* guild technique."

I slammed my clump of bread to the table. "That's not true!"

"It is," Keegan replied calmly. "How many guilders do you have left in the capital?"

I shoved myself back from the table and stood. "There are plenty of guilders. They've just...gone somewhere."

Keegan's look turned pitying. "Gone to get other jobs? They've had to leave here, then, noting how many of them are wandering back across the glacier. Guild jobs are some of the best in the three countries. You think they'd just abandon them all, collectively, to take a trip?"

Her words fell around me like a suffocating blanket. I leaned against a pillar and stared at the ground. I didn't want to hear this. Surely Mother would have told me this was happening! What reason did she have to keep it from me? It's not as if it had just snuck in overnight.

"Do you have any guilders in this town?" I looked back at the booth, which was now empty, the guilders perhaps having turned in for the night. "Guilders that still practice, that is?"

Keegan sat back and blinked several times. "We tore down the trapper's and trader's guildhall over a year ago. We've not had a guild master of any specialty for at least five years, although we see a few scattered guilders from time to time. Travelers mostly. We've had a number of masters pass through, recently, but they never stay. It's been this way for years up here, if not in the capital. We're too remote for the queen to visit much, and we've no real reason to head south. The guilds are dead."

Keegan rolled an egg on the table, her eyes filled with something close enough to pity that I felt heavy. "Not really sure myself how you missed all this."

"I..."

I'd missed it because I was living in Mother's house.

I'd missed it because Mother, who traveled regularly, had conveniently neglected to mention anything about it, and I'd never thought to ask. Why should I have, when Mother had kept me so entrenched in guild culture?

I'd missed it because I'd been too fixated with alchemy to ask, and Magda probably didn't think I was ready to hear it from her. Because guilds were all I knew, and all I had, and I was clinging like a piranha to a dying institution.

I hit my head against the pillar as anger threatened to make me cry for the second time today.

I was an idiot. I was an unguilded, starry-eyed idiot.

What else had I missed while hiding away in the Thujan woods?

Ten: Salt

I walked, shakily, to the private room at the back of the inn. My inner thighs were chafed, my hips sore, and there was a funny tickle in my lower back. Horses. Damn horses. And damn Magda for not telling me how bad the guilds had gotten. Damn Mother, as well, since she clearly knew things were rotten and had never seen fit to mention it.

"Magda?" I pulled my cloak from my shoulders and rapped on the door, trying to settle my emotions. "Are you all right?"

"Come in," I heard through the wood, and though her voice was muffled, it sounded strained.

I pushed the heavy walnut door open and stepped into a small, sparsely furnished room. A double bed sat against the south wall. One sheepskin rug covered half the floor, and an iron table was wedged near the door. A woven hemp partition hung down from the ceiling, concealing another corner.

Magda sat on a short stool in the center of the room, her cloak heaped next to her. Though the room was not overly warm, sweat beaded on her forehead. One of her boots lay crumpled to her right, the other still on, though unlaced—the one on her injured leg. I watched her hands clench and heard the catch in her breathing.

"Might be a little sore from the horse," she said as she looked sheepishly up at me.

I quirked the corner of my mouth. "Definitely not the arrow wound. Here, I've got it."

I tossed my cloak with hers, knelt, and removed the other boot as gently as I could. She hissed only once when the boot snagged on her ankle, but it came off quick enough. Her wool socks were thick and finely knit but smelled the same as any others. I hovered my hand just above her leg, traveling from ankle to thigh. The left side of her pants looked almost entirely dark brown, and the area near her wound felt warm and moist.

"We really need to do something about your leg. You sure we can't ask for a doctor? Surely a doctor would attend to the royal daughter during *tii*."

"No doctor will attend me during *tii* celebrations. Pugins believe each village has a special spirit that guards their lands, and if you don't take care of it when you're supposed to, you know..." She caught my eye and smirked. "Consequently, you'd get along well with them. They also don't like magic as they believe it takes from the natural world and, thereby, takes from the spirits. Spookiness of the unbound guilds and all." She widened her eyes and made a *whooo*ing sound.

"Funny. I don't like magic because it's nonsense," I retorted. I remained on my knees. There had to be a delicate way to get Magda out of her clothes so I could check the wound. All the phrases I could think of, however, only sounded suggestive.

Magda laughed, the sound colored with tightness. "You don't like magic because you don't understand it. It's the intangible part that annoys you. It's *always* annoyed you. That's half the fun."

I muttered and jutted my chin at the wound on her leg. "Royal Daughter—"

Magda nudged my knee with her foot. "No doctors. I'm fine. The week of *tii* is a week of observance. If you go out later, head to the square. Carpenters will be constructing a new house for the spirit, which resides in the center of town. Textile workers will add the cloth embellishments. All adults are expected to attend the building."

Magda eyed the ceramic bath in the corner, which I hadn't noticed until she turned to it. From this angle, I could better see around the partition. Steam rose from the tub. "The inns are the only things open as hospitality to strangers is important in the Puget religion. Would you help me to the tub?"

I frowned at her words, then grabbed Magda's upper arms and helped her to stand. "The spirit house is constructed by free carpenters, no doubt. Wouldn't want to provide jobs to guilders so they'd, maybe, *stay* in the three countries."

Magda snorted as I helped her shuffle toward the tub. "Free laborers are a necessity, Sorin."

"They are *not*."

"You know we've no law against them. That's guild snobbery you have. I've it, too, from the smiths. But rural towns can't import every time they need services, and a town this size couldn't support a guildhall, even before...

this. With the residency ban lifted by my grandmother, most guild members are choosing to remain in their country of license. People still need smiths, and carpenters, and tanners. They may not hold the higher guild secrets, and the work will suffer because of that, but if you need a chair built, or a horse shod, it doesn't pay to be picky. The guilds are still the only places for the finer work. It's not like someone is going to invent a machine to cut veneer or spin cotton. I've heard those rumors. It's ridiculous to think they'll demolish centuries of guild tradition, unless we let them. Our masters are around. We need to find them. Besides, your mother wouldn't just take off and leave you alone. You know that better than anyone."

We reached the edge of the tub, and I eased Magda onto the lip. Relief crossed her face as the bath took weight from her leg. She'd managed a passable amount of pressure on it, which gave me hope that the cut hadn't reached muscle. Or she still hid pain exceptionally well. She'd almost drowned once, when we were five, insisting she could tread water with a broken foot.

I placed the pair of boots in front of the tub and stood back up. There was a distinct scent in the air. Flowers? I followed it to the source and sighed. Peeking through the steam on the surface of the bathwater were rose petals of pink and red and yellow, spinning gently on the surface. A minor enchantment *and* an overpowering scent. Magda wasn't passing as a commoner as well as she'd thought.

"Really?" I asked, abandoning our previous conversation. I scooped a handful of petals and let them fall through my fingers. "The innkeeper is a trade witch perhaps?"

Magda laughed and caught one of the flowers as it fell from my hand. She ran her fingers across the broad surface of the yellow petal before laying it on the rim of the tub. "Perhaps. Even without the toucan crest, an innkeeper can see wealth kilometers away. She knows where the money is coming from."

I frowned, unsure whether Magda was laughing at me or simply being Magda. I argued anyway, because I could, and because the steam from the bath and the scent of the petals set me on edge. "Mother had money, and we did travel some. We even went to Puget once, and no one ever put rose petals in our bathwater."

"If you had taken one of the invitations to travel with me, you could have had your fill." Magda looked pointedly at me. "I would have loved you being with me during our vacations to Eastgate's beaches, or even on some of the diplomatic trips. You're the only friend I managed not to scare off. Well, until you stopped visiting." She frowned. "Why did you stop talking to me, Sorin?"

The room was too hot now to think straight. This was not where I'd wanted the conversation to go at all.

"I—I didn't. I mean, I did, but Mother said she would explain. I needed to focus on woodcutting, and my breasts got, well..." I tugged at my binder through my shirt, hoping she could put enough pieces together that I wouldn't have to continue. "People started talking because I didn't...finish. Because they thought I stayed in between." I paused and considered my next words. "But I'm not, you know— Between. There's no word for what I am. I'm just me."

Magda's next words were laced with hurt. "You think I would have cared about that? I tried to sneak out to see you, dozens of times. People always recognized me. Didn't you ever try to see me? It would have been easier for you, I think. You could have just put on a cloak."

I dropped my gaze to the petal water and rubbed at my cheek. "I needed to get...control of my body. Everything went so wrong."

Magda made a funny little noise, and I looked up to see her staring at my chest. It should have made me feel uncomfortable, but for once, my hands were still, and my skin didn't itch.

"That's why you hide your breasts now?" she asked.

I nodded my head.

"But you don't want to talk about it?"

I smiled sadly. "I don't know how." That wasn't entirely true. I didn't know how to talk about it with *her*.

Magda took my hand from the rim of the tub and held it her own, tracing her thumb over my knuckles. My breath caught; she was beautiful, and competent. And that damn strip of cotton didn't seem to upset her at all.

"Your cut, Royal Daughter," I whispered, although I did not take my hand from hers.

Magda's gentle smile turned to a scowl. "After the bath. Let me clean it first." With exaggerated irritation, she dropped my hand, lifted her tunic over her head, and let it slide to the floor.

I had to remind myself to breathe. She didn't have anything on underneath her tunic. She looked...strikingly feminine. I had steadfastly tried *not* to imagine what she might look like without clothes during our trip here, and now I couldn't take my eyes from her. In what started as clinical interest, I traced the scar tissue that ran across both her sides and, in one instance, over a breast. How soft would the skin be there, at the junction where her breast met her side? As soft as the petals still skating on the water?

That was inappropriate. I turned away as Magda stood and cursed at the ties to her pants and the knotted mess that lay there. I watched her only peripherally in case she needed assistance, my heart thudding in my chest. My mind filled with what-ifs, about what it would have been like to finish growing up together—the dances, the royal parties, the dresses neither of us wanted to wear but would have been forced into anyway. The idea of us *together*...

Magda finally managed to untangle the ties and pushed the material down. She sat again on the edge of the tub, her pants sagging at her knees, and looked up. "Sorin, can you..." She paused when I didn't turn around. I was lucky I heard her over the rushing in my ears, with my mind wandering, as it was, to a past that had never been.

Magda's tone softened. "I'm sorry, Sorin. I didn't think. We just talked about this. Breasts make you uncomfortable, don't they?"

I closed my eyes and tried to clear Magda's chest and everything associated with it from my mind. "No. I don't have an issue with breasts. You're fine. We need to get your wound cleaned and bound."

Magda finished removing her pants, but her movements were slower now, and hesitant. "I can manage on my own from here. You don't have to stay."

Her words brought a different kind of panic. I wanted to stay. My rational mind had steamed away with the bathwater. Gods, I'd have gotten in that bath with her if she'd asked in that moment. I was here to dress a wound, however, not contemplate how we might fit together in a porcelain tub. I had to remain professional. I was here as her guide to all things Mother. I wasn't here as her friend, and certainly not as her lover.

I turned back to Magda, carefully keeping my eyes to her leg and the wound there. I took the small cloth that lay over the side of the tub, wet it, and began to wash near the wound. It was red and puckered, but I saw no pus.

"I'll need to stay for a bit. You won't get the wound closed without me." A basin filled with water sat on a short table near the tub. I brought it down to the floor and used it to wet the washcloth before beginning again. Her skin goosefleshed as I dabbed, and I forced myself to attribute that to her pain and not something else.

Magda snorted. "You're not my servant. Besides, I doubt you're any better with a needle and thread than I am." She gasped on the last word as the cloth brushed the open wound.

"I wasn't going to stitch." I tapped the third satchel on my belt. I had most of the old blood off Magda's leg now. The edges of the wound did look closed and had soft scabs. The center, only, still wept, although the blood beaded instead of ran.

"Would you look at me, Sorin?"

I did, but as my eyes moved upward, they caught again on her breasts. Everything seemed cloudy and felted, with the steam off the water and my heart metaphorically jumping into my throat. The heat came back to my face. Magda had a strange look on hers.

"You're sure that stuff won't kill me? From your demonstrations at the pub..."

Thank the gods we were still talking about the pigments. "I know what I'm doing, Magda."

Magda seemed unconvinced, and my tone had come out harsher than I intended. I tried to mitigate my words.

"Bone oil is my own invention—a really neat new solvent. It's not an alkahest, but it lets me extract things— things from fungi, that no one has ever seen before. This yellow extract, in very small amounts, will form a controllable film that binds to your skin. In a few weeks when that layer of skin sheds, so, too, will the film. In the meantime, it will close the wound. That's what we need right now."

She didn't say anything further, but the quick nod to her head and the way she pressed her lips into a thin line told me volumes about the type of medicine she was used to.

"I wouldn't hurt you," I said, and I did, selfishly, want to touch her skin. I took the yellow extract pouch from my belt and opened it, just enough for my smallest finger to move through. Then I dipped my entire hand in the bathwater, and dripped the excess into Magda's wound.

"I'm forming a barrier," I explained at Magda's quick exhale. "A safety precaution. The extract can't bind in water." A larger towel lay on the floor next to the foot of the bath. I took it and patted the area around the cut dry. Then I again wetted my hand, cinched a small amount of the yellow granules to the top of the bag, and pinched them between my thumb and small finger.

I'd done this before, on viscacha and even an injured cougar once. It was important to work quickly before the water evaporated and the extract had a chance to move internally. Still, the tiny amount wasn't enough to do Magda damage, even if it did get into her system. That I knew from personal experience, and the compound became inert once bound. It was only in loose form that it was dangerous.

I circled the wound in tandem, beginning at the top, then separating my thumb and little finger, running down both sides simultaneously. The extract slid together in my fingers' wake, arching over the water bubble on the wound and closing it off from the air. When I reached the end of the gash, I brought my fingers together, snapped them against one another to dislodge the remaining extract, and immediately dunked my hand in the basin.

"By the gods," Magda whispered as the film closed itself into an elongated, yellow oval. She flexed her thigh, and the film moved with her skin in a seamless layer. "That's extraordinary."

I shrugged and reaffixed the pouch to my belt. "It's just a fungal pigment," I said as I dried my hand. "Extracted from the golden mango fungus, which is a pretentious common name. I've been interested in alkahest work for the past few years. While the bone extract I distill isn't quite there, it does do startling things to fungi that basic alcohols cannot." I patted the pouches. "These three are the most interesting, at least in terms of functionality. I've observed others, however, that have potential. Now the bioluminescent fungi—"

"Sorin."

Startled, I looked up. "Yes?"

"Thank you."

I nodded. Magda was smiling again with that slightly bemused expression I remembered from our youth.

"You're welcome. Ready for the bath?"

Magda stood, experimenting with the weight distribution on her leg. "Still hurts," she said, "though I suppose that's to be expected. It's just a binder, after all. Help me out?" She paused. "If you're all right with that?"

This time I snorted. "Of course I'm fine with it. I don't need the Queensguard coming after me when they hear you've cracked your head open from getting out of a bathtub." I pointed to the wool undergarment she still wore, stretched tight across her hips. Before I spoke again, I checked myself, making sure I could keep my voice even. "Do you need help with those?"

This time it was Magda who looked away. I wasn't quite sure why, since she'd had no problem taking off her shirt in front of me. My heart was still pounding from that, and I couldn't get much warmer. At least a blush wouldn't show through her darker skin as it did mine. At this point, loss of an undergarment was unlikely to further my... Not "discomfort." That wasn't the right word. I didn't like how attraction sounded either. It was too coarse.

"I've got it," she said. I turned my head and heard the brushing of thighs as she stepped from the wool. "Ready."

I kept my eyes on the tub as Magda gripped my arm and pushed into me. Once her right leg was in, we switched grips, and I eased her down into the water. I caught a glimpse of darkness, nothing more, before Magda submerged. She sighed into the petals, and my mind drifted to my own bath, hopefully just as warm, and if Magda had paid enough for each of us to get our own water.

"I'll leave you for a bit," I said. Magda's eyes were closed, and the moment suddenly felt very private. "I'll come back in half an hour to help you out."

I turned to leave, and a splashing of water followed me. I looked back over my shoulder to see Magda sitting forward in the bath and eyeing me intently.

"Which of the rooms will you stay in?" she asked.

My mind blanked. Magda had been an excellent distraction, but now the squirming returned to my gut. I had to remind myself to breathe—that this was a simple thing, and I was a person who could make basic choices, surely.

"I don't know. Anatomically, I match better with the women, but going in there just... I don't know if I can. The men would ask fewer questions maybe. So whichever has the spare bed, I guess. If it comes to it, I can sleep in the stable. I've done it before." It'd be cold, and prickly, but at least there wouldn't be awkward questions.

Magda slapped the water's surface, sending a small wave of petals over the side of the tub. "You're not sleeping in the stable, Sorin. If you don't want to sleep in the commons, then stay here. It's a small room, but we've shared a bed plenty of times in the past." She chuckled. "Most notably during the cold snap when we were eight and the wind was making that ghostly whistle through my fireplace. I don't think I've ever run to another bed as quickly."

"We were a lot smaller then, and you stole all the blankets," I countered, shifting my weight on my feet and turning back to face the door. It wasn't a bad suggestion, although the bed was big enough we would not need to huddle together as when we were children. That had been more from fear, and cold, than the size of the bed. Still, the image of Magda's breasts, and the swell of her hips, would not leave my mind.

I heard her moving in the tub, heard the sound of soap hit the porcelain and Magda submerging herself. When I glanced back over my shoulder, she had moved to her knees, arms resting on the curved lip. Her face had turned from playful to serious, and the intensity of her gaze made me shiver.

"I would never push, Sorin, no matter how much I enjoy your company. You have my word."

Now I was thoroughly confused. It must have crossed my face because Magda laughed and splashed more water at me. "Oh lords, Sorin. You're as dense as when we were kids. I'm done in here. Come help me out and get in while the water is warm. If we share the bath, we can eat sooner. I'll bring our dinners up—well, I'll go down and ask someone to bring our dinners up, so you can bathe in peace. Then, we're going to curl up on our respective sides of the bed and sleep like the dead." She leaned over the ledge and grabbed the towel. "In the morning, maybe, we can have a different discussion if you'd like." Her smile turned to a grin. "I'll even use big words so you feel more at ease."

The ribbing and playfulness slapped away the tension of moments before. I relaxed into the familiarity of our childhood roles and rolled my eyes as I helped her from the tub. Magda dressed and left, neither of us continuing the conversation. I had thought she might come back quickly, so I expedited my bath. But I was dry, dressed, and about to enter the bed when she returned with a woman carrying a tray of food. The serving woman was bustier even than our server at the Sorpsi pub, a fact Magda had not failed to notice.

"Chicken and potatoes tonight," Magda said as the woman placed the tray and left the room. Magda's eyes followed. "I already had mine. I'm going to sleep. Kick me if I move onto your side. It's been over a decade since I had a bedmate. For just sleeping anyway."

I felt silly for getting carried away with the steam of the bath and Magda's direct attention. The joking was back in her voice, and she was Magda again. A friend. Nothing more. I ate my dinner as fast as I had taken my bath, then climbed into bed. Heartbeats after my head hit the pillow, I was out.

My dreams, when they came, were not of Magda, but a tall woman in the trees, a tainted guild mark on her throat, beckoning me to follow her.

Eleven: Fire

Magda was gone when I awoke. I hobbled from the bed and dressed quickly, fingers fumbling the wrapping of my binding so that it slid too far down. I tugged it up, and when it refused to budge, I unwrapped the entire thing in frustration and wound it again. I wished, not for the first time, that I didn't have to wear the suffocating cotton. It wasn't that I didn't like my breasts—they were there, and aside from making it difficult to sleep on my stomach, I didn't mind them.

Not anymore.

It was the way people looked at them, and then me, and the assumptions they made, which were just too exhausting to deal with. My binding dealt with a lot of that, so I was willing to put up with the lightheadedness and poor breathing that came along with it. It was probably a good thing I didn't know how to fight or use a sword. I never could have managed the movement with my chest so constricted.

Mercifully, the rest of the clothes were easier, and I warmed immediately when I fastened my cloak around my shoulders. My hair... The room had no mirror, so whatever state my mop of black curls was in, they would simply have to stay that way.

I'd thought I'd see Magda in the main room, but when I entered, there was only a young man in the corner, sipping tea. He had no guild mark, so he wasn't one of the people from last night either. I scowled. She'd probably already spoken to the guilders or headed out to find them. If she could do this on her own, then why had she forced me along in the first place? I could have been elbows-deep in a cauldron right now, instead of shivering in the Puget mountains.

I stomped from the inn into air so cold it chilled my nose and mouth. I pulled the collar of my shirt up over my nose and hunched into my cloak. It was still early morning, and the sun was not yet over the roofs of the houses. Unsure where to go, I scanned hanging signs as I walked, paying little attention to the frozen dirt road. An apothecary. Another inn. A baker. So many stupid little shops that should have been selling guild wares, that should have been enough to support at least one guildhall. My feet skidded across the frozen dirt as I headed north and turned into the square. Not paying any attention to the road in front of me, I walked directly into the spirit house the town had built last night. The structure was barely taller than my thigh and very pointy, but curtains hung from the tiny windows, and the roof was covered in green felt.

"Gods take this thing," I muttered as I rubbed my bruised shin. "Probably trade-made anyway."

"I'm going to take that as a compliment since you aren't guilded."

I spun around and ended up nose to nose with a man almost my exact height, with the same loose black curls falling into his eyes. The lace man from last night. He was as bundled against the cold as I was, but his eyes were sharp and distinct. He didn't back up, and I couldn't back up because of the spirit house, so I sidestepped, shoving my hands into my pockets as I did so.

"I'm sorry," I said as I took another look at the house. "It's..."

It was exceptional, now that I really looked at it. I couldn't help myself, so I knelt on one knee and ran a finger over the green roof. Each tiny felt shingle was separately made and edged in a delicate lace. The walls of the house were sanded smooth and lightly coated in tar, and the ends all met in gapless joinery. The curtains held a mosaic of patterns I had no name for, and couldn't begin to guess how they had been made.

"You're a master of textiles?" I asked, turning my head to him. "I guess I thought all the masters had fled."

He offered me a hand, and I took it.

"I was on my way out, actually." He pointed to a leather pack near his feet, tied to a narrow-headed axe that was toothed on one side. "I journeyed in the glacial towns, but my master's house was just past Miantri, up until about five years ago. I always come back to help for *tii*, but I don't live here anymore. I'm Sameer, master of textiles."

He turned his head and pulled his cloak down far enough to show me the small cotton boll tattoo on the right side of his neck. It was almost hidden by the thick fur lining of his purple jerkin and the clasp of his heavy wool cloak. He had the same leather pants I was used to seeing on anyone who did guild work, and that brought a relaxing sense of familiarity to the cold.

"I'm Sorin, and I'm a—" I paused, remembering Keegan's warning about unbound guilds. "I was brought up in woodcutting. I know skill when I see it. The house and its textiles are magnificent."

I smiled, hoping the praise might undo my rude comments from earlier, but every trace of friendliness had disappeared from Sameer. The temperature hadn't changed, but Sameer's icy stare made me shiver as he scanned my face, my hands, every centimeter of exposed skin. I crossed my arms over my chest, certain I knew what had prompted this change in attitude.

"I'm sorry," I said as I tried to sidestep. "I really need to get to—"

"Sorin," he said in a sort of high-pitched, stilted voice. "Of Amada the master woodcutter."

I wrinkled my nose in confusion. "Yes..."

"You ended up her heir, then? She kept you and trained you?" The way his brows knit together and the sourness of his mouth blended into a familiar face, but I couldn't place it.

I bit my lip as I tried to remember where I had met this man before. "Yes, I mean, she trained me, but I'm not a woodcutter. I refused the mark. I found these fungal pigments—"

Sameer snarled, grabbed his pack, then spit on the ground. "Go run yourself through with a sword, and take Amada with you. Get out of my town. Seeing you once was enough."

I blinked several times.

"I'm *Sameer* and I'm a master of *textiles*. Fourteen wasn't that long ago, Sorin, when you and Amada visited our guildhall. Are you simple?"

"I..." The memory iced across me. I remembered traveling with Mother—one of the only times we traveled—to the Sorpsi/Puget border. Mother had shopped. I'd gone to find the other children, and there'd been a boy with black hair, only a year older than me, named...Sameer. I remembered him asking who I was, and I could still hear our voices in my head, so sharp was the memory.

"I'm Sorin. I came with Amada."

"Amada is a master woodcutter and doesn't take fosters. So, who are you?"

My arms started to itch, both in the memory and in the present. The glare on child-Sameer's face was the same one I saw now on the adult version.

"Who are you?" he had insisted before pushing me to the dirt. The thought of dust tickled my nose. *"Amada doesn't take fosters."*

I couldn't escape the memory. My binding felt too tight, the air, too warm. The skin on my arms burned, here and on my fourteen-year-old self. I remembered scratching, tearing, shredding, wanting to dig to find the body of mine that had once been there. The body that people understood.

The memory kept playing.

"Well?"

"I'm...I'm her heir."

In my memory, Sameer sneered and kicked dirt at me. I didn't look away. I didn't wipe my face. I didn't stop tearing at my skin.

"You're a boy. A boy can't be an heir. Tell the truth."

But I hadn't been able to tell him. I didn't have any words that made sense. I had whispered "*her daughter*," though the words made me shiver. Then, now, I wanted to bury my face in the dirt, let the earth consume me so I wouldn't have to look him in the eyes.

"I'm not a boy. I'm Amada's daughter."

But he hadn't stopped. Young Sameer had tackled me and pushed my face into the dirt. I could still hear his scream, could still feel him punch me once, twice. Someone had tried to help me up, but I stayed limp, preferring to watch blood drip from my arms onto the floor streaked with dirt and lacemaking bobbins than say those words again.

The sun beat on my face now as the ice of memory melted away. Yet the air felt colder. I breathed deliberately, in and out, letting the memory of the textile shop, the taste of blood and dirt in my mouth, the fear and shame, chill me to the bone.

"What?" Adult Sameer demanded as I stared at him, unmoving.

"I..." What did I have to say to this man who carried such a long, unclear grudge? I rubbed at my arms and tried to push the memory back to wherever it had been hiding these three years. It was best to find Magda and leave. I didn't need to get beaten into the snow, not with a witch following me.

Sameer sneered. "What do you want here, *woodcutter*? You can't possibly have business with our factory."

My arms went slack, and my fingers lay still. "A... factory? There's a factory?"

"Is that why you're here? Digging around other people's business? If that is what it will take to get you out of Miantri, fine." He threw his pack over his shoulder, the strange axe bobbing precariously from the side, then grabbed me by my arm and proceeded to pull me down a street lined with frozen straw. His fingers dug into my jerkin and the skin underneath, and I winced. There would be bruises tomorrow.

"Sameer, wait!"

He growled and kept going. "This is *my* town, Sorin, and I'm going to make sure you leave it."

At least we were in agreement on that. I wanted to pull my arm away, to curse at him in similarly coarse language, but I stopped myself, biting my lower lip as I did so. A *factory*. Probably Magda already knew about it and had gone there this morning. It'd be very Magda-like. It could take me another hour to find the factory on my own. Sameer was a cumbersome, slightly painful guide, but he was still a guide. He hadn't run me through yet, or drawn blood, so that was something. And we weren't children anymore. I could handle a few taunts.

"You didn't see a woman in a blue cloak this morning, did you?" I asked as we passed a run-down smithy with boarded-up windows and a tailor's shop with a simple treadle sitting abandoned outside the door, half covered in snow.

"Would you shut up?"

"Sameer—"

He stopped at the door to a bakery and pulled me up to him, so close I could smell the sweetbread on his breath. "Stop. Talking." He whispered it, his breath hot on my ear. The smell of sweet buns tickled my nose and stirred another amorphous memory. Mother loved sweet buns. She'd made them often when I was very small. I couldn't remember why she'd stopped, but it had been around my fourth year.

The year my older brother had been fostered.

My insides felt heavy. I stared at Sameer. His skin was the same reddish, sepia brown as mine, which wasn't so uncommon in Sorpsi, but his dimples were the same as mine, too, a light pinprick of skin in full cheeks. His eyes were dark brown—almost everyone in Sorpsi had brown eyes—but his had the same orange flecks around the pupil that I remembered from my father, though he'd died when I was very young. Men didn't always stay with the same family, anyway, in Sorpsi. Sameer's nose had a shorter bridge than mine, but was exactly the same width, and ended in the same rounded button shape as Mother's.

"Sameer, your master—"

"Shut up and walk."

It wasn't worth arguing about, not if he wouldn't discuss it. I had more pressing issues. We resumed, though his grip was looser this time, more my sleeve and cloak than my arm. We passed through the business area and finally into more residential construction, with A-line roofs that blended together in the snow. Just beyond the last house was a three-story structure of wood and brick, elongated and rectangular.

I cursed under my breath at the building, forgetting, momentarily, Sameer's grip. Though no smoke billowed from the chimneys, the ground around the building was worn, and the number of outbuildings told me the factory was well used.

Sameer released me at the front door, painted bright green with a cotton boll etched into center.

"Sameer," I began, but he cut me off.

"Get whatever it is you need and *leave*," he spat. "Here." He turned the doorknob and pushed. The door swung inward on groaning hinges. The inside was dark and smelled smoky as if a fire had just extinguished.

"Hello?" I called in hesitantly. "Magda?"

No one answered.

I didn't like how it smelled—like overcooked cauliflower. I wrinkled my nose as I stared into the darkness, then turned back to Sameer. "Is the factory maybe—"

"Just go in," Sameer hissed. "There are plenty of people in there. I can hear the machines."

I couldn't hear anything, except the faint sound of a chair tipping over.

"There's nothing here except rot," I said.

Sameer took my shoulders and pushed me into the room, into the dark and the damp cauliflower smell. His hands dropped away, and I shivered, though Sameer was clearly toying with me. Maybe it was time I spoke with him instead of worrying about a factory that clearly wasn't operational.

Before I could turn, the door slammed closed behind me, clipping my backside.

"Hey!" I yelled as I jumped. My cloak caught in the door and pulled from my throat onto the floor. I grabbed the frozen metal doorknob and tried to twist it, but it refused to move.

"Sameer!" I kicked the door while my eyes adjusted to the dark. The interior of the factory was dim, although light crisscrossed in through the shutters. It wasn't any warmer inside, but there wasn't a breeze either. I cupped my hands near my mouth and blew on them as I looked for the source of the chair noise, or some of the rumored machinery, or Sameer maybe gawking at me through one of the narrow little windows.

But I could see nothing out the windows, not even the roofs of houses or the partially overcast sky. The room around me had no furniture, not even a chair. Someone had scrubbed the brick floor clean and washed the bare, cedar plank walls. No footprints, no embers in the fireplace, and no stairs or other doors. It seemed ghostly familiar, though I'd have preferred the scent of lemon to what was currently assaulting my nose.

"Gods," I whispered. Moats of dust hung in the air, and my breathing, which should have been erratic, came depressed and too even. Then the scraping came again, sounding just to my right. I spun to face the whatever, but again, I saw only emptiness and wisps of smoke...though the smoke quickly solidified into a human shape.

The hair raised on my arms. "Please, let it be another sending," I whispered. "Not a witch. Not a real, living witch."

Again came the sound of wood scraping brick.

"Let me out," I whimpered into the cauliflower air. "I've no business with witches."

Warmth blossomed from the smoke, and my skin tingled as the cold burned away.

"Leave me alone!" I tried to scream it, but my words caught in my throat and came out garbled. So much for bravery. But I *wasn't* afraid. It was just a *witch*. I was an *alchemist*. Alchemists were better than witches. Stronger. More...something or other. I'd defeated the magic in the royal forest. Queen Iana had defeated a king and all his magic with just a short sword and bravery. I had *alchemy*.

But I was definitely still afraid.

"Stay away," a voice hissed. The sound curled inside my head, scalding as it went and flushing my skin. The smoke defined into arms and legs, but no head, and stood in front of me, wisping and curling in the silence. A laugh bubbled from my throat because a shadowy smoke person was plenty creepy enough. Missing a head seemed unnecessary.

"Stay away from *what*?" Now I did sound brave. Or overconfident. I didn't care. At least I was speaking.

"Stay away from the country of Puget!" said the headless figure. A fire surged into the fireplace, blasting heat toward me and shaking off more of the chill. A moment later, it died to ash, and the smoke person dissolved into nothingness. The room was once again bare, but the edges of my vision blurred as though reality had two layers, and the one I could see was curling back to reveal...I didn't know what.

"Stay away from *me*!" I yelled at the fireplace, not knowing where else to direct my words. I was tired of being cold, and scalded, and tormented by some magical ghost in a fairy story. Coming to the factory had clearly been pointless. This town was pointless if it only had a dead factory and none of our missing masters.

"I'll go where I like," I hissed at the room and the witch and the magic. "Stop this game."

The edges of the fireplace softened. The room fell out of focus as rips—there was no better description for them—of light spilled through what had to be some sort of magic veil the witch had placed around me. Laughter erupted from the center of the room, and I heard hands slapping onto a wooden table and a faint hum that sounded almost like a treadle lathe, but higher-pitched. The sound slivered through me. I spun around, looking wildly for the curling smoke that was my witch.

Other voices rose up, of people talking and jeering, sounds of water being poured. I caught the distinct smell of cotton. Patches of brightly lit floor formed near my feet. I saw swatches of leather boots and cotton pant legs as the magic veil peeled back like veneer from a log.

I felt the warmth of a fire.

I heard Magda yell.

Twelve: Fixation

Damn it, why couldn't I *see* her?

"You don't know what you're doing!" I heard her say, both pleading and admonishing. "I know you're angry, but this isn't how we deal with low trade. You can't destroy every other guild just to provide for your town. I'll speak to the queen about your concerns when I return, but you need to shut this down. Now. These water frames will destroy the textile guild!"

My chest tightened. "Magda isn't a part of this, whatever there is between you and I. Leave her alone."

The deep voice whispered around me, and the air rippled. A human form coalesced again, some four meters in front of me and well away from the widening tears in the magic veil. "Go home, Woodcutter's Daughter."

Bile rose in my throat. Booted feet scuffled over bricks, and a chair fell over. Magda growled. "Don't. Put those away."

I clenched my hands into fists and bit my lower lip. "Let me help her!" I yelled into the empty room.

"Go home!"

"No!" I was done with this witch and its threats. If we were the only ones in this subset of reality, that meant I didn't have to aim. I grabbed at my pouches—the first two I could—pulled at their cords, and flung them at the hazy, headless form.

A scream came first—a short, aborted thing that truncated as soon as it started. More surprise than anything, I assumed, because nothing was happening. My pigments, instead of piercing or binding, suspended in the sunlight-streaked air. Dancing, almost, in lazy spirals, somehow buoyed to remain adrift.

That was definitely not supposed to happen. Alchemy wasn't magic, and my pigments obeyed the laws of gravity like any other natural thing. Yet here they were...floating? No. Moving? I squinted. The flakes of pigment *were* moving, albeit slowly, toward the witch. They floated and bound to one another, the red forming crystals and the yellow patches of film. When they met, coming together in a nonexistent breeze, the yellow films coated the long crystal filaments and pulled, as if magnetized, to the witch.

All of it soundless, and beautiful, and horrifying. And too slow...voyeuristic. There was no heat, so it wasn't the witch's doing. That meant, what? An interaction maybe? Was that possible?

The witch's breathing quickened as the crystals bound into a lattice. He had a head now, and a torso, then legs and arms, all yellow orange and patchworked, like he was made of spider webs.

I heard a gurgle. Yellow hands scratched at a throat, and the outline of a mouth that could no longer open appeared in front of me. As the witch's form became more distinct, I could see the folds of his clothes and the shape of his face, all coated in a jagged, hooked, yellow film that would either suffocate him, impale him, or, with luck, both.

"Leave me alone!" I shouted at the silhouette of yellow and red. "Leave both of us alone. I don't know why you want to keep me from finding my mother, and gods take you, *I don't care.* I will find her so I can get back to my life! If you can get yourself doused in bone oil before the crystals penetrate your skin, or the film suffocates you, you might live."

A wave of heat slapped my face, reddening my skin and scalding my eyes. I looked away as I yelled, but the heat passed almost as soon as it had begun. When I looked back, the room was once again empty, save for a slick of yellow slime with red spears sticking out from its surface, covering the center of the floor. The witch had vanished in a wave of his ridiculous magic. Before I could do more than scowl, another wave of heat rolled over me, and light and sound broke through the magic barrier. Forms took shape, of tables and people, as the remains of the magic wore off.

Another moment and the mirage around me shattered.

It felt like I had been dropped into a steamer, so warm was the air inside the factory without the witch's barrier. Blinding sunlight streamed through the windows, brightening the room. The noise increased as people exclaimed over my sudden appearance. I stood a handspan away from a table that filled the center of the room. A system of narrow wood benches made up the table, draped with rough cotton tablecloths. Cotton bolls spilled across the table tops. And the rest of the space...

machines. Everywhere I looked, metal giants spun thread, not a trace of a wood spinning wheel in sight.

The witch had just traded one nightmare for another. I scanned the room of wide-eyed faces, searching for Magda when, from the back of the factory, someone cried "Witch!"

I tapped my pouches with shaking hands. "I'm not...it wasn't me!" I managed to yell back. Where was Magda? I held my hands out to show I had no weapons, though I saw plenty of people reaching for belt knives and scissors.

"Sorin!" Magda pushed between two large women, oblivious to their scissors and scowls. Most of the factory workers were scattered throughout the floor, but a cluster of about a dozen stood at the head of the table, Magda among them. She sounded accusatory, but considering how suddenly I'd appeared, I couldn't blame her.

"Royal Daughter—" I began. I wanted to run to her, stupidly, because I was still shaking from the witch. But a table and people stood between us, and I was too old to act like that anyway.

"You brought guilders, *witch* guilders, to destroy the factory!" a woman screamed from behind one of the spinning machines. "This is our only income. Our village would have died without the water frames. We see well where your loyalties fall, Royal Daughter. Always the guilds over the commoner."

"That's not what I said! Sorin is...unguilded and sometimes messes with things best left alone. We travel together. I apologize for the inconvenience." Magda started to turn, then shook her head and continued to me. She wove her way around a surly-looking gentleman and hopped across the narrowest bench, finally close enough that I could see the worry lines on her forehead.

I stared at Magda for a moment, forgetting the yelling of the factory workers. If she had explained that I was an *alchemist*, it would have sorted everything out. There was no reason to pretend I was just some foolish trade worker unless...she thought of me that way as well?

"Gods, Sorin, what are you doing here?"

"Witch," the woman behind the machine hissed again.

"I'm not a witch!" I yelled to the crowd. Again, I pointed at my pouches. "This is an alchemy belt!"

"Liar!" One of the women sitting at the table piled with bolls stood and brandished her scissors, and other voices followed hers.

"Liar."

"Unbound."

"Witch."

"We need to go." Magda took my hand, and together, we tried to weave our way to the door, around angry villagers and strange, bobbing machines. No one tried to stop us, but no one got out of our way either. When Magda reached for the door handle, I looked over my shoulder one final time and caught sight of Sameer. He leaned against the far corner wall, arms folded. He had a look of frustrated concern on his face, which seemed really out of place. He'd pulled his hair up in a loose tail, and with his facial features completely unobscured, any doubts I had about his parentage vanished. I cursed.

Magda yanked open the door and a bitter gust of snow and wind hit us both in the face.

"You are everything that is wrong with guilds and the leadership of this country," someone screamed. "Get out of Miantri before you destroy more lives."

"The guilds are dead!" a man yelled. "We won't starve for tradition any longer. You tell the queen that. You tell her!"

"Come back here, and we'll give you a sound lesson in Iana's history, and where that fancy sword of yours can go," another man called. "You disgrace her name and her lineage."

Magda stiffened beside me. She cursed viciously, then slammed the door behind us, catching the heel of my boot.

Magda seethed as she stepped into the street. I trailed her, haunted more by her words, and Sameer, than the words of the workers. People filled the streets now, bleary-eyed and bundled well against the cold, busy with their morning shopping.

"Is there a reason you didn't want to call me an alchemist?" I asked her. My voice felt small and the hurt felt petty, but the words were out of my mouth, and I couldn't take them back.

Magda glanced at me briefly. "If they don't like witches, they won't like alchemists either, Sorin. It..." She bit her lip. "It doesn't have anything to do with your skills."

That helped, a bit.

"I don't suppose you saw the man in the corner?" I asked.

Magda paused long enough for me to catch up. When I did, she pulled me tightly against her and wrapped me in the blue cloth of her cloak, for mine was still on the floor of the guildhall.

"I saw a lot of people. We need to keep moving."

She led me through the crowds toward the square, but her arms couldn't warm the breeze, or take the burn from the witch's words, or explain the strangeness of Sameer.

"Magda?" I prodded tentatively. "We need to talk about the factory. Did you find more guilders there? Did they have the snowsickness? Because I found—"

"Later, Sorin. We need to get to the inn. Get packed." Her fingers dug into my arm, and I finally caught the set of her jaw and how narrow her eyes were.

Magda was... She was afraid. *Afraid.* I'd never seen her wear that emotion before. But she had to know; witches were to be expected, perhaps, especially this close to the glacier, but guilders, it seemed, were not. And I knew that man's face as I knew my own—as well as I knew my mother's and father's. He was a perfect blend of both of them, just like me. Unlike me, however, he'd been fostered out at five to a textile guild. All I really remembered about him were hushed whispers and black curls.

I furrowed my brow as I looked up at Magda, unsure how she would react. Unsure how I should react. How many years had I longed for a sibling to ease the isolation of the Thujan woods? How many times had Mother ranted about the uselessness of fosters?

I tried to speak once more as the inn door came into view, just beyond the square.

"Magda."

Magda came to an abrupt halt, released me, then put her hands on her hips. "What, Sorin? What is so important?"

I took a deep breath, practicing his name softly before I said it out loud, as if it might invoke some demon if spoken incorrectly. As if the spirits of *tii* might rise up and take me if I soiled the name of their lace maker.

"There's a master of textiles in this town, guilded. His name is Sameer. He's perfectly healthy."

Finally, Magda looked interested. "Really? Did you speak with him? Are there others around? Has he seen your mother? Mine?"

I shook my head. "No, no, I don't think so. He didn't say anything anyway."

Magda tilted her head. "So why is he important enough to discuss now? I appreciate knowing there are guilders in town, but we need to *go*."

I looked at the ground, suddenly feeling silly for thinking Sameer was somehow more pressing than the witch, or finding Mother. I answered Magda's question regardless, because his presence did bother me, although I wasn't quite sure why.

"It matters because I am Mother's first to be born with the correct anatomy, but Sameer...I think Sameer is my older brother, and he's not happy to see me."

Thirteen: Calcination

I was certain she had heard me, but I hadn't expected, what? Anger? It felt...it felt like she was mad at me, for the guildhall, and Sameer, and the witch. The way that felt— like something melting, or breaking, or seeping away— hurt more than the witch's heat.

"Magda?"

"Not now."

We finally entered the square, where children danced around the tiny house while a handful of older adults looked on. An elderly man played a small woodwind instrument, and the shrillness of the sound pierced the air. The sun was out, the sky a clear blue, but everything around me felt syrupy, as if we were walking alongside reality instead of in it.

"I thought you should know about Sameer," I said as we weaved around the choir of children. "I hadn't realized he was the textile worker from last night, but that doesn't really matter, does it? It was silly. I'm sorry."

Magda stopped again, dead in the center of the square, and looked down at me, deep lines etched into her forehead. "I care, Sorin, especially since he is a master. But he's hardly the most pressing issue right now. I don't need a master of textiles; I need the grandmaster of textiles." Her words were as frozen as the morning air. "Any grandmaster really, at this point. Your mother, gods, even my mother. I need *someone* of guild value before I arrive for the talks. But all I can find is torn-down guildhalls, mechanization, a handful of bewildered guilders with no memory of their trade, and one master of textiles who may not even live in Sorpsi!"

I stopped moving. "The guilders can't remember?"

Magda shook her head. Lines of frustration curled around her mouth. "Half a dozen, at least, in this town, spanning a number of guilds. They all came in off the glacier. None of them can remember anything about their guild or their skills."

"Poisoned?" I asked, flabbergasted.

"Or magic," Magda returned. "The glacier is rife with the old king's magic. But we're still left with the *why*. Why would the guilders all head to the glacier? There are few towns there, and although they used to be part of Gasta Flecha, Queen Iana didn't include them in the three countries when she drew the borders. I doubt they have much to offer in terms of...guild work."

The warmth of the sun couldn't touch the chill inside me. "Factories," I whispered.

Magda nodded sourly. "Being chased out of this town doesn't help either. There are answers here, Sorin. I need more time."

"I'm sorry."

Magda cupped her face in her hands and sighed. "Damn it, don't apologize! Just tell me how you managed to appear from nowhere. Was it witchcraft? Was the witch responsible for that attack in the forest? Was Sameer? You thought you saw your mother...was that a witch thing? Why didn't you tell me?"

I tried to step away, but Magda wouldn't release me. Her arm moved tight around my waist; her hip pressed into mine. Her jaw set in anger. She stared at me as if we were alone in the square, no children singing and chasing one another around our legs, no murmurs from adults or jostling from those late to their destinations. I couldn't gather my thoughts, not with her looking at me like that.

"I...I don't know. The witch and Sameer are different, I think." I kept trying to explain, unsure how to elaborate or escape her eyes. In that moment, she was the royal daughter, grown and angry, and I was ten, my hair in tight braids, squirming in a back-fastened dress.

Magda looked dubious. The children stopped singing, but as they went silent, adult voices took their place. Color flashed in my periphery, the edges of buildings replaced by cloaks and boots, but I kept my eyes on Magda's.

"Should we talk about the witch?" I asked.

Magda did look around, then turned sharply back toward the inn, her arm still around my waist. I had to follow. "I don't have time to deal with a witch either," she muttered.

"Did you find the grandmaster of glass?" As I asked the question, I peered over Magda's shoulder, back toward the factory. A stream of people poured from the wide-open door toward the square, some still clutching scissors or pocketknives. The wind tossed their cloaks into one another, so tightly were they grouped, and they batted the cloth away with curses and slurs.

I heard "witch."

I heard "alchemy."

I heard people invoke Iana's name.

And then the wind swirled, creating a tiny cyclone of snow and dirt in between us and the factory workers. It dissipated almost immediately after forming but blew across my ears all the same, and they sounded like bones snapping.

They're coming for you.

I shivered and turned back around. My stomach tightened. "Magda, the witch is—"

"Enough with that word! Have some sense and keep your voice down."

They will cut you. Hang you. Burn you. The only safe place is Thuja.

I thought of Mother's house. I couldn't help it. All her marquetries, all my pigments, our family's generations of woodwork, burning as I melted a man in yellow. I thought of what it would smell like if I had burned then, too—not just the smell of campfire but the smell of flesh roasting, popping, searing.

I rubbed at my heat blisters from the sending and pushed farther into Magda. "Magda," I warned. My voice bobbed. "The—it wants us, me, to go home. To Thuja."

"Well, you're not going back there without me, and I'm not going back until after the treaty talks. Tell the witch to deal with it."

Buuuurning, Sorin. You don't want to burn.

I bit into my lower lip.

Magda noticed, and she touched her forehead to mine. "Let's focus on getting out of Miantri in one piece. The grandmaster of glass passed through, but it sounds like he kept on, farther north, though apparently, he seemed disoriented. More snowsickness maybe. Or no reason to stay, it seems, since Miantri took down its guildhall last year. For an entire year, that factory has been running in secret, churning out cotton thread faster than any human hand could. No wonder the textile guild disbanded!"

We reached the end of the square, now devoid of children, the spirit house behind us. The factory workers continued their ruckus behind us stomping, swelling, shouting. The words now were for the queen, and the guilds, and lost livelihoods. It sounded like long-steeping anger that finally had a focal point—anger that had forgotten how the guilds had established the three countries as centers of export and trade. How people from other continents sought out our wares because of the detail, because factories and trade work had eaten all of theirs.

"You didn't threaten to burn down the factory, did you?" I asked, forgetting for a moment that we were in public, and I was with the Royal Daughter of Sorpsi and not just Magda. "You can be real quick to threaten burning, like when you told the queen you'd set her wardrobe on fire if she didn't stop those dancing lessons you hated."

Magda glared at me. I curled my lips in and stopped talking. I shouldn't have run my mouth, but I knew Magda well enough—even this new, grown-up version of her—to know when I'd hit something close to the truth.

"Well?"

She scoffed. "You can't tell me you weren't thinking the same thing."

"Yes, but I didn't say it out loud."

Magda's response was immediate. "You haven't been saying anything out loud, recently. At least, not much of substance. I want an explanation later, about the woods, and the witches, and anything else you haven't been telling me. This isn't a game. We will lose land without the grandmasters, and if I don't make it to the talks, we will lose Sorpsi entirely."

Those were the words of the royal daughter, no trace of Magda. I nodded in assent, although a dozen attempts at explanation filled my mouth. Magda released me from her cloak as we entered the inn. Keegan approached us.

"Royal Daughter! Might I suggest a departure? I don't think the factory workers have taken to you. I've saddled your horses and packed you a few meals."

Relief washed across Magda's face. "Thank you very much. Could you bring the horses around? I'll meet you outside. Sorin, with me." She strode toward the kitchen and the hall to our room without looking back.

"Thank you, Keegan," I managed as I marched after Magda, trying to take deep breaths to loosen the tightness in my chest. It was hard to separate a rebuke from the royal heir from a rebuke from a friend. My eyes were threatening to tear because I seemed to meet every emotion with tears these days. Luckily, everything I owned was already on my person, so I needed only to stand near the door as Magda hastily stuffed her belongings into a leather satchel.

"The witch?" I asked.

"If it's not posing an immediate threat, we'll deal with it after we leave town."

"Do you need my help?" I tentatively reached for a shirt, but Magda got to it first.

"No, Sorin. I just didn't want you out of my sight. I'm about done here." Another pair of pants went into the satchel and Magda forced the closure. Curtly, and without looking at me, she said, "Come on. We need to go. No more dawdling or surprises."

This time, her words cut too deeply to pass off as royal orders. I grabbed at her cloak as she reached for the door, thinking I should take just a moment to explain. Her tone cut, and I couldn't ride to Celtis with emotions bleeding all over. I didn't want her to be mad, not at me. Not like this.

"I didn't mean to...surprise you. Um, it's not... A lot of things are happening. Have happened. This...I'm not... If we could just talk."

The eyes that turned back to me were narrow and angry, and the pain there looked personal.

I dropped the fabric. I'd been too forward. Shame flushed my cheeks. She hadn't been talking about my presentation. I was being ridiculous, again. "Royal Daughter, I'm—"

"Look, Sorin, I get that you have a blind spot when it comes to guilds and alchemy. Amada kept you in that damn forest, away from anyone who might have given you some broader look at the world and, in doing so, *became* your world. It's time to come out of your bubble. Gods, Sorin, witches are talking to you. Think about that for a minute."

"I'm so sorry, Royal Daughter. I'm trying to—"

Magda slapped at the doorframe. "Just listen. You don't have any idea what happened back there, do you? You've got them thinking about witches, and old magic, and everything that went along with the king. He *kidnapped* people, Sorin. Women, in particular. He kept them locked up on farms, trained them in all the skills he wanted, and then used...magic—a sword with magic—to kill them and take their skills for his own. He littered the three countries with his magic. Iana broke free. Iana beat him at his own game. But it was a century ago, and that's not so long. And you're a...you're an *alchemist*. You're unbound, the same as the witches." She slapped her chest. "And I may have said some stupid things in that factory indicating it shouldn't be there. Individually, they could have passed. Together, the village is up in arms. We have to go. Now."

"Yes, Your Highness." I walked into the hall.

"Sorin."

It wasn't a question.

I turned and responded without thinking because my mouth had a bad tendency to run when I was nervous or upset. When it did, it was often without consultation with my brain.

"Could we share a room again? In Puget?" I asked.

I didn't know where the words slid from, for I'd not even considered our lodging in the other country. Did they even have inns? Perhaps they slept in the open, or in boats on some landlocked lake. Heat crept to my cheeks, again, but I didn't look away. I wanted her answer.

Magda's eyebrows raised, and she smothered a smile. "I would enjoy that," she whispered into my ear as she passed. She came close enough that her lips just grazed my cheek, but then she was past, down the hall and into the main room of the inn.

It was hard to breathe now, binding or no. Gods, she'd almost kissed me. I'd wanted her to kiss me—it had been in the back of my mind since her bath—but the sudden, tangible reality was overwhelming.

"Are you coming, Sorin?" Magda called from the inn's main door.

"Yes, of course." I followed Magda out of the inn, desperately trying to keep the grin from my face.

Fourteen: Lead

"About half the town is out now," Keegan called from the door as Magda mounted her horse and I the one Keegan had sold us—a short, black thing with a white mark on its nose and front right hoof—and we began toward the road. Keegan had told me its name, but it might as well have been Peanut again, for all I cared. I was way too sore to be riding, and it was difficult to grip the saddle with my thighs.

"You okay then, Sorin?" Magda asked as I gave Peanut the Second a tentative pat. From the back of my saddle, I took a brown, frayed cloak, unrolled it, and fastened it on.

"I suppose."

"They're demanding to speak with you," Keegan called out.

"I'm not surprised. Sorin, stay close, but visible. We'll ride through the plaza. Show them very clearly we're leaving, and our witch is coming with us."

"Hey!" I choked on air, and old, well-honed frustrations about Thujan villagers swelled in my chest.

Magda glared back at me. I pursed my lips to the side and decided against arguing just as we came in front of the stables to face the crowd.

Some fifty people stood in an arc in front of the inn. I recognized many from the factory, but they'd been joined now by men, women, and even a few children from the village. Two in the far back held wooden torches, and at least three factory workers had their scissors.

They're going to kill you.

An elderly woman pushed to the front and addressed Magda. She wore her hair gathered on top of her head, and her fine red cotton dress had stitching so even I wondered whether they were done by machine. Her left hand held a length of rope. The wind batted at my ears.

They're going to kill Magda.

Shut up!

You'll be safe if you return to Thuja.

Magda's voice cut through the wind. "I'm leaving you in peace," Magda called out to the crowd. "I apologize for my statements in the factory. I'll bring this to the queen's attention, as well as your comments about trade. I'm sure we can find a way for guilds and machines to work together."

Promise to return to Thuja and both you and the royal daughter will be spared.

What little patience I had ran out. *How about I melt you into a yellow puddle instead?*

Tinkling laughter scattered through the wind.

I shifted in my saddle, ready to scream out loud at the witch who would not get out of my head. Magda jerked her horse back and put a hand on my shoulder.

"Don't," she cautioned. "One more piece of kindling and the town will go to blaze. They don't care what you are. They just want you, us, gone."

"I just want the witch out of my head," I muttered quietly. I settled, though, scratching my fingernails on the leather of my saddle. I'd pretend it was the witch's face.

The elderly woman stepped up to Magda's horse. She stomped her foot—not the way a child would when not given a sweet, but the way that told us, definitely, who was in charge. It was hard to ignore the implications of the rope she held, and I could almost feel the rough fibers as her fingers stroked the threads. We needed to get out of town, and it didn't look like Magda's royal blood wasn't going to be enough to do it.

"You brought a witch to our village, Royal Daughter. We can forgive your comments in the factory, but you know what a witch means here, guilded or not. He's not leaving."

I rolled my eyes at the pronoun. It didn't hurt the same way "she" did, but it wasn't accurate either. Although if they hung me, pronouns would be the least of my concerns.

"If you can find the witch, he is yours, but Sorin is not." Magda brought her horse in front of mine, cutting me off from the crowd.

The wind laughed.

"Sorin poses no risk to your village, and is an unguilded woodcutter with an interest in alchemy, nothing more. We are, however, being pursued by a witch, and for bringing that to your village, I apologize. As we continue our journey, we will take the north road to avoid more of your rangelands on our way to Celtis."

Another gust of wind, this one without words, tossed around the smell of burnt wood along with Magda's blue cloak. I caught a glint of gold on her head as her hair shifted. She'd put her circlet on, although when I wasn't sure. The added authority didn't seem to be helping.

The old woman looked right at me, her voice calm. "The witch stays, Royal Daughter."

You know how Iana dealt with the king's witches, don't you? The king's witches and the king's alchemists. They tried to take her power with that magic sword, and she killed them all. She hung them, drew and quartered them, then burned them. You could just go back to Thuja. Save Magda. Save yourself.

"I'm not a witch!" I yelled, both to the wind and to the woman on the ground. I tried to guide Peanut II up next to Magda's horse, but he stayed stubbornly behind. "Damn this horse!"

The woman moved toward Peanut. She reached out, first to pet his nose, then went to his bridle, which she tugged. Peanut began to kneel.

I kicked at Peanut, desperate to get him to move or shuffle or do *something*. He steadfastly refused until Magda drew her sword. Then Peanut sidestepped at the sound of the metal against leather, but the woman did not release him.

"Sorin is coming with me," Magda said. Her sword was still pointed to the earth, but if the villagers couldn't hear the warning in her voice, they were idiots.

The woman spat on the ground. "No heir of Iana would protect a witch or alchemist. They are vile."

"Alchemists aren't—"

"No, witches and alchemists are guilded." Magda spoke over me, her knuckles pink with her grip on her sword. "Iana wouldn't condone a lynch mob."

"You don't speak for her," the woman snarled. "*We* are her people. Iana came from a ranch just outside our borders, as the legend says. *We* carry her legacy, not some city-raised descendent."

The woman gestured, and the crowd surged forward. Knives came out of sheaths, and I saw bottles of alcohol opened far too close to the torches. I made a final attempt to pull Peanut back, and failed. Magda's jaw set. Gods, we were going to die here, in this frozen, guildless town. I scanned the crowd, thinking maybe I might see some escape route Magda had missed, when I caught the sight of black curls just to my right.

Sameer. Not holding any weapons, but with fists rammed into his pockets, his brow furrowed, his eyes boring into me. Sameer, who was a guilded textile worker. Sameer, who lived up on the glacier and knew how to navigate it. Sameer, who was trusted by the village.

Damn him for being here, and damn him for being our only way out.

Fifteen: Tin

"The master of textiles will take us." I yelled it into the crowd, ignoring the grunt of surprise from Magda. "He'll escort us to the glacier, where we'll be well off your lands."

Sameer pushed forward, approaching my horse. I sat back in the saddle as he leaned in, his face contorted in rage.

I lowered my voice. "Escort us out of town. Please. I'm not guilded, but the royal daughter is, and Amada—"

Sameer's face looked like an overripe mangosteen. "Fuck Amada."

Maybe Mother had made the right choice in never allowing me to know my sibling. I didn't have the patience for this. "You'd have to find her to do that, and you won't find her with us dead."

His eyes flashed with some emotion I couldn't pinpoint, and then he let out a short growl, mounted my horse, and sat directly behind me in the saddle. Startled, I tried to stand and slide off, but Sameer's arm snaked around my waist and held me down. He whispered into my ear, "You and I need to have a long talk."

"Great," I growled back. "After we get out of the village, okay?"

"Master of textiles?" the lead woman called up to us. "You trust them?"

Sameer snorted. "Absolutely not, but I do know them, sort of. I'll take them to the damn glacier. Let the ice be their executioner. I didn't work on that spirit house to have it trampled by a mob."

The old woman tossed her head in a funny sort of nod. "Acceptable, Master." She sheathed her knife. "Don't ever visit Miantri again." The woman's words might have been meant for Magda, but her eyes glared only at me.

I tried to urge my horse forward while simultaneously elbowing Sameer. He was way too close, and he smelled like old sweat and rotting birch.

Magda gave me a tense, questioning look, but I frowned. "He's fine. Let's go."

"Thank you for your understanding," she said to the woman. She took my horse's reins and kicked her horse to a trot along the path that led from the village. The wind followed us, twirling our cloaks and stinging the tips of our ears as the villagers jeered.

The witch's voice mingled along with them.

You're going to die. You're going to die die die die die.

I spat at the wind, though I'd never been much good at spitting, and all I succeeded in doing was getting Peanut's ear wet.

"Sorin?" Magda asked at Peanut's snort.

I shook my head. "Witches in my head. Trying to keep us off the glacier."

"Possibly the witch isn't as naïve as you two are about ice," Sameer offered, a little too smugly.

"Please be quiet," I hissed.

"Eyes ahead then. Don't want the village to think you're going to hex them."

I slumped. The only other option was to try to land an elbow on Sameer's nose, which the village would definitely not have approved of. So, I stayed silent as we passed through the square at a tense canter, slow enough to watch people shove knives into boots and overhear conversations about guilds and witches and alchemists mingling with questions about lunch. Magda's shoulders progressively relaxed as we neared the city wall, and even Sameer's grip lessened once we'd passed the line of loose gray stones and came to the main path crossroads.

There, while Magda debated which road to take, a soft purple light caught my eyes. It lined the left side of our trail, then cut south, along the road back to Thuja and Sorpsi's capital.

Thousands of ways to die on a glacier. Turn back, Sorin of Thuja. This path will take you home.

Home. The witch meant Thuja, but home also meant the capital, and Master Rahad, and my apprenticeship. A desperate, irrational desire to run down the trail of purple crumbled over me.

"Sorin, what are those? Some of your fungi?" Magda pointed not south, but to the north trail where dotted patches of normal, white foxfire lead into a forest of scraggly firs coated in snow.

I took a deep breath. Magda was the reason I was still here. Magda would release me from my guild inheritance once we finished our trip. Magda, and the northern trail, were what I needed to focus on.

"Those are just foxfire. They're out of season, but maybe this is a winter variety we don't have in Thuja. I don't know. Most glow blue or green in the dark, depending on variety, but it is normal for them to be white in daylight." I didn't mention the south trail. If she hadn't commented on it, then likely she couldn't see it, and now wasn't the time to have another conversation about witches.

Magda backed her horse up so it paralleled mine. "Would you check the fungi? Even though they look normal? This close to the glacier, I'd like to be sure."

Anything to get me out of the saddle and away from Sameer and his stink.

I dismounted my horse, stepped onto the north trail, then knelt at the first fungal cluster. "Okay?" I murmured as I touched the top of one of the little white mushrooms, enjoying the moist, delicate feeling on my skin. In the spring or summer, the texture wouldn't have been strange. For the middle of winter, the fungus was far too alive. "Going to dance or anything? Turn Sameer into a capybara?" I snickered. The fungus, as I had hoped, did not respond.

"It's typical," I said as I looked farther down the trail. "Just some fungi in a fairy trail. A mild enchantment. There's probably an old amulet nearby like Master Rahad said. A broken old amulet leaking some old magic into the duff."

"Is that why it started glowing?" Sameer shot back. "Or is that your magic?"

"I'm *not* a... Glowing? What?" I looked down at the fungi near my knee; they had, in fact, started glowing green. Which was impossible, of course, because it was far too light to see the pale luminescence of foxfire, and the tiny things were so bright I almost had to look away. I frowned and got back on my horse. The glow faded out.

I sighed. I really hated magic.

"Magda, would you take your horse forward? I want to test something."

"The fungi aren't going to kill me or my horse, right?"

I looked over to glare at her but saw a lopsided smirk on her face, and grinned.

"No, Royal Daughter. I promise to protect you from the fungi. Now, if you would please? For alchemy?"

"If it's for a guild, I suppose." Magda uttered what sounded like a well-practiced sigh and let her horse canter a few meters along the northern trail, then turned back. No fungi glowed. She even got off and tried on foot. Again, the foxfire stayed their normal white.

"Uh-huh." Sameer snorted. More loudly, he said, "It's not a bad idea to lose the horses. We can't take them on the glacier, and if Sorin is triggering some old magic, we might as well take advantage of it."

Of course it had to be me triggering the magic. Why couldn't this witch just leave me alone? "You're not afraid of the snowsickness?" I asked Sameer, trying to bring my mind to other pressing issues, like us dying on the glacier.

Sameer coughed. "No. And I'm definitely going with you two to the glacier. I don't want you getting lost and spooking some other village that I contract with. I'm charging for my guide services, though, and it won't be cheap."

"Fine," Magda cut in. "You can name your price after we get to Celtis. Now, Sorin, the foxfire?"

I shrugged. "It's no more dangerous than any other foxfire. Not that I can tell."

Magda slid from her horse and shouldered her pack without argument. She stepped onto the trail as Sameer and I dismounted and took our own packs. She nudged a cluster of foxfire with the side of her foot, and frowned. "Their light is helpful, with the dense canopy. Sorin, you'll have to lead."

Sameer laughed.

"I'm pretty good in a forest," I said to him as I moved onto the trail, and the fungi lit again to their ghostly green. Though the skin on the back of my neck prickled, I took another step, and in the space of a heartbeat, a winding path of foxfire flared to life on the packed dirt and snow of the trail.

"Yes, you're definitely not a witch. You have me convinced." Sameer kicked at a cluster of foxfire. Several caps broke from their stipes and fell into the snow. Color bled from the flesh until it was as white as its surroundings.

There was no point in arguing with him. I tossed my cloak over my shoulder and turned away from the village of Miantri. With a sigh, I led Magda and Sameer down a glowing trail of fungi into the northern wood.

*

Half a day later, the foxfire grew so profuse and thick I had to stomp it down just to stay on the trail. More worrying was that the wind blew milder nearest the foxfire, and the temperature ran higher. The farther we strayed from the path, whether to collect water or to relieve ourselves, the more the actual weather beat upon us until it became a chill that felt like it might break our bones. So we stayed on the magical fungal trail probably made a century ago by the old king for some nefarious purpose, and I fumed silently about magic, and witches, and my brother.

As the conifers around us shortened to head height, then waist, then finally to scrubby bushes, the fungi spun closer together until there was no path, only a thick carpet of stalked green. Underneath that, the ground transitioned to rocky pellets of ice, colored dirty brown from mixing with the soil. Another hour in and I could finally see the glacier, an enormous expanse of white and blue that stretched on into the horizon.

Gods, it was beautiful. It was terrifying. I'd never imagined so much ice, nor the surprising colors that lurked within it. I saw blues and purples mixed with dirty grays and, of course, the omnipresent white. Tall, jagged outcroppings jutted from the surface—hours away, perhaps, but terrifying nonetheless. They looked like spears, like some Puget god had sent deadly icicles raining from the heavens to pierce the ice below.

"We're really going to walk on that?" I asked. I stopped and pointed to one of the ice towers. "Avalanche? Crushing?"

Sameer brushed past me, his shoulder hitting mine hard enough to force me forward. I scowled but didn't push back. If he fell and cracked his head on the ice, witches would be the least of my concerns. Guilders did not look fondly on violence from outside their ranks.

Sameer took the funny axe from his pack and flipped it in his hand. "They're just seracs, and we'll try to stay clear if possible. We're not going past any villages, mostly because they're farther up the glacier, but also, I'm not subjecting them to whatever is going on with you."

He pointed to the path, which ended abruptly at the glacier's edge. I walked to the end of it, then stepped onto the glacier proper. Immediately, the fungi stopped glowing.

"Uh-huh." Sameer came up next to me, followed by Magda. Without the heat from the magic foxfire, the air was almost too cold to bear. I pulled the old cloak tightly about my shoulders and clutched handfuls of the fabric to cover my hands.

"The glacier's preamble here will take us directly to Puget if we follow it, although we'll have to move farther into the glacier some places since there are a few lakes up here we should avoid." Sameer looked back at Magda and held up a hand before she had even started to speak. "No side trips. Four generations haven't been able to find Iana's Lake, and we're not going to either."

Magda stared at Sameer for several moments before shaking her head and heading east. Sameer grinned, then leaned in and tugged at my cloak. I pulled away and kicked a chunk of stony ice toward him.

"I think she likes me," he said. "It's probably my curly hair."

If I'd had a sword, I'd have considered running him through. My cheeks burned. "Why are you still here?" I demanded. "We're at the glacier. Your promise to the villagers is met."

Sameer's grin turned down, into features almost cruel. "Because I've waited a long time to talk to you, Sorin of Thuja. Somewhere you can't run away, and where

Amada can't come to your rescue. And a glacier on the top of the world, away from all the people who love you and insist on smothering you with protection? It sounds about perfect."

Sixteen: Mercury

We walked in a single-file line, sometimes with Magda in the lead, sometimes Sameer, for the rest of the day. Though the view to my north was majestic, my cloak could not keep out the cold, and the ice was too unpredictable to walk side by side, even to share heat. By the time we reached one of the thermal lakes that dotted the glacier—lakes being a generous name for what were often no more than puddles—I could no longer feel my toes or fingertips.

"Take a minute to warm up," Sameer called out. He picked his way over to the bank and took his hands from his cloak to warm them in the steam.

"Sorin, would you walk with me?"

I was looking forward to the warmth, but the catch in Magda's voice, while subtle, was enough to get my attention. I scrambled over to her, crunching the softer, slushier ice that surrounded the small lake. It was easier to walk here, with the added traction, and Magda took my hand and led me around until we were on the opposite bank from Sameer.

"Are you all right?" I looked across the water to Sameer, who watched us with interest.

Magda growled. "Would you come closer, Sorin?"

"Uh, yes? How close?" We were already next to each other, so I stepped in front of her. To my surprise, Magda moved forward until we were only a handspan apart, then wrapped her cloak around us both.

"Magda?" I welcomed the warmth of the double cloak and the tang of metal that seemed to radiate from her clothes and skin. "What are we doing?"

Magda wrapped her arms around my waist and pulled me against her. I caught my breath at the softness of her chest against mine. I tried to find somewhere to put my hands and finally settled on her waist. "Distraction," Magda whispered into my ear. "I need to talk to you, and I'd prefer he think we're doing something else."

I looked back over Magda's shoulder, and Magda turned to look as well. Sameer had started to come toward us but was slowing, his nose turned up.

A look of irritation crossed Magda's face. "Damn him," she murmured and then lowered her head and kissed me just below my ear, on the soft skin of my neck.

Sameer blinked, then stalled.

It was possible my heart was going to stop beating.

Magda lingered, trailing a line of soft kisses up to my ear. I gasped and pressed into her. As a diversionary tactic, it was ideal. Unfortunately, Sameer wasn't the only one being distracted.

"I want to know about witches. Now."

It was hard to find enough air to talk. It was hard to think about anything except her breasts, and her hands, and the way her hip shifted against my thigh.

"They've been after me since Sorpsi, I think—" Magda brushed her lips against mine, enough to tease but not enough to truly make contact. I whimpered, but she'd already moved on to my chin and neck. "That's why we were attacked on the road, I think, as well as the guildhall. There's been one speaking to me and trying to get me to turn back. I don't know if it's affiliated with the men who came after me in Thuja. They were sent by some master witch, for Mother. It's—" I lost my train of thought as Magda's lips brushed my own again. This time, I leaned in, determined for more than teasing contact.

"Keep talking," Magda whispered. She pulled back and moved her attention to my jaw. "I want to get everything out before we talk to Sameer."

"*You* try talking while a princess kisses you," I retorted. "This isn't fair."

Magda snorted and nipped at my neck. "There's nowhere private to go on a glacier. And I'm the royal daughter, not a princess. We're not a kingdom, and I'm not just a well-bred broodmare."

I almost giggled. Almost. "Do you think we'll find any masters through here, Magda? Our mothers maybe? Confused guilders?"

Again, Magda's lips pressed just below my ear, and her skin felt warm and fluttering and perfect. "As far as I know, there is only one path from Miantri to Celtis. If guilders are fleeing to Puget, or farther, then they have to come this way. With luck, we will come across a few."

I touched my forehead to hers. Gods, how I wanted to kiss her, or have her kiss me. Properly, though, no more of this gentle touching that threatened my sanity. It being a ruse would be irrelevant. There were no rules on a glacier, no statuses, no guilds. No one owned this land except those who trod across it. But Mother nagged at my mind and kept me back from what should have been a joyful moment.

"Where are our mothers, Magda?" I whispered into her ear. "What happened? Even if you don't know, what do you suspect?"

Magda sighed. "Witches, sweetheart. I know nothing, but I suspect witches."

I let her words rattle around my head as she tucked a strand of hair behind my ear. "Kidnapped?"

Magda didn't respond, but her eyes turned serious, and her mouth set in a grim line.

"Magda, *tell me.*"

"How about we talk about Sameer instead? Do you trust him?"

"Magda!" I stomped my foot, which nearly slid out from under me. Magda caught me by my elbow, but when our eyes met again, mine simmering with frustration, she did the last thing I'd ever have expected out on this frigid slick of water and death.

She kissed me.

Her lips were warm—so much warmer than the air. One arm wrapped around my waist, the other tangled in my hair. I was so startled I didn't think to grab onto her as well. Instead, I traced her lips with my own, melted into her arms and the thousands of memories we shared. Gods, she was perfect. *We* were perfect. I felt her tongue, her teeth, her hips, her thighs pressed to mine, and it filled me in places I hadn't known were empty.

"Sorin," Magda whispered as she pulled back. I whimpered and grabbed her hand, determined not to resume our previous conversation. I'd waited too long for this. So had she.

"We have to talk about Sameer."

"I don't care about Sameer," I grumbled.

Magda's smile broadened. "I understand, but he's still here and seems unlikely to leave. He's competent on this ice, so I don't mind having him along. But it seems you and he have a history. Do you trust him?"

I blew out a breath of hot, humid air. "I don't *know* him. Not like I'd know a foster that Mother took on. Not that she ever did, of course, guild law be damned." I looked over Magda's shoulder at Sameer, ten meters away now, who was making a very hard study of snowshoe hare tracks just off the game trail. The tips of his ears were red, and I doubted it was entirely from the cold.

"Sorin?"

I turned back. Magda's eyes were serious, so I tried to focus on those, and not her lips, and how one of her hands was stroking the back of my neck.

"He's my brother, Magda. Yet I never had one, not really." I thought about the textile guildhall, and his reaction near the spirit house, and though my stomach churned and my arms started to itch, I shook my head. How many times had I asked, no, begged Mother for a sibling? For her to take just one foster? My blood brother was right here, and I couldn't send him off, antagonistic or not. I didn't know what he wanted from me, but I needed something from him, even if it was just a sense of family. "I...he wants to talk. To me. We have some history. He deserves to be heard, I think, even if he is a jerk."

Magda smiled, then leaned in until our noses touched. "As long as he doesn't endanger us."

"Mmm," I hummed through pressed lips. "I don't really want to talk about my brother right now."

Her voice turned conspiratorial. "More kisses come later—when we're at an inn, and there is a bed, and we aren't freezing. I promise." She stepped back and took my hand, and pulled me toward the lake. "Come on. Let's get warm."

Some of us are already warm, and half a decade is plenty long enough to wait. I didn't say that out loud, but instead, kicked a rock toward Sameer. He sighed and joined us at the lake edge, looking from me, to Magda, then back to me again.

"Was that really necessary?" he asked.

I shrugged and leaned into Magda. "She likes curly hair."

"Could we just warm up and go?"

"Agreed." Magda flipped her cloak back and held her hands out. I started to do the same, then paused when I finally noticed the lake. It was completely still. No waves beveled its surface, and even the air seemed to have ceased all movement. The lake waited to breathe, and I waited with it as warmth crept back into my body. It stretched well into the glacier proper, eating away at smooth walls of blue ice. Mountains rose all around its circumference, buffering and protecting.

No wonder people lived up here, outside the three countries. I'd brave the cold, too, to get a chance to see scenery like this every day.

A snowshoe hare darted across my feet and continued on, tracing the perimeter of the lake. It paused to drink some ten meters away, but while its little whiskers and tongue dipped into the water, the surface did not ripple.

"Magda," I said, pointing to the hare.

"It's a good idea, but I don't have a bow with me anymore, and I can't hit it with a rock hard enough to kill it from this distance."

"You wouldn't want to anyway," Sameer said. "That lake is enchanted. No one knows what the old king used it for, so I wouldn't trust any animal meat from up here. You can bathe in it—people routinely do—but I wouldn't suggest drinking it." Sameer kicked a rock into the water, and Magda and I both watched, wide-eyed, as it sank below the surface seamlessly, not even a small funnel forming in its wake.

Magda ran a hand over her braids, then pulled her cloak back around. "Fascinating and terrifying, but we don't have time for either. Come on. Let's keep going." She walked back to the rocky path denoting the edge of the glacier and continued her careful footsteps east.

I started to follow, but then the snowshoe hare jumped into the lake. It splashed and thumped in the shallows. Each droplet of water that came back down left no indent, made no sound. When it hopped back out again, damp and joyful and completely unharmed, my curiosity got the better of me. It wasn't like Mother was going to come bounding across the landscape and chastise me for wasting time. We had five minutes to spare, and there was no half-finished marquetry or floor that needed polishing. Besides, who was afraid of a lake?

"Hold on," I called out. I'd never had a chance to study magic so closely, and without a witch around, it didn't seem quite so...what? Invasive? Besides, this was old magic. Historical magic. It was degraded and probably completely benign. Some part of me, a younger part of me, didn't want to miss an opportunity like this to study magic without a witch cracking jokes about body parts. It was a historical study, nothing more. Magic had an important place in society; otherwise, Iana would never have let the witches form a guild. If Iana could trust witches after what they'd done to her, so could I.

"Just be quick, Sorin," Magda returned. "It's getting colder by the minute."

I turned back, walked across the desolate patch of earth to the very edge of the water, and squatted down. A strip of old leather lay here, half buried in the slush, with the mark for the Eastgate shepherd's guild stamped into it.

I tried not to think about a master shepherd bobbing, face down, on a glacial lake. Likely, it was from some purchased goods dropped by another traveler. Instead, I let the strange warmth of the water bring feeling back into my fingertips before I picked up a handful of slush and let it melt through my fingers. Nothing felt unusual. I touched the toe of my boot to the water's edge and watched the lake curve around it. I had a wild notion to drop a few flakes of fungal pigment in, but memories of the interactions between them and the witch in Miantri quickly quashed that idea. No, it was time for a proper test. I wasn't going to learn anything by proxy.

I unwrapped myself from my cloak, stuck out a finger, and slowly dragged it across the surface.

Water splashed up at my face. I jumped back and wiped my eyes on my sleeve. My first thought was the hare had come around, but there was nothing living about me, and Sameer and Magda were a good bit away, staring and pointing at a cluster of seracs in the distance. "Just try again," I murmured, and squatted back down, finger out, ready for experiment number two.

But the stillness had not returned to the lake as I expected. I gaped down at the water where concentric rings now radiated out from the point where my finger had touched. The ripples moved into small waves, pushed by some invisible force. The lake frothed. I swore I saw a hand break the surface, then sink back down.

"Magda! Sameer!" I didn't back away, not this time, but I wasn't a complete idiot. If the lake was going to eat me, there needed to be witnesses. Clearly, it had already eaten someone else.

Magda and Sameer's hurried footsteps approached, but I didn't turn to look at them. Where I had touched my finger, the water sank, the focal point dropping away into a funnel of swirling blue. A small brown bulb—an amulet of some kind—spun around the edges of the funnel, rising higher and higher until it floated on top of the foam and glinted in the sunlight.

An amulet. The old king's magic. Why was the lake offering it to me? Would it spew a body at me next?

What in the world was *I* going to do with either one?

I heard Sameer's voice from behind me, laughing. "He's fine, Royal Daughter. Sorin, you want to take the amulet out? The magic has all bled out by now, and it's just a shell with the solvent they used to carry the magic. It'll get a decent price in one of the towns, or we can drink the alcohol in it ourselves. These are as common as the rabbits up here. The alcohol might make tonight more bearable if we don't find a wave cave to sleep in. Or maybe it will turn one of us into a polar bear. Or shrink one of our arms. Either way, fun."

That was too much. Curiosity would take me only so far, and my chest felt heavy from the heat and moisture and the masculine pronouns. I scrambled away from the lake edge on heels and hands, unable to wrest my eyes from the deepening vortex. Any minute now, I'd see the rest of the body, I was sure. Its skin would be wrinkled and saggy. Its eyes sunken. It'd be in high-end leathers with fine stitching and...

Magda looped her arms under mine and hauled me to standing just as foam formed near the edges of the lake, then crashed to shore in a wave. Water soaked through my pants, warm and unwelcome. I pushed us both back again, trying to get out of range of the water, when a twinge pulled at my wet legs. I stopped moving.

"Come on, Sorin. Sameer's right—we were bound to stumble across a few old amulets while up here. I've found them before, with the queen, when we traveled this far north. Mother collects them, in fact. Part of our history, you know? But right now, we have to keep going, and you don't need any more enchanted water on you. Be an alchemist later, when it won't get you killed from hypothermia."

"I'm trying!" I tensed my shoulder muscles until they bunched. My limbs, my *mind*, told me to move back to the water's edge, to look down that supernatural, blasphemous hole, and take the amulet. A sound came from the water, much like twigs snapping and too much like my name. But the wind, with its own words, clashed in discord with the lake, as if the magic was layering on top instead of being a part of the same whole.

Sorin! the water called. Or maybe it was some ghost in the lake. They were both terrifying.

The witch's voice came again. *Go home, Sorin of Thuja, and leave magic alone!*

For once, the witch and I were in agreement.

"Stop!" I screamed at the lake, startling Magda enough that she dropped me back to the ground. On my rear, I kicked at the slush beneath my heels, trying to push back, away from the lake, back to the safety of the ice. Another two meters and the water on my pants evaporated. The waves stopped. The foam sank and dissolved in gliding burps. The concentric rings fell still, first at the widest circumference and then collapsing in until there were only tight circles where my finger had broken the surface. The bottom of the vortex rose back up, and finally, the lake exhaled. The water stilled back to glass. The amulet disappeared. There was no trace of the body.

"Sorin?"

"I'm really, really tired of magic, and I think it's creepy that the queen collected those things. Also, why are there bodies up here?"

"Bodies?" Magda wrinkled her nose and scanned the lake. "All I saw was the amulet. But up here, who knows? There are a lot of ways to die on a glacier. And I don't disagree with you. If the lakes act like that, no wonder the Miantri villagers were spooked when you appeared from nowhere. There's a lot more active magic in this area than

I remember. We'll stay out of the lakes from here on out."
Magda got me to my feet once again, and together, we
walked back to Sameer.

He shook his head. "Get it studied then? You could
have at least taken the amulet if you were going to waste
time," he said. "Just because they're common doesn't
mean they're not useful. The king stored spells and such
in them. They're worth money, even if the magic is long
gone. They're hard to make, and the witches' guild will
buy them back if nothing else."

"I don't need to get drunk, and I have no interest in
magic," I retorted. I brushed my pants one more time,
then pulled my cloak around my shoulders again. It
probably had just been the froth on the water. I had a
witch whispering to me, after all. My imagination was
overactive.

Sameer kept talking. "You don't care for magic, but
you have an interest in alchemy? That makes no sense. So,
instead, you persist in being useless. I can see why the
royal daughter travels with you."

Was he going to be like this the entire way to Puget?
Maybe I didn't need a sibling after all. Maybe next time,
the lake could attack *him*.

"*Magic* is useless. Why do you want an artifact from
something the old king cooked up in this desolate, treeless
place? I just wanted to have a look. I'm done. We can go.
I'm not going to be wooed by a lake, no matter how many
amulets it offers me."

"Stop it," Magda snapped. "Both of you. Please. Let's
just keep moving."

I grimaced but nodded, and fell in step behind
Magda. "My apologies."

"Did you have a destination in mind for when we set down for the night?" Magda's lead foot slipped out from under her before she had put her full weight on it, and she steadied herself on my shoulder.

"Take short, cautious steps from here on," Sameer advised. "And yes, I have thoughts on where we can camp. We'll have to move onto the glacier proper soon, but there's a small lake just up here, perhaps twenty minutes away. It has one small wave cave, or at least it did on my journey out. The weather has been consistent. It should still be there. The lake won't be frozen, either, unless the thermal vents gave out." He pointed southeast. "This line of vents will take us directly to Celtis. We have one, maybe two more days of travel ahead of us, assuming Sorin can keep from triggering any larger spells."

I scowled. "I'm not doing it on purpose."

Sameer tightened his cloak and pushed ahead of Magda on the trail. "I know. That's why you're so damn dangerous."

Seventeen: Silver

It was evening before my temper cooled enough to speak. Sameer and Magda hadn't had much to say, either, as our movement onto the glacier brought us closer to the towering seracs and the ground under our feet turned from pebbles to ice.

Our destination—the wave cave—was a short ice outcropping, maybe only a handspan taller than Sameer, that arched partially over the ground. It did indeed look like a frozen wave, although how anything that size could have come from the tiny little lake it butted up against, I didn't know.

"We'll stay there tonight. This is a common waypoint stop. The cave is stable."

I eyed the ice critically. If it wasn't stable, it'd kill us all when it caved in, since it was deep enough that even our toes wouldn't poke from the entry.

When neither Magda nor I moved any closer, Sameer tossed his pack forward. It slid the remaining distance to the cave, ending in a rattling sound.

"I'll just relieve myself then," he muttered and disappeared behind the cave.

Magda's hand ran across my back, not slow enough to tease but lingering enough to tell me she was still thinking about the last lake as well. I looked out along the never-ending sheet of ice to a looming serac around fifteen meters away. Were the crackling sounds I heard coming from the glacier itself, or the serac? I couldn't be sure, not with the wind pushing kernels of words at my ears I was determined, this time, to ignore. I told myself there was no sound in the wind. The dotting greens and blues I saw in the distance were lights reflecting off the ice, not enchanted foxfire. I told my mind to shut up and forced myself to stare at the endless expanse of white, and at sheets of ice so blue they looked like the ocean. Nothing to see. Nothing to think. I just needed to go to sleep.

"How long will the talks take?" I asked Magda as she put down her pack and removed her sleeping mat.

"A few days at most. I don't have much to negotiate with anyway. The census already came around. None of the rulers—not the triarchy from Puget, nor Eastgate's king, nor I—get to see them before the talks, but I know what ours will look like. We're going to lose land."

I laid my pack next to hers, then sat down to fuss with the lacings on my boots. I didn't look at her; she didn't need to see the concern on my face that "a few days" could be long enough for Master Rahad to forget. To find another apprentice. That a few days was already too late for that body in the lake and, maybe, too, for the other missing masters.

Magda misunderstood my frown. "We'll find them, Sorin; I promise. Your mother wasn't at Miantri. We know that now. Do you have any thoughts where she might be in Celtis? Does she have any contacts there? Former clients?" Her hand covered my own, and she scooted up behind me.

"Amada's missing?" Sameer had returned. He put his canteen down and wiped his face with his sleeve. "Is that why you're traveling with Sorin and not a bunch of knights? Some sense of obligation?"

"Why Sorin is with me is none of your business, Sameer," Magda said tersely. "You're here because Sorin wants you here. I've traveled the glacier before. I don't *need* a chaperone."

Sameer knelt next to Magda and scratched at the ice. The sound was horrid, and I winced. "She's my mother, too, Royal Daughter. I'm allowed to have feelings. This isn't a political game."

"Good, because I'm not going to negotiate."

Sameer's jaw set into a hard line. "I only want to talk with Sorin." He paused and narrowed his eyes. "Alone."

Magda scoffed. "Thus far, all you've done is mock Sorin. Why? You're guilded. You know the rules. You're not the only firstborn son to get fostered. You became a master of textiles. You could have your own hall if you wanted. Life hasn't been cruel to you, so what is the problem? Sorin isn't responsible for the matrilineal inheritance laws."

"I'm not arguing with matrilineal inheritance." Sameer glared at me, and then, in an action that broadcast itself in a hundred familiar ways, his eyes fell on my chest. I pushed into the side of the cave until ice dug into my spine. I wrapped my arms around my bound breasts and tried to breathe, clutching at fabric instead of skin.

"Stop it," I said, though I wasn't sure I was loud enough for him to hear me. "I can't help this."

Sameer rolled his eyes. "I don't *care* that you strap your breasts to your chest, Sorin. But the rights of matrilineal inheritance are clear. They've always been clear, even with the unbound guilds. The problem is, of course, that you are Amada's goal and Amada's masterpiece, identity be damned."

The air tasted, suddenly, like guilt. Matrilineal inheritance laws were as old as Queen Iana's reign. Pervasive across every guild, and even the tradespeople followed them. I wasn't perfect; I just had the right genitalia. It was no more complex than that.

Magda shuffled beside me. I needed to respond if only so we could get some sleep, but I didn't understand. Sameer should have been happy in his textile guild. He should have never known who his biological mother was, who *I* was, outside of some distant childhood memory. What was there to say that wouldn't drive his hurt deeper? He had his parents. I had mine. My mother had encouraged me. Trained me. Supported me, even when I wasn't the daughter she'd thought she had.

The daughter she'd thought she'd had.

Oh.

Sameer's bitterness snapped into focus. I leaned toward him, unsure of what to say but wanting to do *something*, but he mirrored backward, his face contorting into distaste.

"I remember when you came to the shop with Amada. I was almost fifteen, so you'd have been fourteen. Dressed in woodcutter's leathers. Not a trace of a chest. Your hair so short it stuck up from your head like a porcupine." He pulled his cloak tighter around his shoulders, enveloping himself in cloth and memories. "I hated you. I hated you when you were born because you were a girl, but then you were there, in front of me, and you looked just like me. A boy, just like me. Still, Amada kept you." He whispered the last sentence. The wind caught it and carried it deftly to my ears.

I drowned in memories. The guildhall. The boy barely taller than me, pushing me down. Hitting me. Rubbing my face into the dirt. It was the last guildhall we ever visited. There were scars on my arms. still, from that day. My right hand moved of its own accord, back to my left arm. My fingertips curled into my skin.

Magda stayed silent but took my hand, steadying it. I couldn't uncurl my fingers. My skin wouldn't still.

"I'm not a man," I said, as if that would somehow heal the rift between us. I didn't know what else to offer. I hadn't given his existence more than a precursory thought. He was fostered. He wasn't really my brother, not by guild law. I hadn't known Mother was in contact with him or his foster family. She never should have been. There was no reason to be. This torture he carried should never have happened.

Well, if his desire was inheritance, of being Mother's heir, the solution was simple. Maybe it would ease some of the ache for both of us. "You can have it if you want it. The guild line. I have no desire to be a woodcutter."

Sameer's hand sprang from his cloak and slapped me. I fell back into Magda's arms, stunned, my head spinning.

"I can cut his hands off with my boot knife," Magda hissed into my ear as she helped me back up.

"You don't even care for what she's done for you!" Sameer yelled now, glaring at me though he made no further move to strike. "You toss it aside like a toy. Without respect for your guild or our family's history."

I rubbed at my cheek as my own anger bubbled up. "I didn't choose to be this way!"

"I didn't say that you did," Sameer countered, his jaw clenched. "Don't make this about—this." He gestured at my chest.

"Well, what in the three countries *is* it about? I don't know why Mother kept me, but she did. I had no say in the matter. The decision wasn't mine. I was assigned to woodcutting from the moment of my birth. However, you—" I pointed a finger at his chest. "—have chosen to travel with me. To mock me in some perverse desire to find every fault I have, obsessed about inheritance rights over which I have no control. If you want some admission of guilt, that I tricked Mother or the guild, you won't get it."

I swore I heard Sameer growl. "Fuck Amada," he spat into the wind.

Though part of me agreed with him, the words still burned. "If you plan on finding Amada, to have her acknowledge you as heir due to some deficiency on my part, well, we have to find her first. So, you could help, instead of taunting." I unclasped my cloak and tucked it around my legs. "I was never able to convince her I wasn't suited for woodcutting." My voice turned bitter. "Maybe you will have better luck. Maybe you could ask *her* about her motivations, instead of assuming I was ever party to her decisions."

"You're a disgrace to woodcutting," Sameer whispered.

The sun had finished setting during our argument, and I couldn't see his face in the dark. That didn't matter because I was too angry to respond with anything coherent. Sameer stormed into the cave, pushing me as he went. I slid back into Magda. Though her hands were warm and she tried to talk to me, I twisted against her words, crouched down on the ice, and brought my cloak up over my head.

You should have stayed in Thuja, the wind whispered in my ear. *You'll die on the ice. You'll die, and freeze, and your friends will be unable to take your body back. It will be found by ice harvesters, and they'll cut you free, and they'll see you're a woman. All anyone will remember about you is that you are a woman.*

SHUT UP! I yelled into my head as my fingernails found purchase on my arms.

"Sorin?" Magda's voice was soft, but still more than I could manage. "Come inside. We should get some sleep."

"Not yet." Sameer emerged from the cave, a frown on his face and a candle in his hand. "You'll have to lend me a hand, Royal Daughter. A former occupant never quite made it out."

My head shot up, though my nails did not leave my skin. "Guilder?" I asked. "Snowsickness?"

Sameer simply glared at me. "It's a dead body, Sorin. You can alchemy magic it or whatever you want after we get it out of the cave."

I stood as images of Mother, frozen and stiff, danced in front of my eyes. I took a step forward, but Magda put a hand on my shoulder.

"Let me get it out. We can check after."

I nodded and backed away. Although the sun had set, the sky was alight in greens and yellows, which, with the help of Sameer's candle, allowed me to make out the bundled form Magda and Sameer pushed from the cave. It was human, certainly, but curled into the fetal position, its head tucked low to its chest. It didn't appear to be very large, and at first, I worried that it might be a child. It was certainly far too small to be the queen or Mother. But as I knelt, Magda moved the hood back to reveal gray hair and a thick beard. When she pulled down the collar, exposing the man's neck and half his face, our gasps came in tandem. I didn't need to see the guild mark. I'd know the man's face anywhere.

Master Rahad.

Eighteen: Separation

"He's dead. He's dead on a glacier. What business could he possibly have had here?" Magda pawed through the pockets of his cloak. She tore his belt from his pants, cracking the frozen leather. She unstrung his pouches and opened them before I could warn her otherwise, and tipped them upside down. Every one was empty.

"I don't understand," she murmured. "Why?"

Empty was exactly how I felt. Empty like Master Rahad's pouches, like his vacant eyes. I fingered my own belt and the pouches there. I thought about his offer of apprenticeship. I thought about how joy had threatened to burst from my chest that day. About how I'd made it to this point only by telling myself that eventually I'd be back in Sorpsi and in Master Rahad's workshop. That I'd be his apprentice. That my life was finally starting.

"I take it you know him?" Sameer unrolled his sleeping pad and pushed it into the cave.

"He was my future," I said, too softly for anyone to hear.

"He was my mother's guild alchemist." Magda draped his belt back over his hips and arranged the pouches in a neat line by his face. "He'd never left the capital, at least not in my memory. There's no reason for him to be out here."

"Well, that does explain his clothes." Sameer picked at the edge of Master Rahad's green hood. "No fur in the hood or the body of the cloak. He has no mittens, and his boots are worn and not insulated. No wonder he froze to death. He was an idiot."

"He was anything but." Magda sighed and pushed her own pad into the cave. I wanted to do so as well, but I couldn't stop staring at Master Rahad's body, and his empty pouches. "Perhaps it was snowsickness. But that doesn't explain why he was here to begin with."

"You'll get no answers from a dead man," Sameer called from inside the cave. "Sleep. We can give Sorin a stick to poke him with in the morning."

I didn't rise to the bait. Master Rahad was *dead*. There was nothing to go home for, now, and no reason for me to continue on this stupid trip, either, outside of my promise to Magda. Did Sameer have to be so callous? Did he see so many bodies up here that he'd become numb? How many of those bodies were guilders, I wondered, as I let Magda lead me into the cave. It was marginally warmer in there, with the help of the heat from the thermal lake and the natural windbreak. She rolled out my pad, and I sat heavily, my eyes planted on the body.

"Don't give up hope," Magda whispered as she crawled into her pad and wrapped her body around mine. "We will figure out what happened. Remember, there are other alchemists. I'll help you find another master; I promise."

I closed my eyes and settled against her. Magda's arm wrapped around my waist, and though my body stopped shivering, all I could think was that at the rate we were finding bodies and addled minds, by the time we found an answer, I might very well be the last alchemist in Sorpsi.

*

I awoke to an overcast sky and drops of seashell-pink ice around my pad. The skin on my arms was rough with scabs, but I hadn't managed to do much more than superficial damage. I sat up, let my cloak fall from my shoulders, and took a minute to breathe, deeply, purposefully. To try to relax into the moderate warmth of the cave and our shared body heat.

"Good morning." Magda turned over and rubbed her eyes. I yanked my sleeves back down and offered her my hand. She smiled as she took it and sat up. "Better this morning?"

I let out a long sigh. "Master Rahad's body is outside, likely frozen to the glacier, and Sameer is an ass. No, I am not better. But I suppose I will have to be."

Sameer rose as well, reattached his cloak, and slid out of our wave cave. "We can't take him with us, so say your goodbyes. We have a long day of walking ahead. We'll stay on the glacier's edge most of today. Move to the ground if you can, as we'll make better time that way, and it is safer."

Goodbyes for a man I'd barely known but whom I'd fantasized about since I was ten. Goodbyes for a future I was likely never going to see. I crammed my pad back into my pack and sighed silently about another day spent with tiny steps, and Sameer, and his anger. "I'll be ready in a moment. I need to relieve myself."

Sameer waved me off. I stood and looked for a natural formation that might give me privacy on an otherwise white, snowy plane when Magda approached.

"Magda, please," I said without turning around. "I'm tired, and my insides are knotted enough. Any more and I will dissolve like paper in water. Leave it alone. I just want to find Mother and go home."

"Home? To Thuja?" There was so much surprise in Magda's voice that I turned. She had worry lines across her forehead and a mark on her cheek from where her cloak had bunched during the night. She was unkempt, her hair escaping its normally tight braids, and her clothes wrinkled. The knot inside me softened.

"I don't know. But I suspect Mother will move to the grandmaster's building. She was his heir."

"And this?" Magda asked, cupping one of the pouches on my belt. "Will you go to her, or to the alchemists, when we return? Or something in between?"

So we weren't, in fact, talking about alchemy. It was an inevitable question. It wasn't like I was unused to it, but the whole thing was incessantly exhausting. I pushed her hand away. "There is nothing *between*. I hate that word. I am whatever I am, but I'm not some halfway point between only two options. Maybe that makes me a bastardization. Like those pseudoalchemists who only use chemicals. I don't know."

Magda's eyebrow quirked up. "There's no law against being...what you are." She reached for my arm, but again I pulled away.

"Except being like this hurts people." I pointed at Sameer who was some distance off, relieving himself. Magda scoffed.

"He's angry at inheritance laws. At Amada. Not you, not really. And I, Sorin, I want to get to know you because childhood caricatures are clearly not working." The smile that played at her mouth was hesitant. Inviting. I struggled against my rising desire to kiss her, right there on the glacier. Gods, she was trying, but it felt like kilometers between us. "Please?" she asked.

"I have a gender," I whispered, although I don't know why I cared if Sameer overheard. If anything, it would save me from additional awkwardness later. "It's not yours, or his, and neither is it wholly made up of those two options."

I reached up to her face and ran a finger across the rough, weathered skin of her cheek. The heat of the smithy and years riding with the Queensguard had molded her with a strength and purpose I envied. I wanted to see myself mirrored there—a master of alchemy, the weathering of my skin informing my trade. Even more so, I wanted to see her understanding of me. Of who I was, who I had always been but, as a child, had been unable to express.

I trailed my fingers down her neck to her collar, the fine leathers and cottons she wore still smooth despite the mud and ice. I stopped at the top of her breasts, catching their subtle push forward. I lingered under the clasp of her cloak and let my eyes travel back down to her breasts. There was where we could never be the same. There was something I desired, had desired since the moment sexual feelings blossomed, but which was also an unabashed indicator of femininity.

"They suit you," I said, finally raising my eyes back to Magda's. "Breasts— On me, they clash." It was more complex than that, of course, but I didn't know how to explain that Magda's hands would be welcome on my chest, that, in fact, when I looked in a mirror, nude, I saw nothing out of place. Rather, it was the reactions of others when they saw my breasts, their assumptions of gender, that hurt.

Magda took my hand from her cloak clasp and wrapped it in her own. She didn't speak, but she brought my roaming finger to her lips and kissed it. I wanted to melt in that moment, into her, into the glacier. She didn't understand; I could see that in her eyes, but the confusion didn't seem to matter to her either. I wished to sweep the entire issue aside. To just kiss her, or rest my head on her shoulder. How easy it would be to tell her I was a woman. That there were no barriers between us, cloth or otherwise.

How easy, and how utterly violating.

A skittering, slipping sound came from Sameer's direction. Magda and I turned, my hand falling from hers, to see Sameer kick a cream-colored lump of what looked like cloth into the lake.

I hadn't realized how still the glacier had become until Magda's voice broke through. "Did you just drown a blanket or something else that could have helped us keep warm? Are you an idiot?" She stormed toward Sameer, around the thin, jagged circle of water near where we had slept. The area was just as small in the daylight as it had been under the stars, perhaps some ten meters across. "Lake" was a very generous term.

"We should go." Sameer tried to move past her, but Magda grabbed his arm.

"What did you put in the lake?"

"Trash. Nothing more. People shouldn't leave things on the glacier. Nothing decays at these temperatures."

Magda dropped his arm, pushing it away as she did so, and called over to me. "Sorin, would you come over here please?"

My stomach jumped. I'd no need for another lake, enchanted or not. "I didn't see what it was either," I said cautiously. "Maybe we should just—" Magda's look shut my mouth. I picked my way over to her and a scowling Sameer.

"Ask the lake," she commanded.

I crossed my arms over my chest and blinked. "Ask... the lake? Ask the lake what?"

"For the fabric," she responded, her voice filled with frustration.

"Magda, I can't. I'm not a witch. I can't make the lake vomit something from inside it!" I chose to ignore the lake that had offered me the amulet. That had been an isolated incident, surely.

"Would you please just try?"

And risk having another dead hand rise from the water? There was no way I was going to seek that out.

"Sameer?" I asked, thinking he might confirm the ridiculousness of the request, even if only to get us moving again.

"It's just a blanket, Royal Daughter. If we're going to get off the glacier by nightfall, we need to move, or we could end up like your dead alchemist.

"It was more than one blanket, and all of them looked identical. Like they'd fallen from a pack of yet more identical blankets." Magda took a threatening step toward Sameer. "Forget the snowsickness. What is going on in the glacial towns? Do you have factories up here too? Is that how they made it into Miantri? Is that why all my guilders are here?"

"What the glacial people do is not under your purview, Royal Daughter." Sameer spat the words into the wind. "We're not bound by your guilds, nor your laws. That Iana came from our land but chose not to include it in the three countries when she defeated the old king and divided up his territory was her decision. You are her descendant, but you have no say here."

Magda spun to me, speaking through clenched teeth. "I want to see those blankets, Sorin."

It was an order, but I couldn't follow it. I did not want to put my hands in that water. Did not want to touch the magic-infused relic of the old king's reign, did not want to see body parts reaching for me, and did not want to see another lake spread open before me like a bride.

"I can't, Royal Daughter. I won't."

"Damn it, Sorin!"

"No!"

Magda stomped her good leg in frustration. "You're the only one the magic responds to! I need to see those textiles!"

I wrapped my hands in my cloak to keep them from my arms. The command in her voice was hard to ignore, and she knew that. I swallowed my apology because I *wasn't* some Thujan villager she could command at will, and I spoke to Sameer instead. "Sameer, were the textiles factory-made? Just tell us."

"Yes." He said it defiantly, with unblinking eyes. He was challenging me. Challenging Magda.

"How many factories are there on the glacier?" I asked.

"Dozens. More. Factories with power looms, factories with metal lathes for making threaded screws. Factories that can mechanically separate cotton. Every one of them is staffed by guilders who are tired of not having work, who are tired of seeing their guildhalls close. Guilders from Puget, from Eastgate, and especially from Sorpsi. Apprentices, journeys, masters, and even some grandmasters, I've heard, have come through this way. They don't all make it, as you've seen, but some do. Some did. They're all seeking what is new. They don't care about old secrets anymore. They refuse to be left behind by mechanization."

He might as well have slapped me again. Slapped the both of us, for Magda took a step back, almost into the lake.

"No." Magda had her hands over her mouth and nose. "You're a guild master."

"What has that got to do with anything?"

Magda looked incredulous. "This doesn't matter to you?"

"Why would I use a treadle machine when I could use a steam-powered one? Why should Sorin cut veneers by hand? The queen may have some notion that the guilds are infallible, but some of us refuse to be left behind by history."

"You don't care about tradition?" Magda pressed her hands into her braids now, alternately clutching and rubbing the strands. "Our history?"

Sameer looked pointedly at me. "Tradition is clearly flexible."

Everything inside me felt numb. There had been a person, then, in that lake. There was likely one in this one, if not more—some poor guilder following false promises. Or maybe Mother was in this lake, although I doubted she'd flee the life she'd been so devoted to. And Master Rahad was here. Dead, and my future with him.

"The factories are inevitable, then?" I asked, my voice flat.

Sameer shrugged.

"You're a part of this, aren't you?" Magda asked Sameer. She looked dazed. I helped her sit on the ice and knelt next to her. I felt dizzy, and the wind was whispering to me again, about Thuja, and safety, but I didn't listen to the words.

"I travel to Miantri when they need a textile guilder for festivals. For *tradition*. I don't haul factories on my back. People talk. They visit. They spread ideas. I don't know where your queen is, but I doubt she is working as a laborer in a factory. This isn't anyone's fault; it's called progress. If you wanted to save the guilds, you'd work *with* the new technology, not against it. It doesn't have to be a choice—fine embellishment and skill over mass production. We can have both. There's more than one option. Gods, there's more than two options, even."

"We're going to lose Sorpsi because of that progress!" Magda raked her fingers over the ice, then punched it. I tried to lean in to take her hand, but my thigh slipped across the ice. My fingernails tore as I dug for purchase. I slid back, down across the slush, and into the lake.

I gasped. The water felt too warm, and the smell of it fizzed in my nose. I took in large gulps of air, convinced at any minute that a hand would drag me down under. I scrabbled at the slushy shore.

"Sorin!" Magda had my wrists a heartbeat later before the warm water made it past my waist.

Something firm and round connected with the bottom of my foot, and I yelled. "Get me out! Please! Magda! Sameer!"

With Sameer's help Magda pulled me up the slush bank, my clothes dripping that stupid magic water that evaporated in steaming clouds the moment I was out of it. I shivered, then sneezed, and my shaking had nothing to do with the temperature.

"How have you survived woodcutting all these years?" Sameer asked, exasperated, as he wrung water from his sleeves. Water that wasn't evaporating from him, though I was already completely dry.

"I'm sorry!" I pointed to the lake—the suddenly frothing, swirling, vortexing lake that was pushing an oval *thing* toward me on an unnatural wave. I reached for it this time, determined to throw the amulet as far as I could, or at least have the satisfaction of smashing it on the ice before the lake presented me with any other "gifts."

"I'm sorry about the guild law, and about Amada, and about *falling into an enchanted lake*, which was clearly not planned." I wrapped my fingers around the amulet, pulled it from the water, and thrust it toward Sameer.

"Here! Didn't you want one of these last time? This, this stupid piece of..."

Wood.

Not metal, or stone, or even glazed ceramic.

Guilders, and bodies, and enchanted lakes fled my mind. The rational side that sounded too much like Mother took over.

"It's *red oak*," I said, dazed, as I turned the amulet over in my hands. "Were the witches uniformly simple? What moron uses porous wood for holding magic and alcohol in a *lake*? These were supposed to *store* magic."

"May I see it?" Magda asked. She was far too calm noting the utter failure of magic and wood anatomy in my hand. Too calm noting how she'd been ready to strangle Sameer only moments ago.

"Magda, it's a *red oak amulet*."

"Sorin, I don't know what that means." She held out her hand. "It's an important piece of Iana's history—my history—and it would be nice to see it before Sameer and his factories erase everything."

"They're just factories, Royal Daughter." Sameer took the amulet from my hand and tossed it at Magda's feet. "And that is just transmuted wood."

"The...wait, what?" I blinked at Sameer. "Transmuted wood? Alchemists made this? Red oak is porous. The magic would have seeped out. This isn't storage; this is a...a wooden tea bag. Alchemists aren't this dumb."

"But witches are?" Sameer asked, one eyebrow raised. Magda stifled a laugh.

I rolled my lips in, then blew out a puff of air. "I didn't mean it that way."

Sameer balked. "You are not this ignorant. Lakes have been opening up to you since we arrived. You've triggered magical foxfire everywhere we've walked. Did Amada not teach you anything about basic history? Do you cherry-pick what you want to hear?" He pointed south, back toward Miantri. "Do you think the villagers chased you out because they were bored and had nothing better to do? Do you think foxfire glows for everyone?"

"Sameer," Magda cautioned, though her voice sounded more tired than irritated.

"No." Sameer kicked the amulet. It skittered to the side of my boot. "With all that time alone in the woods, studying and reading and woodcutting and dreaming of alchemy, you *have* to have thought about the parallels. Or, damn it, *look* around you, at how every earthen thing seems to bend natural laws when you're around."

"They're *different*. Magic is...alchemy is..." My face felt flushed. I balled my hands into my cloak and glared at Sameer. "Alchemy has rules. Alchemy doesn't distort the natural order of things! Alchemy doesn't..." I couldn't find the right words. I wanted to say that alchemy didn't try to take your breasts, or pretend to be your mother in a frozen forest, but that sounded petty and not at all logical.

I looked to Magda for some confirmation or backup, but her eyes were on the ground, on the slick of ice beneath us. That stung.

"Magda?" I asked more testily than I meant to.

Magda closed her eyes and rubbed at her cheeks. It was Sameer who answered.

"Time to listen, woodcutter. Alchemist. Whatever you are. Lead to gold is transmutation. So if you transform a rock, it's alchemy, but if you transform, say, a prince to a frog, that's magic? A philosopher's stone is alchemy, but a healing spell is magic. So...the difference is rocks, basically. Alchemy uses rocks for magic."

I bit my lower lip and refused to meet Sameer's eyes. His words burned in my ears and rattled around my head. I swallowed, my throat sore from the cold.

"It's not the same," I returned. I heard the hitch in my voice. Saw how my arms started to tremble as I stared at the blasphemous wooden amulet near my foot. "Woodcutting isn't the same as carpentry or cooperage, though they may look like it on the surface."

Sameer threw up his hands. "They use the same damn material, Sorin! Gods, think about what you're saying! How do you not have a more intuitive understanding of this?"

Wood wasn't magic, damn it! I shook my head, my insides squirming.

"You're wrong."

Magda touched my hand.

"He's wrong! Isn't he?"

"You were always so determined about the distinction, but, Sorin...both witches and alchemists were penalized by Iana when she took the kingdom." Magda's words were warm but apologetic. "They're the two unbound guilds. Their paths and histories are intertwined. Witches alone could not make an amulet like this, or rather, they could if they broadened their scope a bit. Witches and alchemists have always worked together. They're two sides of the same leaf, like carpentry and cooperage. They're the same line, just different places on it."

"Magic isn't alchemy." I whispered it because I could barely form words. If alchemy drew on the same principles, the same elements as magic, then there was no alchemy at all, and I would not accept that there was...magic and slightly more rule-based magic. What was it that I did with my bone oil and my fungi if not alchemy?

Go home. Gohomegohomegohome. Witch-alchemist. Go home.

Something inside me broke.

I could shake off the cancelled alchemical fair. I could mourn Master Rahad and know that I had been good enough, at least, for him, and that if I could impress the royal alchemist, there were other masters out there who would take me on too. But I could not rationalize participation in...magic.

I'd pushed away woodcutting, and my family, and my birthright, to define myself into a trade that I loathed. How long had I fought against other people's semantics, only to have fallen into my own?

The ice shifted under my feet. A sound like breaking glass shattered the air. I heard Sameer yell, felt Magda tie a rope around my waist and order me to run, but their voices seemed surreal. Where was there to go? What was there to run to? I was no alchemist, nor witch or woodcutter, not man or woman, not guilded, and not skilled enough to be a trader in any profession.

"Sorin!" Magda yelled.

I was nothing.

"Sorin, *please!*"

The ground opened up at my feet.

Nineteen: Stone

The ice beneath me gave a final, deafening whine. Just under my feet was a crack that had been well encased beneath the top layer of ice. It now squealed upward, sifting rock and snow, and creating hairline fractures. I slid to the left on wobbling legs, Magda pulling me in by the rope. The fissure hit the surface, cleaving the ground in two. Sameer tried to jump, to reach us before he was caught on the other side, his ice axe held out like a javelin.

The glacier was too fast, and Sameer's jump too short.

His axe caught the edge of the crack and implanted with a sharp crunch, but it was the hollower, rounded sound of his head hitting ice that reverberated across the glacier. The rope around Magda's waist pulled her forward, and she landed on her wrists. I scrambled to find a brace—some outcropping, some large rock—as Sameer's unconscious form slid into the widening crevasse. Magda caught herself just before the edge, her fingers pulling at the ice, but there was so little slack between us that she brought me down with her.

The ice near the crevasse shuddered and crunched. Another fissure formed due north, separating us in one quick, fluid motion from the nearby lake and its thermal vents. The cold slammed into me, and I coughed from deep in my throat as I fell to my stomach. The dry air burned and the wind tore at my eyes.

"Brace!" Magda called up to me.

"I'll try!" I had no gloves, and the ice around me was sheer and speckled with stones. They might not be enough, but I didn't have any other option. My fingers and nose stung as I pulled rocks and small boulders from the snow, praying I could find one large enough to hold us all. There was one larger rock here, wedged well into the ice, but it had a smooth surface and barely protruded from the ice.

"Sorin, hurry!" I heard Magda clawing at the ice, and a low groan from beneath me that meant the edge of the crevasse was soon to expand again.

"Is there anything down near you?" I looked back over my shoulder and instantly regretted it. All I saw was deep blue ice and Magda's terror. Tears gathered in my eyes. She had managed to scrape out divots in the ice big enough for the first parts of her fingers, but her lower torso dangled from the precipice.

"My foot is on Sameer's axe, but it's not enough. You've got to find something more stable. I can't hold his weight much longer, and I'm too far down to pull myself, and him, up."

"I'll keep looking. Just hold on."

I slapped at my clothes as I desperately tried to find something to anchor with. Sameer could fall down that crevasse, for all I cared after our last argument, but I would *not* let Magda die. But my pigments—those stupid, worthless, *magical* pigments—were no good here. They couldn't bind to water, much less ice, and even if they could, none of them formed anything akin to a rope. What else...?

My palm contacted my foraging knife at the same time I heard Magda unsheathe hers. I pulled a knee under myself and drove the blade into the powder and, finally, into the ice. A *clang-crunch* from behind told me Magda had done the same. I grabbed the handle of my blade just as the rope went tight about my waist. It felt like my heart jumped into my throat. My knees slid out from under me, and I fell, belly first, onto the glacier.

Magda yelled up at me, the wind tossing her words so they sounded scattered and distant. "Axe is broken! The metal head is still wedged in. My knife is in a little higher. If you slide right just a bit, you can use it as leverage for your foot."

"Okay!"

I used my knees and belly to slither to the right until my boot found the handle. Tears leaked from my eyes at the strain, and my nose ran from the cold. The knife brace helped, but the strain on my hips shot sharp jabs through my thighs. I'd dislocate or break apart if I didn't get Sameer and Magda over the edge soon.

I heard Magda's feet kicking the inside of the crevasse, searching for a hold. Gods, we couldn't die here. Not like this! If only there was a larger brace! The knives would only bear the weight so long. Mine was already bending under the strain. What else could I do? Alchemy? Magic? I had only the tiniest amounts of the yellow and red pigment left. The green would be of no use. I couldn't poison a glacier. The yellow—the golden mango—had the most potential, but what would be worth binding, except maybe...

The rocks. Of course.

"Can you pull up a little, Magda?" I called back against the wind. "I need a bit of slack. Just for a moment."

Magda grunted, and I heard the sound of scraping, scrabbling ice. It was enough. The pull on my hips eased, and I snaked one hand from the bending knife to pull the yellow pouch loose. The leather belt, cracked and old, broke apart as I yanked the pouch from it. I crammed frozen fingers into the pouch opening, not caring if it got on me, and pushed the gathering apart. Only a light powder of granules remained, there was so little left. Nevertheless, I flipped the pouch inside out and rubbed it over the rocks. Hoping, praying to the gods of Sorpsi, there was enough left.

You're going to die out here. You should have gone home.

"Shut *up!*" I yelled at the words tickling across the wind. The bits of yellow coalesced. Two rocks joined with a film, then three, then four. I rubbed the pouch furiously over the remainder until a hole came through the leather. The pile fused together to the base rock lodged into the glacier, but so, too, did my hand.

I both praised and cursed my recklessness. My skin wasn't enough to pull us up, and the knife wasn't enough either. I needed another rope!

"Sorin?" Magda's voice squeaked with pain. "Please tell me you are done? I can't hold anymore."

There wasn't time to think. If we slid down, better all together. I let go of the knife and screamed as the skin of my hand bore the weight. I slid for a moment on the ice, knocking the remains of my pouches and my belt down toward Magda, and the crevasse, and death. For a fleeting moment, I mourned the pigments, but they were magic, and I'd be a woodcutter before I'd be a witch. Let the glacier have them, instead of us.

I still had the knife beneath my foot, and Magda's partial brace, but the pain that shot through my arm made me wonder if the yellow had penetrated farther than my skin and filmed to the bone. With my free hand, I pulled the knife from the ice, slit the side of my shirt and the ties of my binding. The cloth unraveled quickly with my torso so stretched. I sank the knife into the ice near my waist, then wrapped the end of my binding three times around the rock closest to me and the rest around as much of my arm as I could.

"Magda! I'm pulling up! Try to climb the wall if you can." Tears froze to my face. I dug torn nails into the rocks and pulled against the cotton. My joints cracked. I heard a ripping sound near my right hand, the one bound to the rock, and looked away. It was so cold the pain there had turned to a dull throb. There was no blood, but that didn't mean much. I pulled and shimmied, bringing my knee to the knife near my hip and pushing off there. The rope tore at my hips even through the leather, but I was moving forward, which meant Magda was too.

"I've got it!" Her triumphant call was broken by a fit of coughing. Hers or mine, I didn't know. The wind howled now against us, and in it, I swore I heard something scream my name. But all I could do was keep trying to pull myself forward, eyes tightly clenched against the pain and the cold, praying Magda could do the rest.

"I've got the knife. Sorin, hold on!"

I heard scraping, then cursing, then finally, the rope eased. I gasped in relief and got to my knees, unwinding my arm as I did so.

"Sameer?"

"Yes." Magda's face was a mask of pain as her bloody fingers sank my knife next to hers on the ice. She put one foot on each, squatted and braced, and began to pull the rope that held Sameer dangling below.

I didn't know what to do, so I held back. It hurt to move. It hurt to breathe. My right hand was stuck fast to the rocks; if she slipped, my skin would be our only remaining safety.

But Magda didn't slip. She was a master smith, and although she grunted and coughed as she pulled, and although her blood stained the rope a bright red, Sameer did appear over the edge. He didn't hit his head as I imagined he would. He blinked and fumbled instead, grabbing the ledge as it came near and drawing his legs up to safety. Alive, and ready to argue with me again the second his wits came back, no doubt.

Magda pulled him all the way to the rock cluster. The rope went slack, and I slumped to the ice and bit back another scream, managing a whimper instead. My hips ached. My shoulder and elbow felt out of joint and seared in pain. My palm... I looked. It was still firmly connected to the rocks, no blood in sight. But the stabbing pinpricks in my hand told me a different story lay under the skin. The pigment had bound to muscle, at least partially.

Magda shook, from the stress on her arms likely, and her fingernails were torn and bleeding. Sameer, on the other hand, looked stunned but mostly unscathed. He sat up slowly. It was first to his elbows, then, with a groan, to his rear. He still blinked at us and the ice, but he was focusing for longer intervals.

"Sameer?" Magda put a hand on his shoulder.

"I'm all right. I just need a minute." He gingerly prodded the back of his head and winced at the contact. "Thank you. Both." He looked down at my hand, then the rock. "Your magical alchemy comes with a pretty high cost."

I stared at him indignantly as Magda helped him to stand. My belt was gone. My pouches were gone. I could live without a hand. I couldn't live without a future. He could at least have had the decency to mourn with me, even if it was magic.

"Next time, I'll just let you fall," I muttered.

I expected a cold retort, or a glare, or maybe even a handful of pebbles at my face. Instead, Sameer looked at me, and my hand slimed in yellow to the rock, and offered a small smile. "Whatever it is you did, it's nice to see you're not horrible at everything. Maybe Amada wasn't completely vapid."

There was no place inside me for anger to burn. I rested my head on the ice and groaned.

"Could we just deal with our lingering problem?" Magda asked as she rubbed clean snow into her wounds.

Sameer recovered my knife, handed it to me, then, after a moment of thought, took the amulet from where it teetered on the edge of the crevasse and slid it into my pocket. "For you to study. Later. I know you like that sort of thing."

"Sure. Later. Have to deal with this first," I said with a dry laugh.

Sameer stared at the yellow mess of the rocks. "Can we dissolve it somehow?"

I looked up at my hand. Yellow film seeped around the edges of my palm. When I pulled against it, I felt a sharp ache, dulled, no doubt, by the cold. It wasn't to the bone at least. I could have dissolved it using bone oil distillate, but that was in short supply on a glacier. Reluctantly, I handed Magda my knife. "Only one way. I don't know how much muscle you'll have to remove."

"What?" She looked at me, horrified.

I shrugged. The air was frigid. The pain in my heart cut far worse than my hand.

"It'll mean a good scar." Sameer tapped my shoulder, and though his words were tight, I heard the attempt at empathy. "Wood people like scars."

"Something to look forward to." I nodded at Magda's hands, which were well marked from the smithy. "Guilders always have great hands. I do have some catching up to do."

"Sorin!"

"Please, Magda. Just do it, while my hand is still cold."

"But—"

"Sameer, hold me down."

Sameer wrapped his arms around me in a bear hug. From his pocket, he brought a thick piece of jerky and pushed it into my mouth. I bit down. "I am an ass," he whispered into my ear. "You're an ass. Amada's an ass. Must be a family thing. You might make a decent alchemist if you can get over the magic part. Or you could just take the parts you like and do something else entirely. It's not like you haven't done that before. Sorry for pounding you to the dirt when we were kids."

"You'd make a gwate woofcuffer," I said through the jerky.

"I doubt Amada would be all right with that."

I grimaced as the wind gusted against my cheeks. "Can't argue. I'f only one handf."

Louder, Sameer said, "Magda, you'd better do this soon, or Sorin will lose the arm from frostbite."

Magda got to her knees. Her hands were steady, but I could see her jagged puffs of breath as she gripped her knife. "Are you sure?"

"Do it."

She still looked ill, but she nodded and kissed me lightly on the cheek. "I'm so sorry," she whispered into my ear, just before she plunged her knife into my palm.

Twenty: Aqua vitae

I trembled as we walked, even with Magda next to me. My hand tingled more than hurt, but I'd already bled through my binding, which now covered my right hand. The pigment had only gone to the topmost muscle, part of which we'd left on the rock. I could still make a fist, though it took a lot of cursing to do so. If I didn't get an infection, I'd likely only lose some range of motion. Sameer had offered no words, but I could see on his face that he knew what such an injury meant. Even an alchemist was of little use with only one working hand.

Go home before you lose another hand. Your pigments are gone. You are useless. Go home go home go home.

The voice in the wind was relentless, but the tingling in my hand helped drown it out as our sad procession continued. My unbound breasts swished against the cotton of my shirt, chafing my nipples. That pain was no more significant than any other, but it was the thought of entering Celtis without my binding that blanketed my thoughts and swamped me with a convulsive desire to peel myself from my skin. Here on the ice, with two people who had maybe used up all their awkward questions, it wasn't such a problem. But each step brought us closer to Puget, and closer to assumptions that would cut my heart from my chest.

The thermal vents turned south again, and we followed as the ground morphed from sheer ice back to dirty snowcaps and, finally, a mix of pebbles and snow. Even with the added traction, Sameer was more circumspect, constantly scanning the ground and the horizon. Magda, too, kept her eyes forward, but her hands clutched at her bright cloak, pulling the wool tight around her shoulders. Occasionally, I thought I saw another human figure in the distance, but when Magda and Sameer said nothing, I stayed silent. Who knew what was the witch, or the magic of the glacier, or a pain-fueled mirage?

Instead, I tried to focus on Magda. I looked over at her when my thoughts allowed, searching for some distraction from the pain—a conversation, or a smile even. With her wrapped cloak, she was suddenly the blue of the ice around us, with sections of her black hair chasing the wind.

"Magda?" The words were sticky in my mouth and congealed with pain. "Talk to me? Not about the crevasse."

Leave Magda. She will be safer without you.

Magda returned a tight smile, tempered no doubt by her own injuries. I refused to acknowledge the wind words.

"Thank you for saving us, Sorin." She reached a hand from her cloak and grabbed my left. Although she winced, she gripped tightly. Scabbed fingers traced the top of my knuckles, and it was warmer and more intimate than anything had a right to be on this glacier. I unclenched my jaw.

"Would you distract me? Tell me about your apprenticeship with the smiths?"

Magda blinked, then smiled. "That's pretty boring. How about a story of the first ball the queen made me host, and the outfit she made me wear? That'll keep you laughing for hours."

I chuckled, although doing so made my hand throb. I could almost picture the gown the queen would have picked for her, and I could clearly imagine the look Magda would have had on her face the entire time. "I think that will work just fine."

Magda looked up to her left at the aching whites and blues around us. We were at the base of a small ice hill, and just at the top, I saw a black-cloaked figure. It turned when it caught sight of us, then fled down the opposite side of the hill, and out of sight.

This time, fortunately, Magda saw it too.

"Sameer?" She pointed. "Friend of yours?"

"No idea. Keep walking and...distracting. Whatever keeps Sorin upright."

"Magda, if they're a snowsick guilder..."

Magda smiled tightly. "We're not going to chase after them on ice. The edge of the glacier isn't far. They probably just wanted to meet us on more solid footing." She tugged at my hand. "Focus on me."

We kept walking, Magda all but pulling me up the slope. We paused at the crest of the hill. I couldn't see the traveler, but the end of the glacier loomed ahead—only a few hundred meters away—and beyond that, the start of the shrubby trees that would eventually transition into a real forest.

Sameer walked back to me and pointed at my hand. "When we make the sharp transition to temperate forest, the cold that's keeping your pain at bay is going to snap as well." He turned to Magda, his forehead wrinkled in... worry? I scoffed. "Maybe keep at that story," he said. "Add a little...huzzah. I don't know."

Magda chuckled. "Something dirty?"

The tips of Sameer's ears turned red.

Magda leaned in conspiratorially. "The most recent ball, well, the last one we had before the guilder situation started... I was fourteen. I begged to have you at that party, but the queen shot me down so many times I thought she'd gone mad. *Then* she invited most every noble-blooded female in the three countries, I think, as some sort of apology. My gods, the amount of silk. You don't think about it with everyday clothes, and we're so fond of cotton in the three countries, but fifty people in a ballroom with swirling gowns? You could drown."

Sameer changed direction without warning, and I sidestepped to follow as I tried to imagine Magda in a silk gown, with the lace trim of her shift flaring from the sleeves. The pebbles gave way under me, and my foot slid out. It was only Magda's hand on mine that kept me upright. She pulled me up with a yank on my wrist. I found my footing again, and then Magda was right next to me, one hand holding mine, the other around my waist.

"Yes," she murmured next to my ear, "I ended up in one of those horrendous dresses. Yes, it had a low-cut front. But that's no reason for you to kill yourself daydreaming. No more injuries."

My heart skipped, and I turned to her windswept face, her forehead wrinkled with worry. Magda pulled back before I could say anything, refusing to release my hand, and we continued walking. A distraction. I'd wanted a distraction. With my heart thudding in my chest, it was easier to ignore everything else, including the stupid wind.

Except my hand would not stop throbbing. No redness dripped from the soaked bandage, but the pain was deeper now, joining the ache in my heart and head and hips. I *could* have been at that party with Magda, cracking jokes and being just as uncomfortable in silk as she was. We could have grown up together. I could have seen more of Sorpsi, and the guilds, and maybe gotten a reasonable education. And here I was, having given up everything, *everything*, chasing the mother who had assigned me this life in the first place.

Maybe Sameer was right. Maybe Mother... I shook my head. Second-guessing a woman who was likely wandering the glacier, confused, or dead, would get me nowhere.

Eventually, the seracs faded behind us. It wasn't until we hit the glacial edge—perhaps two meters raised from solid dirt below—that Magda spoke again.

"Here?" she asked Sameer.

"Here, or in a few meters. We will hit the full forest in less than half an hour. By the time we reach Miantri, we won't even need our cloaks." His eyes flicked to mine. "You ready then, Sorin?"

I couldn't imagine the pain being much worse, so I shrugged.

Magda hopped down from the glacial edge and had her arms under my knees and arms before I could squeak out a response. The temperature change was immediate. Warm air that blew in the breeze and the sun—blinding on the glacier—were hot enough now to make me break into a sweat. As Magda set me on my feet, sharp little pinpricks dotted my arm, then into my hand as the warmth filtered back to my fingers.

I cried out and fell to my knees onto the hard gravel. I retched once, twice, and finally had to lie, belly first, on the stones until my head stopped spinning.

Magda's hand brushed across my back and neck. Her soothing words and Sameer's gruff encouragement buffered around me, but it all sounded felted, like my whole head was wrapped in cotton.

"Sorin?" It was Magda, and even through the haze, I could hear her worry. "Can you sit up?"

"Ehh," I groaned. I pulled my knees underneath myself and managed a hunched position, keeping my head tucked to my chest. It kept the world from spinning quite so much. On the bright side, the nausea and vertigo were excellent distractions from my hand. So was the crunching sound coming from the south. Sameer handed me a tincture of laudanum from his pack, which I quickly downed. The relief was immediate.

"The other traveler," Sameer said. "Heading our way. And that's all I've got of that, so hopefully, we find a doctor before tomorrow."

"It's enough. Thank you." Instead of looking at him, I watched a woman in a long, embroidered dress and brown cloak approach us. Mud stained the hem of her cloak, but the remains of white lace peeked out beneath it. A leather strap crossed her front, and the top of what looked like a lute or violin poked over her shoulder.

"Whoa," Magda called out. "Who are you?"

The woman stopped and knelt a few paces away. She looked up at the sharp blue sky, then down to the ground, then at herself, as if she couldn't see how she fit into the world around her. Curls of thin, black hair tumbled from her hood, and her fingertips were red and scabbed. "Watchara, of Puget. You?"

"Sameer, master of textiles," Sameer said, cutting Magda off. "These are my traveling companions. I live in Ankatt, on the glacier. What business do you have here?"

Watchara stared at Sameer for a long moment, her lips moving but no sound coming out. I managed to sit up a bit more, leaning heavily against Magda.

"I'm Watchara of Puget," she repeated, more slowly this time.

"Are you a musician?" I managed to croak, pointing at the whatever she carried on her back.

Watchara's eyes fluttered to me before she looked back at Sameer. "Yes. No. I...was. I think."

Sameer cocked his head to the side and studied Watchara. "Are you sure you want to go on the glacier? You seem...disoriented."

"Can you still work?"

Her words took Sameer by surprise, and he stepped back a few paces. "Yeah. Yes, I mean." He glanced at Magda, whose face had turned grim. His voice sounded deeper, or more serious, or the laudanum was mixed more strongly than I'd thought. "You can't? Were you on the glacier long?"

Watchara shook her head and looked down at the pebbled ground. "No, only just now. Just the preamble. I thought... I'd heard there were guilders up here. I wanted to find other guilders because this—" She pointed to the wood strapped to her back. "My violin. I know it's mine. I remember making it with my father from a half-rotten log." She pulled it from the strap and placed it between Sameer and herself. It was a beautiful piece of wood— highly polished with a mother-of-pearl inlay. I was certain if she pulled down her hood, I'd see a guild mark.

A sob rose from Watchara's throat. "I can't play it. I know I did play. I must have because when I see this violin, I remember clapping, and laughter, and the smiles of my parents. But if I draw a bow across, it only screeches. My fingers fumble on the strings. I don't know where to put my chin or how tightly to hold it."

"It's a beautiful instrument. We had a guild violinist at court for most of my childhood. I remember him so well." Magda moved her arm from my waist, making sure I'd not topple, and scooted close enough to Watchara that she could stroke two fingers over the violin. Jealousy bloomed, unexpectedly, in the way she touched the instrument, like she was caressing some Puget god. I berated myself. Jealousy of a violin was about as stupid as walking across a glacier.

"He's there now?" Watchara asked.

Magda shook her head and sat back. "He left two years ago. Said there were better jobs, though I can't believe he found work for more than what the queen paid him."

Watchara wiped her running nose on the sleeve of her cloak and put her violin away. "I haven't seen another from the musician's guild in over four months, and I've been travelling." She pulled down her hood, exposing a bass clef tattoo just under her chin. "Before this...I was a master. I remember getting my tattoo. I remember how proud my parents were of my journey piece, but...I can't remember the piece itself."

She bit her lower lip and tears swelled in her eyes. "I can't remember music!" Her eyes moved to the glacier. "There's supposed to be magic in the glacier, right? Old magic, old amulets, leftover from the old king's reign? A woman in Celtis said maybe I could find my memories there. But I saw you three, and I...it suddenly seemed stupid, walking on a glacier alone."

"That's because it *is* stupid," Sameer said. "You're not dressed for it at all. You'd have died within an hour."

Watchara hung her head. "It seemed really important that I go. A woodcutter woman said the glacier was where others went when they forgot."

I snapped my head up. "What did she look like?"

Watchara started to sob.

"Not the time," Sameer said. He stood and then knelt next Watchara, covering one of her hands with his own. "Come with us, back to Celtis. You should see a doctor. Preferably one who doesn't buy into this snowsickness nonsense."

"I tried," she argued as Sameer helped her to stand. "No one knew anything. They said it was pandemic, without a cure. But I...appreciate the offer to take me back to the village. Maybe it's best I'm not walking alone."

I managed to get back on my feet as well, although I didn't mind Magda's assistance in the matter. "Why would Mother be in Celtis?" I asked no one in particular. "There's no reason."

Sameer snorted. "Except for magic. Everything about this reeks of magic. Has no one seriously thought of that? Gods, do the doctors as well as the guilders have their heads up their asses?"

Magda let out a low sigh as we continued walking, Watchara guided by Sameer, Magda at my side. She had her arm around my waist, and her fingers stroked my hip bone just enough to keep me from floundering in pain— what little there was left—or conjecture.

"There are too many parallels to ignore, anymore," Magda said. "I need to get these treaty talks done. After that, I may need to hire you to take me farther up the glacier, Sameer. Something is rotting up there."

The ground transitioned smoothly from pebbles to moss, which Sameer kicked at. He shot back at Magda, "If something is rotting, try the woods of Thuja. No part of me is surprised about this."

Magda gave him a sharp look. I groaned.

Sameer stopped walking and spun to face us. He crossed his arms over his chest, and with the way his jaw set, he looked exactly like Mother. A shiver ran down my spine.

"Apologies, Watchara, but you two"—he pointed at Magda and me—"let's talk about Amada the master woodcutter. *Really* talk about her. I'm tired of dancing around the devil. Even if she isn't the same master woodcutter sending guilders off to die on a glacier, do you really think she'll let you go, Sorin? How do you think she'll react when you end up in Celtis instead of hiding away in the Thujan woods?"

I decided to look up at the canopy of conifers that now engulfed us, instead of my brother. Everything he was saying was ridiculous, even with my mind fuzzy from the laudanum. Mother was domineering, but she wasn't cruel, and there was no way she was a witch. Mother hated witches as much as I did.

"She doesn't control me, Sameer."

Sameer laughed. "Yeah, she just kept you penned in a forest for your entire life through guilt and fear. I'm sure an injured hand will be enough to keep her away."

"Enough, Sameer. *I* made the choice to come here. *I* left our home, despite what Mother wanted. She does not control me!"

"Sure." Sameer eased Watchara over a moss-covered log and shook his head. "She doesn't control you, or our futures, or the wandering, magicked guilders of Celtis. Keep telling yourself that. See if it keeps you from the wrong side of Amada's sword in the end."

Twenty-One: Separation

There were no witches near the old stone wall of Celtis, but enchanted foxfire fairy trails lit the stone an eerie green as we approached. It was just after sundown, and the nagging weight that I'd carried in my stomach since the crevasse and the loss of my binding surged up past the opium that fuzzed my mind. I choked on air, coughed, but waved Magda, Sameer, and Watchara off when they looked at me with concern. They'd forgotten, likely, the origin of the fabric wrapped around my torn hand. I had not. I forced myself to look at the town, the old wall not good for anything anymore save perhaps keeping out ranging cattle. Anything to take my mind from our walk to the inn and the eyes that would see me and make assumptions. Only one walk, at night. Surely no one would notice. And if they did, would it matter? They didn't know me. What did pronouns matter, especially from a stranger?

It did matter, of course, and denying the effect it would have on me was foolish, but I'd never get the courage to enter the city otherwise. It was best to focus on the mundane. The wall was easy enough to climb even with one hand. We wandered first through the outlying houses of the poor, myself once again with an arm crossed and pressing my chest down. The shacks were of wood beams and bark walls, but as we progressed in, the buildings changed to stone and, finally, clay. Every house we saw, from the smallest hovel to the grand guildhalls, was decorated in green lanterns for *tii*.

Woodwind instruments could be heard from all around. Watchara swayed with the music. Her eyes, when I could catch them, looked distant as she tried to force memories that would not come. Multiple times, she reached for her violin, just to draw her hand back and stare at her twitching fingers.

A spirit house, fully built from birch and cedar and inlayed with silver, sat prominently in the city square. Well-lit with candles, its walls did not meet at ninety-degree angles. The roof sloped too gently. The silver inlay sank too low beneath the wood. It had not been guild-made, and it hurt to see something so sloppy in an otherwise cheerful festival.

The people were less formally dressed than in Miantri and, while friendly, not even passably interested in our haggard appearance. That helped settle my nerves, but I kept my arm high, regardless. Magda did notice when a young girl's eyes stayed too long on us and I turned to a sideways shuffle.

"We'll get some cloth tomorrow morning," she whispered into my ear. "And a doctor for your hand. I think *tii* ends tonight."

"You'll be hard-pressed to do that *and* negotiate a treaty, I think," I returned, though I smiled at her. She had the same look in her eyes now that she'd had on the glacier, right before we'd kissed. If she looked at me like that much longer, I wouldn't be able to hide my blush.

"Just because the talks start in the morning doesn't mean you can't see a doctor right away," Magda said. "You and Watchara. I'll be tied up for at least two days. But for right now, let's focus on getting some...some sleep."

Get sleep, after she'd looked at me like that? After everything that had happened on the glacier?

Magda winked. "A meal, and a bath, and a bed. We will go from there, assuming your hand isn't bothering you too much." She touched the back of my neck—a surprisingly intimate gesture—and we once again fell to silence.

We passed easily through town to the Celtis Inn—a two-story stone structure with a clay tiled roof and pigs mucking in a side pen. The inside of the inn was bright but still smelled somewhat musty, likely from Puget's ranching heritage. The tables were of a formed silver metal, and across them lay tablecloths of woven grasses in a multitude of colors and textures. Ornate tapestries of wools and silks covered the walls, all brightly dyed and expertly woven.

The people wore cotton almost exclusively. Magda, Sameer, and I stood out in our leathers, but the dinner guests again took little notice. The air was thick with the smell of beef bouillon and onion, and my stomach growled loudly. Sameer's did the same a moment later.

"Rooms for the night?" Magda asked a girl, perhaps ten, with her hair in looped braids. The child had three bowls of soup and a loaf of bread balanced on her arm, which she deftly spread onto an empty table.

"Not me." Sameer sat in the bone chair next to me, slipped his cloak from his shoulders, and let his head fall back. "Just dinner."

"Obligation fulfilled?" Magda patted her pocket where I knew a fat satchel of stones rested. "I can pay you a bit now, and more fully when I return to Sorpsi."

Sameer rolled his head to the right and scanned my face. "Come with me, Sorin."

I looked at him, so taken aback by his request that for a moment I couldn't speak. "Come... You don't want to find Mother? Talk to her?" I rubbed my forehead. "Why would you want to travel with someone you hate so much?"

Sameer's stomach growled again. He put his head down on the table briefly before speaking. "No, I don't want to meet Amada the master manipulator, and you shouldn't want to either." His nose turned up. "I don't need Amada's permission to be a woodcutter, Sorin. I can take a dual affiliation as easily as any other master. I wanted to meet you, to try to understand Amada's choice, but that doesn't change anything. She picked you, not me, and if you stay here, you'll end up locked back up in that forest hovel, thinking it's your own choice. At least in a glacial town, you'd be a person, not a possession."

"And alchemy?" I asked. That dream still clung to the back of my mind, despite its magic taint.

Sameer threw up his hands. "Forget damned alchemy! You could have a *real* life. And no one will ever even notice this." He gestured at my breasts. "You'll be in too many layers of fur and hide. Be a man. Be a woman. Be whatever. Just don't be Amada's pawn."

I clamped my mouth shut. Emotions and rebukes and denial that Mother was involved in any of this swirled on my tongue. Sameer's offer was too much, and I was too tired, and it was too warm in the inn after days on a glacier. And I couldn't leave Magda. Wouldn't leave Magda. Not again.

The little girl cut into the conversation. "Could we finish the transaction before you start yelling? Three rooms and four dinners. Fifteen stone per head."

I blinked, and Sameer coughed. Fifteen stone per person? That would have gotten us rooms at the palace!

Magda pulled her smaller purse from her belt and toyed with the closure. The girl put her hands on her hips and tilted her head, looking every centimeter a grown proprietor if not for her dimpled cheeks and braids. "Seems high for soup and a bed. And we'll only need two rooms, I think?"

My cheeks burned when Magda turned to me. We'd slept together on the glacier. We'd slept together as children. There was no reason for the fluttering low in my belly, unless I thought about Magda's lips, or the way her fingers had stroked Watchara's violin. There was no way the fuzziness in my head was entirely from the laudanum.

"Um." I swallowed half a dozen responses before managing, "Yes, that would be fine. It's just, uh, pricey."

The girl sniffed. "It's *tii*, and we're the only inn with space left. We have a lot more visitors than usual this year. If you don't like it, you can leave."

The idea of leaving the steaming soup behind hurt my stomach more than the hunger, but that many stone would likely wipe Magda's purse clean. Yet she pulled the stones out and handed them to the child with no further hesitation, then sat, ripped a third of the bread from the loaf, and bit viciously into it.

"Thank you, Royal Daughter." Watchara, who had remained quiet and withdrawn for the trip to Celtis, finally sat. She took her violin from her back, cradled it for a moment in her arms, then set it on her lap and started in on a bowl of soup.

Sameer gave a heavy sigh. "You're not coming, then, I take it?" He downed his soup, although I could see from his wincing that it burned his tongue.

I shook my head as I sipped my soup, pleased with the richness of the flavor. "I can't, Sameer." I didn't look at Magda, but he did, and I could tell by the expression on his face that he understood. He didn't like it, but he understood.

The girl brought us wine and water glasses. I drank both immediately, which further fuzzed my head. It didn't matter though. We had spent enough time together in the past several days, and were certainly hungry enough, that we forwent conversation almost entirely as we ate. I didn't know what to say to Sameer, so I didn't say anything, and although Magda twice tried to engage Watchara in conversation, the master musician remained quiet.

I listened to the conversations around us instead as I chewed the hard rye bread. Excitement buzzed over the final two days of *tii*. A festival to celebrate returning spirits was planned for the day after tomorrow, and people were making food preparations already. And tourists. There were a number of conversations, both amused and frustrated, by the larger-than-normal crowds of tourists, especially those with guild affiliations, and the unusually warm weather the region had experienced of late.

After three days on glaciers and in forests, the conversations around me were quick to overwhelm. I finished my meal first and stood. My arm immediately went to my chest, but when I swept the inn, no one was looking. I pressed my arm in anyway. "I'm going to the room. See you both tomorrow?"

Magda looked up at me with a tired smile. "Good idea. I'll be along shortly. Tomorrow...tomorrow we'll have a big breakfast once the kitchens are up. We'll get you and Watchara to a doctor, and then I'll have to leave you and present myself at the castle."

Sameer fished the last bit of broth from his bowl with a chunk of bread. "Good night, Sorin. Magda. Watchara." He stood as well and managed a funny little smile. "I hope you both find your mothers. And good luck, Sorin, with your alchemy, or whatever you end up calling what you do. Preferably nothing with an unbound guild. Maybe tell Amada to shove her head up a donkey's ass. From me, from you, whomever."

Gods, if I told Mother that, she'd have a heart attack. I snickered. "Um. Sure. Thank you for your help on the glacier."

He nodded, the edges of his smile threatening to break into any number of other expressions, then turned and walked away.

"You okay?" Magda asked as she motioned for another bowl of soup. I considered doing the same, but the idea of a warm bath and soft bed appealed more.

"Yes. No. There's too much going on, and it's hard to think. I'm going to bed." I paused as I picked up the long key on the leather strap. "It's...you're okay with sharing with me, right?" I don't know why I asked. She'd been the one to suggest it in the first place. But my insides were still jumping, and I wanted to be sure. Had to be sure.

The young girl brought over another bowl. Magda flipped her another three stone, then put her spoon on the table and stared up at me. "I was looking forward to it. Besides—" She pointed at my bandaged hand. "—my turn to tend a wound. Mine is still sore but mending fine on its own."

That pushed the last wisps of Sameer from my mind. "I'll bathe first, then," I said, turning away from the table so she wouldn't see the stuttering of my chest as my heart pounded beneath it. I remembered the warmth of her hand on mine, and the earthen taste of her lips, and walked purposefully to the stairs—wooden and skillfully made, the banister carved from a single writhing tree—to my, our, room.

The bath, already set up and steaming, was mercifully free of petals. I undid my clothes, sticky with dried sweat and my own blood, as best I could. I waited until I was in the bath to attempt to unwrap the cotton on my hand. The steam helped ease apart the strips of fabric, but as I got closer to the wound, the very act of unwrapping brought tears to my eyes. Gods, it felt like I was peeling off layers of skin, though I was still four or five passes from the wound itself. The more I tugged, the more the remaining skin underneath pulled and the farther the ache spread up my arm. I'd have to prioritize a doctor tomorrow, or whatever infection had started would only spread. If I left it alone, the opium covered the pain well enough. Best to just leave it for the evening.

I puffed air up, blowing curls from my face, and rewrapped the cloth. I had nothing new to wrap my hand in anyway. I scrubbed the rest of myself with the coarse soap as the last of the wine fuzziness cleared from my head, then stepped from the metal tub and toweled dry.

Two sets of sleepwear lay on the bed, both old, boxy cuts of white linen. The man's had a turned-down collar and single button. The woman's dress had buttons as well, but they were on the sleeves, near a gather in the cuff. The double bed made sense with paired clothing, but I still paused, considering both. What a bother. I suppose I'd have chosen one with a button and ruffling somewhere else if given the opportunity. The hemline, perhaps, although a button there would be silly. Certainly, I wouldn't want one without any embellishment. That would have been just as problematic as what was currently before me.

In the end, I took the man's nightshirt and slipped it over my head. I placed the nightdress over the high edge of the tub just as Magda came into the room. She immediately took me in and fought a smile of her own.

"Sorin—"

I laughed and ran a hand through my damp hair, pulling at the curls to straighten them. "My choices were narrow, and I thought you might prefer the woman's dress." I had a brief thought to cross my arms and hide my chest from her, to make the shirt look more appropriate, but it bled away as quickly as it came. There was no need, not with her.

"It will work fine." Magda shed her clothes without preamble and sank with a groan into the tub. I let my eyes follow her as I climbed into the bed, lingering on areas of her body I had strenuously tried to avoid in Miantri.

"Can I ask you a question, Sorin? What...what is it that you like? In people?" Magda turned to her stomach and slid beneath the water. When she came up it was to face me, arms wrapped around the tub's rim. Droplets of water fell from her hair and nose to the floor below, and beaded on the tops of her breasts. She was pressed against the tub side, but my mind readily filled in the gaps. It was hard to look only at her face, and I heard a small chuckle as I tried to rein in my eyes.

"I don't mind. It's not like you've not seen me in a bath before."

But this was different, and the way her smile faltered near the corners of her mouth told me she was aware of that as well.

"I like—" I paused, trying to choose the right words. "I like how the smithy has shaped you." There. That was flattering without being too specific. I didn't know what parts of herself Magda valued, and which she was disliking of, and I was perhaps too conscious of how the wrong words could injure.

"You like arms?" She moved one from the rim and eyed it critically. Muscles sloped from shoulder to wrist, but they were padded in softness.

I propped pillows behind my back and leaned against the wall, the blankets still under me. "I like a lot of things, including arms," I returned.

"On men as well?"

I exhaled audibly. There it was. She had asked, to be fair, and it was unlike Magda to ask permission before an onslaught. I knew where this conversation was headed, and we'd put it off long enough. Still, I was tired, and while the wine had worn off, I didn't trust myself or my words. I wanted her with me in this bed, without the silly nightshirts between us, but that couldn't happen until we dealt with the intangible.

I crossed my arms, pressing my breasts to my body, as Magda took a quick scrub to her skin with the soap and washcloth, rinsed, and stepped gingerly from the tub, her wound still tender. This time I did avert my eyes, but needlessly, as she came to sit next to me on the bed after toweling off. It was impossible, then, to not see her, and the splay of her breasts, and the flare of her hips, and the triangular patch of hair between her legs.

"I do like men, sometimes," I said as I reached for her hand. What I wanted was to run my hand across her thigh, to slope down to the inside where her muscle eased to suppleness, but Magda did not settle next to me. She scooted instead, and I followed until we both were propped against the headboard. Our hips pressed together, and I took her hand. "I like women more, I think." Warmth crept across my face and down my neck. "I, uh...didn't get to meet a lot of people in the forest. I, um, don't have experience with either."

"Hmm." Magda squeezed my hand, then let go.

What in the world did that mean? She'd had every gender paraded in front of her since menarche, but as helpful as it would be for one of us to have some idea of what was about to happen, the idea of Magda having slept with another person did *not* settle my nerves.

"Magda?" I prodded, hoping she might offer more.

Magda smiled and reached for the hem of my nightshirt. She cupped her hand and tugged, bringing the fabric up to my midthigh. There, she released, and ran the backs of her fingers in circles across my skin. Goose bumps followed in her wake.

"I've had a million fantasies about this, Sorin. Since we were young." She cupped my cheek and leaned in until our noses touched. "And I don't have much experience either. You don't need to look so terrified. Not about that."

I pushed forward, and our lips met, just for a moment. Magda inhaled sharply before she stroked my cheek—not deepening the kiss, but not breaking it either.

"You taste like the forest. Like maple sap," she breathed when I pulled back. She bit her lower lip, and I mirrored her, fighting a smile. I wanted to lean in again, but we'd delayed this conversation for too long already.

"You prefer women." It was a statement, not a question, but I needed to hear her affirmation.

Magda's eyes opened in surprise. Her fingers stilled, and she sat upright. "Yes. I have forever. I know I didn't talk about it when we were children, but I suppose I never thought it was an option for me. We have courtiers like this, of course, and men who love men." She gave a small laugh as her gaze fell back to the nightshirt, and my thighs.

I'd have taken the woodcutter's mark, the witch's mark, anything in that moment if Magda's hands would have followed her eyes.

"Sorpsi's entire textile district is run by those who were born one way...or born presenting one way, but changed later. That's different than attraction though. More a body thing. Makes sense why they'd congregate in the textile district. It's nice to be able to make clothes that fit when your body isn't shaped like you want, right?" She looked pointedly at my breasts. "Except you don't mind yours, I guess. Still, it's not like this, or you, are new, or revolutionary. It's...I mean, you haven't really picked one or the other. People don't just, just stop in the middle, I guess."

Again, her eyes found mine. The earnest confusion that swam there tugged at me and drew me to my knees. I wanted to kiss her, and wipe away all the questions and doubt and have us be two people exploring two bodies, without all the awkwardness of, well, me.

But Magda needed an explanation, and I didn't know what to say. I didn't have the words either of us needed. Instead, we stared at each other for an indefinite amount of time. Her gaze remained steady, but mine flicked from her eyes to her chest, lower, then back up again. I saw old scars and burns, lines of thin pink and wide patches of red. I saw lines from swords, pinpricks from chainmail, and on the hand resting on the blanket next to me, a dozen smooth areas on her knuckles.

I wanted to touch every mark, hear the story of every encounter. Hundreds of pale lines from knives and saws marred my own skin but did not contain nearly the same richness of story. I ran fingers over her upper arm, tracing the musculature. She was warm, from the soup or the fireplace, and her skin rough with experience.

"Sorin?" Magda asked tentatively, her younger self echoing through. I brought her hand to my waist and gathered the fabric there.

"Go ahead."

Magda bit at her lower lip again, hard enough that I saw a bead of blood form.

I touched my fingers to her cheek, then brushed our lips together. She exhaled as I did so, letting go of some enormous weight. Still, she seemed almost withdrawn. She pulled back, just centimeters, but enough to give me pause, as if she thought her body might frighten me away.

"I'm not caught in the middle. I'm distinct. And I like women." I moved my lips to her jawline. I trailed my hands along her arms, reveling in the complex skin. I'd read her correctly, for Magda renegotiated the space between us until I was on my right hip and she was kissing near the collar of my nightshirt.

"So do I," she murmured and deftly undid the small button. The neck of the shirt spread, and Magda's lips followed. Her hand slid up under my nightshirt and grabbed my rear, pushing me into her.

"I'm not a woman," I reminded her. I lifted my hips enough to pull the nightshirt from under my hip. Magda did the rest, gliding the linen off my shoulders and to the floor below.

Her eyes didn't leave mine, but her hands explored. The sides of my breasts. The hollow of my hips. My collarbone. The skin where my thighs became my bottom. I held on to her shoulders, wanting to touch her as well, but knowing if I let go I would fall into memories and desire, and I wanted to remember every moment of her touch.

"Take my hand?" Magda asked.

I took her hand as she moved to the center of the bed. She remained sitting, so, with my heart pounding against my rib cage, I sat on her lap, wrapping my legs around her. The intimate position surprised even Magda, but she only smiled when I leaned forward and kissed her.

Her arms went around my waist, drawing us closer together. I gasped as her breasts touched mine, then pressed, and then there was softness and heat, and her tongue tracing my lips, demanding entrance, and one of her hands pushing down past my belly, sinking into dark, damp curls. It was hard to remember the conversation, to see if she really understood my words, when all I wanted, in that moment, was for her fingers to press in or her thigh to come up. Anything to provide counterpressure for the desire she drove inside me.

Instead, she pushed forward, and I fell onto my back, Magda between my legs. I lay on the white sheets, with skipping breath and hips pushing upward as Magda, finally, looked at me.

I didn't know if she admired the same things as I did—musculature built from dedicated repetition, scarring earned from tumultuous apprenticeships and experimentation. I watched her begin low, with my legs, pausing long enough over the dark patch of hair for a smile to curve on her lips before moving to my stomach, then breasts.

Here, she changed. What had been hesitant and curious became laden with desire. Magda didn't move, didn't bring her hands or mouth to me, but suddenly I was the barmaid in the capital, the server in Miantri. My skin itched, and I had to clamp down on the urge to move, to roll, to dress and hide and be something, anything, other than what she saw.

"Magda." It came out a whisper.

Her eyes came to mine, and she pulled back with a questioning look. "Sorin? Are you all right?"

I swung my leg from around her and sat back, on the far end of the bed. *I'm not a woman!* I wanted to yell, but I kept control of my voice, even as the pain of her eyes stabbed at my heart. "I'm not a woman," I managed to say as my throat thickened.

Magda's eyebrows furrowed, and she pulled her legs under herself. "Sorin, I never argued that point." I crossed my good arm over my chest, crushing my breasts. Magda sat next to me, our hips just touching. She moved to place a hand on my knee, then placed it on her own instead. "Sorin, whatever I did, I'm sorry!" Again, she looked at my chest. "I thought when they were unbound...that with me..." She fumbled for words, grabbing at the blankets as she did so. "However you present yourself, I don't care."

"And if I didn't have breasts?" I challenged her, determined now to drive the point home. "If I had a penis?"

"But you don't! If you don't want to be touched there, on your breasts, that's all right." Her voice turned pleading. "I don't want to hurt you. I want to understand."

Wanting to understand and trying to, unfortunately, were very different things. I slid to the edge of the bed and off. Cold, and fighting tears, I struggled with my old clothes, cursing that I had nothing to bind over my breasts. It was night, and no one had cared before. Hopefully, no one would now either. Only when I was dressed did I turn to face Magda. She clutched the bedsheets, her knuckles white, her face searching mine for an explanation.

"You can like breasts," I said firmly, for I needed her to hear the pain behind the words. "You can like my breasts, for being mine, or because it would give me pleasure to have you touch them. But when you look at me as you just did, as you do to *women*...you're not seeing me. When you look at my breasts like that, you call me a woman, even without saying a thing. I need you to see *me*, not just the parts you find attractive. I am not a woman because of my breasts. I am me, despite them."

Magda didn't speak, but I could see from her face, from the *V* between her eyes, that she still didn't understand.

She didn't understand me. And that burned.

The misunderstanding, the precursory, marginal attempt at empathy, the well-meaning misgendering burned worse than steam from bone oil, cut deeper than the pain in my hand. It was uncomfortably hot in the room, between the steam from the bathwater, arousal, and anger. I fixed my cloak around my neck and went to the door. The night air would go a long way to easing what felt like a punch to the gut, and hopefully calm the prickling on my skin that made me feel like I had to get *out*, get *away*, or somehow take off this false exterior into which I had been born.

"Sorin!" Magda called out to me as I turned to pull the door shut.

"Some other time," I returned. "Not tonight. I'll see you in the morning, Royal Daughter."

Twenty-Two: Ceration

I fled to the square, to the small spirit house of cedar and birch. Flickering candles surrounded the wooden structure, and between the candles and the house lay hundreds of dried flower petals in orange, yellow, and red.

I wanted to kick the petals, step on the candles, light the flowers on fire, and burn the house to tar and ash. I needed to *destroy* something, and not just for the pleasure of breaking. Wood could be distilled to tar. Honey to mead. Iron to gold, with transmutational alchemy. Why was I so different? Why couldn't I be changed as easily into a form that truly represented who I was? If I burned this spirit house to ash, no one would still call it a house. No one looked at a sequoia and saw only the seed it came from. One admired marquetry for its beauty of form, not the component pieces, or the trees it had been. Why? Why why *why* couldn't the same happen to me?! Why did the parts of me, the parts that meant *female*, have to be used in my definition?

I fell to my knees, knocking over a candle. I didn't bother to pick it up, and the flame quickly extinguished. My throat prickled. My chest hurt. I dropped my head forward, and my wet hair fell into my eyes, and I let it hang there. Maybe it was time to pick between two ends: male or female, magical alchemy or woodcutting. Why try to make something new? That would make things easier, surely, and then maybe, with Magda...

Again, I saw the change in her eyes when she looked at me, and again, an anvil fell on my chest. But this was my fault, wasn't it? I'd put off the conversation. I had avoided every opportunity to discuss who I was. I had thought...I had thought she might come to understand, intuitively, that I wasn't male or female, but another option entirely. That I was a part of both worlds, but somehow also removed from them. That there was something else to me. I had thought her feelings for me would be enough to glean understanding.

I pushed my palm into the stony dirt. I was so tired of the questioning, so tired of having to explain. I had thought I was enough. I had wanted to be enough, for her, and I felt crushed under the weight of knowing that somehow, I had come up short.

A hand smoothed across my neck at the exposed skin there, the fingers warm, calloused, and intimate. I shrugged my shoulders and leaned away.

"I'm not ready to talk about this, Magda. Tomorrow, or the day after." I wiped at my eyes with the back of my hand, embarrassed and upset that she'd followed me. I didn't want her to see me like this. She hadn't earned the right to see me like this.

"I'm not pleased to see you crying, Sorin. Especially with the royal daughter's name in your mouth."

My emotions stopped. My heart stopped, although I knew it had to still be beating. That was Mother's voice. The deepness and disdain mixed so perfectly together into the familiar. I cried out in surprise and sprang to my feet, pivoting around.

It was Amada the master woodcutter. Grandmaster woodcutter, I corrected myself. She wore loose-fitting brown cotton pants and shirt, with a purple wool cloak around her shoulders. Her boots were still the same leather pair she'd had in Thuja, but they were well worn and muddy. Under the gibbous moon, I could make out the familiar cleft to her chin, the shape of her jaw, the tight pull of her hair back into a tail. Her woodcutting tattoo was prominent as well—distinct and without a halo. She was neither conjuring nor imagined. We were reunited, and my heart leapt. I had found her! Or, perhaps, she had found me?

"Mother!"

She smiled at me, and it held the warmth of my childhood bound with the more rational thoughts that wondered about her calmness, and Sameer's predictions, and that she was here, alone, near a magical glacier and the pivotal treaty talks.

"You shouldn't have come, Sorin. You need to leave. Now."

"Leave?" I stood and brushed petals from my pants. "I've only just found you. Mother, where have you been? Do you remember woodcutting? Are you afflicted with the same thing as the rest of the guilders?"

Mother sighed. "Come with me. There's a trail I can put you on that will keep you off the glacier and get you back to Thuja that much faster." She offered me her hand, and I instinctively reached for it with my right. I touched my fingertips to her palm, wincing at the pain. Mother noticed, grasped them, and raised my bound hand toward her face. "Damn it, why hasn't this been attended?"

I was surprised at the bite in her words. "Because I've been on a glacier, and because we arrived here at night, and because it's *tii*." I pulled my hand from her grasp, ignoring the pain that followed. "My hand isn't important. I was worried about you."

I hadn't expected some overly indulgent embrace, but neither had I expected this brashness. Mother was never affectionate, but she was also never dismissive. I was old enough to take care of myself, and to journey with the royal daughter if I so chose. Her words flustered me and were far too reminiscent of the voice on the glacier, and of Sameer's warning. Still, I wasn't going *anywhere*, especially not without her.

"Mother, *where have you been*?"

"I was detained."

"Witches?" I asked. I had to know because all I could hear was Sameer in my head. Baiting me. Warning me. His words battled with memories of Mother, of her hatred of witches, of her dismissal of magic. She couldn't be a witch. She *couldn't*.

Mother stared at me, then, a frown pulling at her mouth. Her hand fell away, and she tilted her head—like she was seeing me for the first time.

"Sorin, you *have* to go home. Now."

"No!" If both my hands had worked, I'd have crossed my arms. As it was, the best pose I could manage was one balled fist. "The grandmaster woodcutter is dead, and grandmasters from across the guilds are missing. There are *factories*, Mother. Factories in Miantri, and on the glacier. The guilds are dying. Guilders are dying on the glacier. They're losing their memories and skills, just like in the king's time. It's not safe here. You need to come with me, to Magda. With you, at least, she has the woodcutter's guild. She can save at least part of Sorpsi at the talks, and then we can try to sort out what is going on."

Mother squeezed her eyes shut and let her head fall back. "Damn it, Sorin," she muttered. "Damn it damn it damn it."

"Mother, would you please just—"

Mother's hands moved then, fluid like water but with a speed I'd never seen before. She muttered words I couldn't hear, and heat descended, first around my ears, then to my neck and shoulders. Sweat erupted across my brow. The candles extinguished, and the flower petals lifted despite the stillness of the air. I batted at them in confusion. Witches? Here? Where? I looked about the square, but I could see only Mother and myself. What was she doing? Some type of witch defense?

Calm down, Sorin, or you'll end up with a nasty headache.

Had I heard the voice out loud, or had it been in my head? I couldn't tell, but it was Mother's voice, so surely that meant she had spoken. Mother was no witch. "Mother, what—"

It's time to take a rest.

The light from the moon waned as the edges of my vision fuzzed. I tried to speak again, but the heat scalded my tongue and held it prisoner while petals clung to my clothes and skin.

Just lie down.

I clawed at the swirling petals, frantic to clear my vision, but everything before me spotted into drops of moonlight. I fell onto my side on a bed of petals, surrounded by the remains of white candles. Every intake of air coated my throat in stinging dryness, and my eyelids felt like sandpaper. I tried to stand, to speak, to beg for an explanation, but my vision turned black. Finally, I gave into the pressure on my mind telling me to relax. To follow. That I was going home.

*

"Do it again," Mother said with that infuriating calm she always had when we argued. She pointed to a perfectly fine spot on the wood floor where the fresh finish gleamed. "Do it right this time."

I clenched my jaw. "If I can redo it to your specifications by tonight, could I meet up with Magda tomorrow? She said Master Rahad would give me a tour of his laboratory, a real tour, and I—"

Mother stepped past me without speaking, into the forest.

"Mother!" I called out after her. "Mother, I haven't seen Magda in months. Mother, why are you keeping me here?"

"Mother?"

"Mother!"

I awoke, naked, atop a pile of wool blankets in the middle of a fairy ring. Snow coated the branches of the ash and fir forest around me, yet inside the circle, it was warm and the ground clear.

"Hello?" I called out as I tried to shake the dream from my mind. That wasn't one of my better memories of growing up, and I had no desire for it to linger. "Mother?"

I stood, wrapped one of the blankets around my body, and walked the perimeter of the ring. The fungi were strange and not a type I had seen before—candlestick-shaped and branched, almost like antlers at their top. They glowed, too, the faint green of foxfire, despite the daylight.

That spoke of magic, and I frowned and dug my fingers into the wool. The rough fabric scratched my palms, and when I pulled my hands back, I startled enough to drop the blanket.

My right hand was no longer bound. It was healed. Whole. I gave an experimental kick to my legs. My hips no longer popped, and not even the scabs from my wounds from Thuja were still present.

"Mother?" I called out tentatively. It was one thing to enchant foxfire. To repair muscle was...extraordinary, and unwanted. I ran my hands over the unblemished skin. I'd earned no scars from this. Magic had taken them away, it seemed, this chance to look older and more experienced. I gathered the fallen blanket, sat back on the pile, rammed my fist into the dry ground, then spat.

"Mother? Whoever did this? I didn't ask to be healed!" I yelled into the bright morning sun. "You should have asked!"

My answer was the song of winter birds and the rustling of foragers. I clutched at my blanket and screamed, at my nudity, and the healing, and because I was tired of witches intervening in my life. I'd have rather lost my hand than this unnatural healing that left no scars.

I wasn't going to be a woodcutter or an alchemist. What did I really need a second hand for anyway? For that matter, where *was* I, and how far from Celtis, and where was Mother?

"Come out!" I screamed it hard enough to scratch my throat and launch myself into a coughing fit. Birds flew at my voice this time, but still no one answered me.

I muttered a string of curses I'd once heard Magda use. "Fine. Maybe I'll crush a magical amulet and see if that gets your attention."

Except...the amulet was in my pants pocket. Unless it had fallen out while the witch had disrobed me... I clawed frantically at my hips, then at the ground. I flung the blankets from my legs and searched through them. Nothing. I sat back down, pulled the blanket over my lap, and looked up at the canopy. Everything was gone, from the amulet to my bloody binding, to my foraging knife. What in the name of the gods was I going to do, sitting out in a forest clearing like some maiden or lost prince in a fairy tale?

Soft footsteps came up behind me. I didn't need to turn around to know the aroma of cedar on Mother's cloak that no laundering could remove. I clutched the blanket to my chest and turned. The air warmed as she approached, the snow melting from her footsteps until she entered the ring of dry ground where I sat. Mother had a satchel slung over one shoulder. She slid it from her arm and placed on the moss next to me.

"Some old blueberries inside. Desiccated, but nutritious anyway. Help yourself, since you're apparently staying a while."

"Witches, Mother." I curled my legs up to my torso as I tried to cover myself with a blanket. Too many questions coated my tongue, mostly about how calm she was in a forest filled with witches, and magic. But only one came out. "My clothes. Mother, I'm not—"

"You've been out twelve hours. You're healed. You need to eat. Your clothes were filthy. Master Walerian is conjuring you new ones, or stealing them. He wasn't clear on which, and I don't really care." Mother knelt next to me and turned my head from side to side, inspecting my neck. Her fingers were as cool and rough as they had been since my earliest memories. I wanted to sink into her, to drown myself in the smell of cedar, but how could I when we were both in so much danger?

"Did you not attend the fair then, Sorin?"

Her words took me by surprise, and I blinked several times. "The...the alchemical guild fair?" She'd remembered? She'd never remembered before, which was why I'd missed the event five years in a row.

Mother smoothed a wrinkle on her shirt. "Was there another one running at the same time?"

"I—no. It was cancelled. I'd have missed it anyway."

"Why?" She sat on a patch of moss next to me, her eyes expectant. Like she knew my answer but wanted to hear my humiliation when I spoke it.

I clutched the blankets tightly to my chest and stuttered. "I had to go looking *for you*. And when I arrived, the grandmasters were all missing and the fair had been shut down." *And you were missing, and I was worried about you!*

Mother crossed her arms over her chest. "So you did not become an alchemical apprentice."

That was what this was about, then. Her words had no inflection, but I could hear the statement underneath, and it varnished me in shame. I was still unguilded, and that was worse, somehow, than witches, and being in a ring of enchanted foxfire. It was an embarrassment, both to her, and to guild tradition.

"I don't care much for alchemy anymore." I looked intently at the moss. The words were hollow even in my own ears. The pride from the fungal pigments that had once swelled in my chest had left only a deflated, hollow space.

"So you are still considering which guild to join?"

I did catch something in her voice, that time. Something that sounded very suspiciously like excitement.

"I suppose."

Mother's hand stroked my shoulder, once. She again peered at my neck, then sat back. "Would you consider woodcutting then? There is a welcome place for you here."

Her voice lilted. She was *hopeful*. That was almost worse than excited. "Not witchcraft? You seem...cozy with them. The witches."

Mother laughed and didn't take the bait. "No, Sorin, not witchcraft. You belong in woodcutting. Your skills are in woodcutting." She took my chin in her hand and stroked the skin with her thumb. "You are a woodcutter, by birth and by skill. It's time to join the guild, and thus gain every benefit it offers."

There was so much warmth in her voice when she spoke of woodcutting that it momentarily filled my chest with a feeling very akin to love. I let my vision blur.

Woodcutting was as good as glass or smith or carpentry. At least in this, I had a history and some skill. It mattered to Mother that I was guilded, one way or another, even if the guilds eventually disbanded. If I couldn't have what I wanted, at least one of us would be happy, and I wanted... I did want her to be happy with me.

"It is decided then. Once Walerian is back, we can have your guild mark placed." She scooped a small handful of wrinkled blueberries from her satchel and handed them to me. "Here. Eat."

I took the berries and held them in my hand, letting their desiccated forms roll about my palm. "Walerian is...a witch? He healed me?" I asked, not meeting her eyes.

She evaded, as skillfully as ever. "A woodcutter can't have just one hand, Sorin, especially not a master."

I looked up sharply and frowned. Heir or not, that wasn't how the guild system worked. I was surprised at her for even suggesting it. "I'm not even an apprentice. I'm not a journey. I've not earned a mark, much less a title."

"A child can declare at twelve, Sorin, or after one year of service to a master. You are well past both. This mark is your birthright."

"But what does that matter?" I dug my fingernails into the ground. "You must have seen what happened in the capital. You must have met some of the afflicted guilders. What about the machines? What about the woodcutter's guildhall, the smiths, the textile workers—all those empty guildhalls? What about...what about Sameer?" That last part tumbled out uninvited. I mumbled then, for my throat was tightening with emotion. "You've got a firstborn son who wants this. A son who is already a master. If you want to carry on a dying tradition, he should be the one you guild, not me."

Mother's voice held a familiar cord of tried patience, though her left eyebrow arched. "The guilds aren't lost, just changing. The guilders are changing, too, although slower than one might like. And Sameer is a textile worker, Sorin, and he is a man. He can be a master or grandmaster through skill and training, but he can never be my heir. Of my two children, you were the one fit for woodcutting. I've too much work invested in you, and your skill level is above my own with veneer work. Female or male, or lurking on some other axis as you do, you will inherit from me, regardless."

Mother's words sliced me as expertly as a fretsaw. I'd always thought her accepting of my identity, but here we were with her casual rejection of Sameer and coveting some base part of me over which I had no control. Just like Magda.

There was nothing left inside me to break.

"Is the queen dead?" I snapped. I would not fall apart in front of her. I would get the information Magda needed to save the guilds, and Sorpsi, and I would leave. There were no ties anymore, between Mother and me.

Sameer would be so proud.

Mother blinked, then laughed. It came out a thin, tinkling sound that felt at odds with the conversation. "A few days with the royal daughter has you making demands."

"Damn it, Mother. The queen will cripple Sorpsi with her absence! Where is she?"

Her eyebrow raised. "Hardly, child. Calm down."

I threw a rock at Mother's midsection that she sidestepped without a second thought. She tsked, but that same damn smile stayed on her face.

"You've never been one for a temper, Sorin."

I fumed. I had every right to be angry, especially considering I'd been abducted in a swirl of flower petals and was currently sitting in a ring of enchanted, false foxfire.

"I've been calm for too long. You've cost me apprenticeship after apprenticeship, and now you and the queen are, what? Lurking with witches in the northern forests? Doing...hurting, guilders?" That was a jump, perhaps, but she had to give me something, anything, before my mind spun so far I became unhinged. "You can't just—just muddle about in state affairs like this!"

Mother shook her head. "I had thought both of us proficient at muddling about in areas we shouldn't be. You should be at home, in Thuja, and well away from all of this business. I don't begrudge you alchemy, Sorin; I just wish you had explored more than wood finishes. A dual affiliation could suit you." Mother smiled, and it chilled me. "Rather, it does suit you." She turned at a sound I did not hear and pointed.

A man approached from the north, two thick leather bags slung over his shoulders. "Get dressed. Walerian will have brought the inks. We can finish your guild mark before sundown. Tomorrow we depart. I'll take you home myself, to ensure you don't wander back." Her voice had returned to that separated coolness that I loathed. I bristled, more out of habit than anything else.

I wrapped a hand around my neck, making sure to keep the blankets up around myself with the other. "I don't want a tattoo," I stated as Walerian dropped the bags at Mother's feet and grunted.

Mother pulled a roll of cotton from the first bag and handed it to me. A flash of softness swept across her face before she turned away.

It was enough to steady my fingers so that the binding went on properly the first time. The other clothes were leather, and the cape and boots trimmed with a fur I didn't recognize. Still, the thought of the tattoo ate away at all that brash confidence I'd had moments ago. "Mother, are you all right? Really?"

"Hmm?" She looked up at me finally, then wiped dirt from my pants with the back of her hand. "Yes, and so are you." She gestured with a fragment of bone she'd pulled from one of Walerian's satchels. "The life you want is right here. You went out looking for it, and it's found you. Excellent work, and well worthy of a journey piece. Now *sit.*"

Too many years of bowing to those words and that tone froze me to the ground. The heaviness from the Thujan lake, from Magda's eyes, and Master Rahad's words, settled across my lungs like a wet blanket. I couldn't sit. I couldn't run. I could only stare at Mother, and that piece of bone.

Walerian placed the ink container on the ground and grabbed me by the arm.

"Hey!" I startled into action and yelled, images of the not-guards from Thuja slamming across my vision. Walerian's fingers chilled my skin even through the layers of leather. I hissed at him and yanked my arm from his grasp. They couldn't force this. There were *rules.*

Walerian moved to grab me again, but Mother raised her hand.

"It's time, Sorin. No more running." Mother tilted her head and raised her eyebrows. "You can still get an alchemist tattoo one day, should you find a suitable apprenticeship. Making one choice does not preclude you from making another, later on."

My heart pounded. It was one betrayal after another, but this...Mother *couldn't*.

She stepped toward me, and I stepped back in tandem until I backed into a jack pine. The narrow trunk dug into my back, but Mother was close enough to me now that I could smell the sawdust on her clothes. I hated the way the familiarly helped me remember to breathe, even as I thought my heart might break through my chest.

Mother stroked my cheek, the bone still in her other hand. "It shouldn't be like this, but it is. You will need to trust me. You know yourself, but I know your skill." Mother's fingers trailed down to my neck and thrummed on the spot where the guild mark would be placed.

I needed to run, or scream, or stop this entire chain of events, but the pine felt too big to get around all of a sudden. Mother was a woodcutter, and a woodcutter only. She supported me. She loved me. She'd chosen me. I was her heir and...and...

The tip of the bone, now black with ink, hovered just over my skin. The wetness dripped down, cold and slimy, and made my skin crawl.

"A mark can't be placed without consent, Sorin. You know that. You've earned the mark, and your place with the woodcutters."

Again, the ink dripped onto my skin, and in the damp, I saw a future of saws and veneer, dust and glue. I saw my pigments used to dye royal crests that Magda would wear as she sat on her throne, ruling with a regent by her side—a regent with black curls and wide hips, but who wasn't me. I saw Sameer in his textile shop, curling ribbon between a thumb and forefinger and dreaming it was veneer. I saw the factories come, the machines, and take it all away.

I didn't want this future, not for any of us.

"Stop."

I met Mother's eyes. In them was a childhood of strong guidance, of directed patience, of love and partial abandonment. I saw her guide my hand as I cut my first veneer, and her strike me across the face when, in an act of defiance, I threw her favorite knife into the fireplace. That same unyielding love was on her face now.

"I don't want it," I whispered, finally. I moved my head, so the wrong side of my neck faced her, and felt the bone tip smear ink across my skin.

"Hold Sorin down."

I jerked against Walerian's hands as he pulled my arms back around the tree trunk. He held my wrists with one hand and my head with the other, forcing it back to face Mother. I pulled against him and screamed, but he had my wrists smashed into the bark.

"Stop! Please!"

Heat flared near my feet. Mother stepped away from me, leaving footprints of burnt sorrel in her wake. Desiccated leaves puffed from existence in a flash of sparks. Vines slithered from the ground, from the base of the tree, and wound around my body, cementing me to the jack pine.

Mother smiled but did not speak, and in her smile, I saw no warmth.

And it had been warm when she'd found me last night, though we were in the middle of winter.

It had been warm, and petals had floated in the air, and I had fallen to unconsciousness at her unspoken words.

She had been alone and unharmed despite being sought by witches.

And the sorrel burned at her feet.

And her voice called from my memory, telling me to stay away from unbound guilds. I remembered her warnings. That if I left Thuja, a witch might find me and take all my extraction knowledge and the guild secrets she'd trusted me with. I remembered her chilling words. "There are witches everywhere, Sorin," she'd whispered into my hair. "They are everywhere, and they don't need to impale you with a magic sword to take your skills. Not anymore."

Gods, I was an idiot. A sheltered, unguilded moron.

I pulled against the vines, against Walerian's hands. I screamed. "NO!" It was a plea—a childish, desperate plea—to the woman who had sheltered me, taught me, cherished me when I hadn't been a girl. It wasn't a plea for a witch.

"Calm down," Walerian said.

A shiver coursed down my body. It was the voice from the glacier. The voice from the guildhall. I froze like a hare. My witch tormentor was here, now, and he worked with Mother! Betrayal intertwined with confusion. She'd worked so hard to keep me away, just to end up here? Forcing a tattoo for a guild I'd never wanted? It didn't make any sense!

"Sorin has not consented," Walerian said gruffly.

Mother met my eyes. We stayed locked together for several long breaths. She'd had him follow me the whole way here. She'd tried to send me back, but even then, we'd have ended up in this place, Mother and I. There was a stifling inevitability to this moment, bred from being her heir. I could run, or reject the mark outright, but I could see in her eyes that she would follow me, witch or not, and she would keep asking until my answer was yes.

I let my head drop forward.

"All right."

The vines fell away.

"Steady now, Sorin." Walerian's grip tightened on my wrists, and his other hand forced my head back against the trunk. The bone, when it pierced my skin, felt like the nails from our roof as they rained down upon me, except there were thousands of them now, and they would not relent. I swallowed screams, and pleading, and I yelled at myself to stay still, to not toss my head and pull at Walerian's hands. A poorly done guild tattoo was grounds for execution under suspicion of forgery, so I forced the shaking from my body and thought of being at home, or at the alchemist's fair, or back in bed with Magda and her bluntness.

"Halfway done now, Sorin. Just a bit more." Wetness dripped down my skin and stained the white leather on my shoulder. I pressed my back into the tree bark. I wanted to draw blood there to rival the pain in my neck. When that didn't work, I tried to imagine what my life would be like after this. What would it be like to enter a guildhall with my mark? Would eyes fall on my neck and smiles return, instead of frowns? Would there be warm greetings and invitations to join tables, instead of aloofness and fear?

I searched for some joy in the images but came up empty no matter how I brought them together. What should have been a mark of pride, earned and submitted to willingly, instead corrupted and tainted my flesh. Each prick felt like a deep stain that even a solvent could not remove.

"It's done." Walerian released me as Mother pulled back. She tossed the bone and the ink tray to the ground, where the black spread across the snow. I took a step from the tree and prodded the swollen area of my neck with two fingertips, wincing at the pain. When I brought my hand down, it was stained black and red, the colors swirling into teardrops.

"It hurts," I managed. They were a child's words, but what else was there to say? It felt almost like a burn, the skin around the area raised and too warm despite the temperature. It throbbed, it seared, both on my skin and deep inside me, but saying as much would not change its presence on my throat.

"Take care to let it scab over properly, and let the scabs come off on their own," Mother instructed as she cleaned her hands in the snow. "Otherwise, we shall have to do it again."

She stood back up and pointed west, farther into the woods. The sun had fallen beneath the canopy, and the forest beyond loomed dark. "We're less than a kilometer from my camp. We will spend the night there, and you can meet the queen. Tell her about Magda if you like. Show her your tattoo. Tomorrow, we will return home."

Walerian held out his right hand. The snow around his boots melted, and the bite to the air fell away. "Follow me," he said as he turned and headed farther into the forest.

Mother hesitated before following. There was no joy on her face, but pride crackled all around her. I wanted to capture it for my own, for her pride in me was seldom so visible, but my mouth tasted like ash and my stomach clenched into cramps.

"Sorin?" she asked. "It's just a tattoo. The discomfort will soon fade. I'm... It was the right thing to do, for you."

"I came here to find you and bring you home."

Mother nodded and gave a terse smile. "And you have. Well done. If the pain in your neck becomes troublesome, you can think about how we can best rebuild the house. Walerian and I had...a discussion about his men's tactics in trying to find me, so I do apologize for that. Come. It's time to see the queen."

She held out her hand to me. When I still didn't come forward, she stepped in and wrapped an arm around my shoulder. I closed my eyes, unable to move. The queen. I didn't care. All I could think about was the throbbing of my neck, and the woodcutting tattoo, and that it was over. Everything was over.

My choice had been made.

Twenty-Three: Multiplication

The queen was Magda, some twenty years older. She was stretched taller than the royal daughter, but without the musculature to fill her out. Where Magda was strong, the queen was elegant. Where Magda sneered and smirked, the queen's face was sharp. Her lips still idled in neutrality as they had in my youth—neither smiling nor frowning, neither approving nor disdaining. She had far more wrinkles than I remembered, but that could have been due to the passage of time. Regardless, I still thought she looked, not burned, but desiccated, like Mother's blueberries, and like the dry, browned sorrel that covered the camp.

A camp filled with guild witches.

Magic was apparent when we crossed the boundary line. Following Mother, I stepped toward an enormous ring of false foxfire—the same funny black candlestick structures from before—and into a forest of charred tree trunks and crunching leaf litter. Snow still hung and glistened on the pines outside the ring, and nuthatches called, and turkey tail fungi sprouted their blues and greens from the stumps of thin hardwoods. Inside the ring, everything was burned and hard, and while it was warm, I did not want to take off my cloak.

"Come along, Sorin," Mother said when I lingered near the false foxfire, well away from the queen. My foot rose to comply, more habit than anything, and it took concerted effort to slam it back down onto the burnt sorrel. What was I doing, willingly walking into a fairy ring with witches? The tattoo still burned on my neck, but it hadn't addled my mind.

"I want to go back." I took a deep breath, then added, "I am going back. To Magda."

"She can wait a bit. Please come here, Sorin and Amada."

Orders from the queen. My queen. My feet moved without my permission, but there was no magic involved. Years of listening to Mother, of doing what she asked so I might earn a chance to see Magda again, or go to the alchemical fair, overrode my common sense.

I walked to the center of the camp, which was small, perhaps sixty meters across. Scattered within the fairy ring were hide tents and short timber frames, and on the trees... I blinked, then sidestepped to a needleless pine. An old, transmuted amulet of oak swung from a low branch. I reached to touch it, but my hand couldn't get close. The thing radiated heat so intense it scalded my fingers even three meters away.

"Sorin!" Mother said sharply.

I pulled away and kept walking. Amulets on trees. Mother, a witch. The queen in an enchanted foxfire ring. It felt like a dream, almost. Here, I was approaching a ruler I'd not seen since—since when? Since I was small enough to try on her shoes while Magda giggled from the queen's bedchamber door. Since Magda had broken the queen's favorite teapot while showing me some new sword maneuverer. Since just before I had started wearing my binding.

"You're pleased with all this?"

"Huh?" I'd been smiling at the memories. It'd been enough to momentarily distract me from Mother, and the ache of the guild mark, but now both slammed back into my mind, and I flinched.

"Apologies, Your Highness." I bowed and made sure to wipe my smile away. Did one bow to a runaway queen? Kidnapped queen? She didn't look kidnapped, but then again, Mother didn't look like a witch.

Mother came up to the queen's side and inclined her head. "The healing took more time than Master Walerian and I had planned, Maja. Otherwise, we'd have come sooner."

Maja? Have I ever heard Mother use the queen's name before?

The queen laughed—a honeyed, candied sound—and my jaw dropped as she stepped out and embraced Mother. Mother thumped the queen on the back, much harder than she ought to have been able, given the thinness of her frame. It wouldn't have been strange at all if they weren't of such severely disparate stations and, well, witches. At least, I assumed the queen was a witch. She didn't bear the witch guild mark, but what other reason was there for her being here?

"Sorin?" The queen broke from Mother, and her unwavering, neutral gaze fell back on me. "Thank you for coming."

"I wasn't given an option." I wasn't often given options. I remembered Magda's plea for me to join her on this quest, and Mother bringing me into the woods and repairing my hand. I thought about my tattoo, and my childhood in Thuja. If I'd had a knife in that moment, I'd have impaled my hand, just to spite them all.

"You were given plenty of options," Mother retorted. "You ignored them."

The queen waved a hand, then stepped forward, took my chin between her thumb and forefinger, and turned my head to the right, exposing my tattoo. Her fingers weren't calloused like Magda's, but she smelled of the same soap. I closed my eyes. I hadn't forgotten about the tattoo, but I hadn't seen it yet, either. Somehow, that made it less real. I was afraid that if the queen spoke about it, the mark would become a tangible thing. I wasn't certain I could handle that right now. One more mark of absurdity and reality might crumble to pieces around me.

"Never mind that. Sorin is here now. Sorin," the queen began.

"Magda is in Celtis looking for you!" I blurted out.

"I'm aware." The queen frowned at my neck. "I'm surprised at this, Amada. I doubt Sorin decided to declare for the woodcutter's guild on the sole delight of finding you." She canted her head. "Was this mark freely chosen?"

Mother, for the first time in my memory, looked uncomfortable. She shuffled back a step, and her eyes flicked to the ground before returning the queen's stare. It was comforting, in a way, to think the queen might have stayed Mother's hand with the tattooing. At least someone could control Mother's reins.

"It's done. Sorin chose this. There is no need for a debate."

"Hmmm." The queen nodded and smoothed the front of her thick silk tunic. "No more alchemy, Sorin?"

I shrugged and tried to look indifferent. "I guess." I couldn't get out the rest of the words. They stayed stuck in my mouth. *Why are you lurking in the woods of Puget? Why did you abandon Sorpsi? Why are you staring at me like I'm a tasty little bug?*

"Pity." She pointed to the north end of the camp. "Amada, would you join Walerian in his preparations? I'd like to have a chat with Sorin about Magda, I think. Sorin, sit by the south end there and wait for me." She turned sharply on her booted heel and went back inside her tent.

Mother paused only long enough to squeeze my hand. It was a surprisingly affectionate gesture. She leaned in and kissed my cheek, which was terrifying, and slipped a...stone, maybe, into my pocket. I pushed her away, letting my fingernails dig into her leathers. She'd never kissed me, not in my memory.

"I do love you, Sorin." Mother whispered the words, and a heartbeat later, she turned and headed farther into the camp.

Love. The word tasted chalky. I sat on a downed hardwood log and rammed my heel into the side. A fist-sized chunk came free, revealing a vein of red stain from the flaming dragon fungus. Out of disgust, I went to my knees and gouged at the wood with a stick, dislodging several red fragments. I'd find a fire and toss them in. Let the fire burn the wood. Let it cauterize my memories. Break apart my life so that I might reassemble it, properly this time.

"Always playing in the dirt, you woodcutters."

I startled and dropped the wood as the queen knelt before me, a bucket of steaming water in one hand and a hard roll in the other. Now queens were kneeling before me? Maybe I had fallen unconscious near the spirit house and this was some petal-infused nightmare. I wiped my hands on my pants and sat so she would still be above me. "Your Highness?"

She offered me the roll. "Hungry?"

"Yes. Thank you." The roll was too dry and hard to be part of a dream, but I demolished it anyway in three bites while the queen pulled a white cloth from the bucket. I eyed the sopping thing warily. "Is there something in there?" It smelled faintly of wintergreen. In a camp of witches, it was logical to assume herbs and potions.

The queen laughed. "Just water, alchemist," she said smoothly. "You have my word."

"Do queens usually wash guilders?"

The queen clasped her hands behind her back. "Is it a problem? I cleaned your bottom, too, when you were small."

I looked away. "No, Your Majesty, of course not." I really had no reason to refuse, and the tattoo *was* still seeping. I turned my neck to her and bit back a scream as the queen dabbed the cloth around the tattoo, careful not to touch the actual mark. Combined with the heat of the campsite, the hot water made me to break into a sweat. The queen's washing was attentively gentle, but I still hissed in pain when she got too close to lines.

"I trust my daughter is well?"

I didn't know what she was looking for and had no idea how to respond. My argument with Magda from the day before seemed so far in the past as to be intangible, and Magda was clearly not "well," since she'd had to make an emergency trip to Puget in place of her missing mother.

"As well as can be expected."

The queen rinsed the cloth in the bucket and came back in for a second pass. "Magda is capable of running Sorpsi in my absence, Sorin."

I jerked my head at her words. I'd had common sense once, and an understanding of how one spoke to royalty, but that had bled away, it seemed, into this ridiculous setting. "Ruling, maybe, but the treaty talks?"

The queen rinsed the rag a final time, then began to clean the dirt from my face. It should have felt patronizing, but instead it reminded me of the times the queen had wiped our tears—Magda's and mine—when we'd fallen in the courtyard, or scraped against some log on the outskirts of the forest. Mother had often left me at the palace for days on end, and I couldn't remember a time when she had been as gentle as the queen was now.

"The first day is merely the presentation by the census," the queen said. She sat back and dropped the cloth into the bucket. "There now. You look like a human again."

"But it's a census for which Sorpsi has no guilds." I wanted my words to have more sting to them, but they only sounded tired.

The queen chortled. "For which none of the three countries have guilds. Do you think industrialization is solely limited to Sorpsi?"

"I..." Of course it wasn't, but wasn't it Sorpsi we were trying to save?

"I'll join her tomorrow when the negotiating begins." The queen tilted her head to the side and tucked a thick lock of hair behind her ear. In that moment, she looked so much like Magda that a lump rose in my throat. "Is that the only issue you take with me, that I've abandoned Magda to the treaty talks? I'd always thought we got on well enough, you and I. Do you not trust me?"

I glared at the queen, partly because she was baiting me like some stinkhorn fungus, and partly because I was frustrated with the calmness of everyone around me. Sorpsi was going to fall apart, apparently all three countries were going to fall apart, and the queen was washing my forced tattoo like we were at tea and I was a ten-year-old pouting over sweets.

"Magda came for you because of the missing guilders, and what is happening to Sorpsi. I came looking for Amada. That's all."

"And you've found her. Well done." She made a diagonal motion across my torso. "You lost something along the way, though, didn't you?"

"My knife," I muttered, for I missed the weight of it on my belt. *My sanity, possibly.*

"I was thinking of something more substantial." From behind the bucket, the queen pulled a strip of worn leather that dangled three small leather pouches. "Yours, is it not? I would very much like to know more about your alchemy."

My eyes went wide, and I snatched my belt from her and cradled it in my lap. How? Why? Had Walerian found it as he'd trailed us on the glacier? Why couldn't it have stayed there and been merely another relic to the king's old magic? The pigments were *mine*; that they had been handled by anyone else, especially witches, made them feel that much more tarnished. I clutched at the middle pouch, still full of blue-green pigment, and tried to even out my breathing. They'd meant so much to me for so long. I missed their familiar weight and the reminder of the one thing I was truly good at.

"They're just toys, Your Highness. I'm not an alchemist."

She sat forward and braced herself on her thighs. "No, you are not. But you'd like to be, wouldn't you?" She tapped the first pouch and smiled. "I've watched you for years, Sorin. Don't think I haven't noticed, even with Amada insisting it was only for wood finishes. I've wanted you training with Rahad at the palace since you were twelve. Your mother would have none of it. She didn't want you involved in any of this. Didn't think you had it in you. And now, here we are."

Twelve? Twelve was the year we'd stopped visiting the palace. Twelve was the last year I had seen Magda, and the last year we'd run through the square and climbed the old king's statue. It was the year I'd snuck into Master Rahad's laboratory at night on a dare and read his notes on how to dissolve gold in an acid mixture. It was the year I'd made my first solvent, and the year I'd started to turn from woodcutting.

The skin on my neck burned, though nothing had touched it. Forget magic and all its implications. Forget the history of the unbound guilds that I no longer wanted anything to do with. The trade I'd wanted had been *right there*, and now that I had found it, I was marked with another guild's symbol because Mother couldn't let me go. She would never see me as anything beyond a woodcutter, and her heir. Her deliberate cruelty pierced my heart like thousands of tiny bone fragments. The queen had been watching, and the future I'd wanted had been there, perfect and formed and more than anyone had a right to wish for, and Mother had kept me from it. She had kept me locked in that forest, away from Magda, and the queen, and alchemy, so I would have no choice but to follow her.

I touched a finger to my new tattoo.

And I hated her.

Twenty-Four: Aqua regia

In that moment, in that forest rotten with magic and burnt sorrel, I pushed away all of Mother's words about acceptance and heirship. I wanted to scream, and throw, kick and punch and demand *why why WHY* Mother had seen fit to cripple my future.

"Sorin?" the queen asked, both gentle and impatient. She sounded like my childhood, like the woman who had brought Magda and me hot tea late at night when we stayed up telling each other ghost stories. Like the woman who'd chided us for playing too long by the river, thereby delaying her dinner because she'd not eat without us.

"Mother kept me from you." I'd meant to ask, but it came out as a statement.

The queen nodded. "She did."

"She kept me from Magda." My voice caught as if Mother's hands were around my throat.

"She did."

"Why?"

The way the queen's fingers spread across her thighs, and the look of hunger I saw as she eyed my pouches, pushed me to sit back. I rammed my balled fits into my hips and clenched my jaw. "Why?"

"Because you belong to her, by guild law. Because she covets your skills. Because she would not see the guilds die—would not have you wander off like so many guilder heirs to factory jobs that require less skill."

"I would have stayed!" I pounded my fist into the ground. "I would have stayed for Master Rahad, for alchemy, for..." *For Magda*, I finished, silently.

"I know." The queen moved the bucket to the side and wiped the back of her hand across her forehead. "So let's talk about that, you and I. I have a position open, it would seem, for a royal alchemist, but Walerian tells me this is perhaps no longer what you want." Half of her mouth turned up into a smile. "Are you afraid of alchemy, Sorin, after that trouble on the glacier?"

"You know about Master Rahad?" I asked, although, really, if Walerian reported to her, he'd likely seen the body as well. "Do you know how he died?"

Irritation flashed across the queen's face so quickly I almost thought I'd imagined it. "He and I had a disagreement. He was supposed to go back to the capital, but it seems the ice took him instead." She frowned, and it highlighted the lines around her mouth and the hollowness of her cheeks. I was not, I reminded myself, simply talking to an older version of Magda. "He'd never been the best of apprentices either." Her eyes bored into mine, and I couldn't bring myself to look away. It felt like she could see all the way through me, to the trees beyond the burnt circle in which we sat. "You'd be much better, I'd think. Especially after all of Amada's training."

"A...apprentice," I stuttered.

"Mmm." The queen nodded and smiled, although it didn't quite reach her eyes.

"You an *alchemist*?" I asked. I searcher her neck for a tattoo, but the skin was as smooth and brown as it had always been. "Does Magda know? Does the *kingdom* know?"

"I doubt it. But don't look at me like that, Sorin, like I've just killed your pet monkey. Iana was an alchemist, a guilded alchemist at that. Most queens have to be, after a fashion. We've a legacy of old magic to contain, and that's hard to do with no knowledge of the unbound guilds."

"So you're all witches." It wasn't a question, and the disgust was more than evident in my voice.

"Your mother is a witch," the queen returned with a biting tone. "I am an alchemist."

"They're both obscene."

The queen chewed on her lower lip for a moment, contemplating her answer. Good. Let her wrestle with the same definitions I'd had to since the glacier.

"Not obscene, necessarily," she said finally. "Alchemy is a bit more...efficient. You've found that out, haven't you, with your explosive fungal pigments."

The way she looked at my belt felt almost predatory. I put a hand over the full pouch of the blue-green and scooted down the log.

The queen laughed, startling a nuthatch on a barren branch above our heads and sending it flying into the afternoon sky. She reached into the pocket of her leather pants and pulled out a satchel of yellow-brown powder. "Foxfire spores. Come now, do you really think you're the only alchemist to ever play with fungi?" She shook a thimbleful onto the cap of a nearby amanita mushroom, and then blew across the top. The mushroom began to glow a sickly yellow. "Just a small change. A reaction, as you say." Her eyes danced. "But this bone oil of yours, now that is interesting. Master Rahad walked me through the steps as you showed him. It's opened up a new world for us, and for alchemy."

The queen leaned in. Her breath gusted over my face, hot and humid in the dry air, but I didn't back away. I was desperate for her words.

"Who knows what other secrets you have? I've watched you, Sorin, and I've wanted you for a long, long time. Consider what being my apprentice would mean for your future, not just in alchemy, but with Magda."

"I..." I stood, my mouth still agape. The queen stood as well. We breathed in tandem for what felt like hours as I wrestled with the data. To study with the queen... I let my mind drift toward that future. I'd be close to Magda. I would have access to the royal libraries and Master Rahad's laboratory—my laboratory. I would be close enough to see Mother if I wanted to. But...but but *but*.

"Why are you here?" I whispered into the dry air. "Why are you here when there are dead guilders? Missing grandmasters. When Master Rahad's body is frozen to a glacier, and you *don't even care*. And why am I here, with alchemists and witches in a desiccated forest, probably surrounded by the amulets the old king used to seep magic into the glacial melt water, to poison the population of Gasta Flecha?"

"Alchemy, my young friend." This time when she smiled, I saw her joy, and when she clasped her hand to my shoulder, warmth filled my body. With Mother, moments like this had always been hard-won. Here, with the queen, her affection came so easily I felt drunk. I wanted to submerge myself into her enthusiasm, and acceptance, perhaps not of my body, but of what I had achieved with alchemy. Did it matter, really, if magic and alchemy were different points on the same line if the Queen of Sorpsi controlled both? I had no interest in magic—never would—but it was hard not to be enticed. Every part of my life to this point had been about my pigments and their potential. Maybe it didn't have to be thrown away after all.

"You'd really take me as an apprentice?"

The queen offered me her hand. I searched her eyes, thinking I might find some deeper truth, but all I saw was the woman who had raised me as much as Mother had. I put my hand in hers, and we stood, the soft smile never leaving her face. She took my belt from the ground and fastened it around my waist, taking care to refasten each pouch in the front where I could easily reach them.

"You are brilliant, Sorin," she murmured as she knelt before me, the burnt sorrel crumbling into her pants.

Tears collected in the corners of my eyes. "My queen," I mumbled.

She rose, took my hand again, and together, we walked into her hide tent. The inside was sparse, but a pile of thick wool blankets clustered in the center. I recognized the purple-and-red one as the top covering of the queen's bed. Magda and I had played under its enormous width more times than I could remember. Made from baby alpaca, the soft fibers felt like a bed of tulip petals. The sense of familiarity was so strong that I closed my eyes and inhaled. I caught the familiar scent of woodsmoke, a base note of cedar—no doubt from Mother—and the faintest bit of the lemon soap the maids used to wash the palace textiles.

The queen led me to the blankets, and I sat without being asked. I slipped, effortlessly, into the oasis the queen provided. The tension from the glacier, the tension in my muscles, my mind, evaporated. There was no magic about, for I felt no heat, but time seemed slower. Even my heartbeat calmed.

"Sit with me tonight, my new alchemist," the queen said. She wrapped the purple-and-red blanket about my shoulders, and her tenderness knit together so many wounds that still seeped in my heart. "Tell me about my daughter, and your journey here, and your pigments. Tomorrow, I'll show you why you left home, and why you have no reason to return. An industrial revolution is beating at our borders, and I intend to welcome it, with you, and your alchemy, at my side."

Twenty-Five: Projection

Mother had read me stories when I was little—before I turned from woodcutting. The most common were fairy stories about enchanted woods, and elves and snakes that talked, and old men who guarded magical glowing trees. The mystic nature of the forest had faded away as I grew older, but as I followed the Queen of Sorpsi across ashen earth and burnt grasslands devoid of trees, as we left Mother and the witches behind, all those old stories came back to me as the forest sprang back to life.

The sky was just starting to peak with the oranges and reds of sunrise. Light caught on the dew and scattered rainbows across my legs. In only a few short minutes, saplings choked the game trail, and the bracken became high as my waist. We pushed through until hemlocks towered over our heads, and the scent of pinesap filled the air.

Then we broke into a clearing, into another camp, and my world cracked apart again.

Before me was an alchemical dream. My dream, now again, after a night spent with the queen. She'd talked to me for hours of alkahests and transmutation—never the guilders or the talks, but I'd been too caught in her words to ask. Now we were in a camp of metal poles and finely woven textiles. Small fires dotted the clear areas beneath several old oaks. Cauldrons hung over fires, and long tables took up the center of a ring of tents, covered in glassware and metalworking and slices of branches. Rolls of parchment and cords of wood lay stacked in heaps all about the camp. People milled about or hunched close to the earth, mumbling and mixing, the air thick with the smell of fish—the smell of my bone oil, in dozens of cauldrons.

I had died, surely, or I was hallucinating. I had no idea this many cauldrons even existed, much less alchemists to work them. There had to be close to a hundred people about, all engaged in some form of alchemical pursuit, and they were all working with my alchemy. My discovery.

Was this what Mother felt when a patron purchased a marquetry? When the queen commissioned an inlayed ceiling in the royal ballroom? The feeling of—of being *valued*, intoxicated me.

"They're yours," the queen said. She swept into the center of the clearing and beckoned for me to follow her. "All of it is yours. Direct them. Command them. They follow your recipe."

My head spun, and it wasn't just from the bone oil fumes. I needed a minute to respond. I knew what to do in a small laboratory, but with dozens of cauldrons and other alchemists?

"Not enough?" the queen asked coyly. "Tell me what else you want, and I will find it."

"I want..." What I wanted at that exact moment was fresh air. The other alchemists here had much stronger stomachs than I did. I looked up, thinking I might be able to see where the fumes were the thinnest, and gasped at the thousands of pinecones dancing on the branches over my head.

Except...they weren't all pinecones. They were... amulets?

"My queen?" I asked, pointing to an amulet hanging directly over me. There were so many of them! Heavy amulets that dragged down the branches. Tiny amulets that bobbed in the wind. All of them oak and graying, the same as the amulets from the lakes.

How many years had it taken for the queen to dig up all of these old relics? How many more were there, waiting to emerge at the slightest hint of magic or alchemy? Was she actually using them as the old king had? And if so, what did they store?

I slipped my hands into the deep pockets of my pants, attempting to ground myself. I'd forgotten about the stone Mother had slipped in there, and I'd been too tired last night to care what she'd been about. Now my fingers wrapped over a warm and slightly sticky oval clearly made from wood and likely no different from the hundreds that swayed above me.

"Do you like them?" the queen asked. "Your mother found most of them. Her time away from you wasn't wasted."

I pulled my hand from my pocket and wiped off the alcohol residue. "You needed her magic? To pull the amulets from the glacier? Why couldn't you do it yourself?" I asked sourly.

The queen chortled. "I have a queendom to run."

I flexed the hand Mother had fixed. As interested as I was in the queen's version of alchemy, reminding me of my mother and her frequent trips turned my mood further south.

"Why bother?" I asked as I moved to the center of camp, next to a long oak table littered with amulets releasing so much heat they'd scalded their outlines onto the wood beneath them. "The magic is mostly gone, isn't it? And we can make ethanol easily enough."

"Ethanol. Yes, hmm." The queen led me to the table in the very center of the clearing. A tall glass beaker sat on it filled with a clear, syrupy liquid that I knew far too well. Three triangular amulets weighted it at the bottom. The queen plunged a pair of metal tongs down into the solvent and pulled out the smallest one. A tall alchemist in Queensguard red toweled the wood dry, then handed it to the queen. She let the amulet swing down from her hand, the wood suspended on a thin string.

"We've decided to call it pyridine," the queen said as I leaned in to inspect her amulet despite its smell. "Although if you're opposed to the name, we can change it. Bone oil sounds too...sinister."

"That depends on what you use it for."

"Yes, well, aside from its unique solvent properties, pyridine is an excellent lubricant between magic and alchemy. Between a number of things, really. You solved a very large problem for us, Sorin."

The lightness I'd had since meeting the queen, since spending the evening talking about the academics of alchemy, began to drift away. Why did it have to be magic? Why did it *always* have to be magic?

"So you are using them for magic."

"I'm using them for storage," the queen said flatly. "Would you put your ridiculous grudge against magic away for a moment? You're speaking with Amada's voice." The queen's tone was cool as she let her fingers rest on my shoulder. One came up and brushed my neck, over the irritated lines of the tattoo. I winced and pulled away. I didn't need the reminder. The skin still stung, and it'd be years before I could forget the feeling of the bone in my skin.

"I'm not afraid of magic because of Mother."

The queen's voice turned sharp. "Will you make excuses for her your whole life? Were you ever going to grow up and do anything of your own?" She pinched the top of my binding through my shirt. I tried to jerk away, but she'd dug her fingernails into the cotton, and there was an instant pull against my chest. I stilled, and fumed. Whatever her business in alchemy or magic, it had *nothing* to do with my binding.

"You let her, and this, be an impediment when both were well within your sphere of control."

This time, I spun hard enough to tear her hand away. I slapped at her fingers, my teeth ground so tightly together I couldn't speak.

Warmth fled her face.

"Your future is here, Sorin." She held out the amulet.

And because I'd spent years following rules, and Mother, and Magda, and because I didn't think I could survive having another pillar from my childhood taken from me, I stepped forward and touched the damn thing.

"What are you storing? Tell me the truth," I said, though I could barely hear my voice over the sounds of the mortar and pestles and boiling cauldrons.

The queen softened again. The tension around her eyes and mouth drained away until she looked like a mother, not a monarch. My heart wouldn't tolerate being tugged in another direction. I needed her endgame before the fumes of the bone oil ate away my senses.

"I'm ensuring our history isn't lost. I'm protecting the guilds since they refuse to protect themselves." Her voice lowered. "That's important to you, too, isn't it?"

I looked up into the queen's eyes. "Your Majesty, our guilds are dying. Dead. Old magic won't save them. People have to care about the skills guilders offer. Their work has to be valued. Nothing else is likely to help."

The left side of her mouth twitched. "The guilds have been dying for a long time, alchemist. But the skills of the guilders haven't been lost." She tossed the amulet to me, and I caught it, though the wetness made it slippery. "The one in your hands, in fact, came from the grandmaster of glass."

I dropped the amulet. It slipped underneath the leaves of a bunchberry, its string coiling on top of the short sedge. "Inside the amulet?" I croaked. My hands were wet with bone oil. Too much on my skin and I would pass out. What in the name of the gods was the queen playing with?

"Just his skills. Not the man himself. We have had the knowledge to transfer skills, obviously, since our last king. Iana herself committed the spell to paper. But what good is transferring skills, even if you concentrate them in a few individuals? People die. They leave. They're too unreliable. No, what was needed was *storage*. An extraction if you will."

She took my hands in hers. I hadn't realized I was shaking.

"You used my bone oil," I stammered, "to do this? To...to rape guilders of their skills and...store them?" She might as well have stabbed me with a magic sword. The queen had taken my work, my *life*, and transmuted it into this *perversion*.

The queen tsked as a cloud of emotions raged across my face. "We store them for people who are loyal. Like you. Like Amada. Let the factories come. We can have the best of both. These skills are for people who will help me build Sorpsi into a powerhouse of trade. We are in a bit of a bind, however. We can get the skills transferred in, you see, using your pyridine and the old king's magic, but we can't quite seem to get it back *out*. That will be the first task for my new master alchemist."

"This..." I looked up at the swaying amulets above me, all glinting in the scattered sunlight. There were hundreds suspended in the trees. Thousands. I felt heavy. I thought I might fall into the earth and be consumed by soil and fungi.

"Your logic is flawed," I told her, told my queen whom half an hour ago I'd have followed off a cliff. "None of this helps the guilds. None of this helps the census. Losing guilders means losing boundaries. You should be at the treaty talks."

"It doesn't make sense because you don't understand it. You're caught up in Magda's disdain for our old king and your mother's sense of guild loyalty."

"I'm caught up in not repeating history!" I yelled, loud enough that the alchemist at the cauldron to my right looked up, startled, before the queen waved her back to work.

"Shut those voices out. The guilds are dead. There is nothing to be done about that. Guilders have been fleeing the three countries for years. Now they're paying a toll before they leave. I won't lose generations of knowledge because we can manufacture nails on a machine."

Bile rose in my throat. Guilders heading to the glacier, the queen trapping them and taking their skills and leaving them to wander and die, forever missing part of themselves—because of *my* bone oil.

I rubbed my forehead and looked away from the queen and the amulets, to the tree above me. The breeze rippled the branches of the tall oak, rustling the brown leaves that still clung to their beds and knocking swaying amulets against one another. I tried to count them, but there were too many strapped across tree boughs, scattered on tables, littering the ground near my feet. There weren't this many grandmasters, or masters, or even journeys in Sorpsi.

"They're not just from your queendom, are they?"

The queen looked at me, and as I met her gaze, a smile crept across her face. "No. They're not. Just in case something changes. Just in case the guilds try to recover in Puget and Eastgate. We have everything now, my alchemist. Every skill, every trade, every craft. Sorpsi is safe." She stepped into me and lifted my pouch of elf's cup with one long finger. "I need another bone oil, Sorin. You will find me one, to get the skills from these amulets so we can give these skills and this knowledge to people who truly deserve it."

She couldn't be serious. This would destroy the guilds faster than factories ever could. Industrialization was terrifying, but it wasn't...it wasn't guild genocide! I wouldn't be an alchemist if it meant ripping people apart. The queen was no better than my witch mother. This entire forest was poisoned. *Sorpsi* was poisoned. Magda had to be told.

"I'm not an alchemist," I said. I felt defiant. Brash. Like all the words and all the anger I'd pushed aside when living with Mother were scrambling back to me, demanding to be voiced. I put my hand over my woodcutter's guild mark. I would not be forced again into something I was not.

The coldness of iron swept into the queen's voice. "This wouldn't be just your own laboratory, Sorin, or a building of laboratories. If you can pull the skills out from these amulets, you could rebuild the guilds however you wanted. Change their layout, give yourself all the skills you could never master. You could be grandmaster of them all."

She was delusional. The heat from the amulets, the smell of the bone oil, and the ambient magic had boiled her mind.

"You have to be joking."

"No one would question *this*." She eyed my chest.

Damn her! My anger bled into tightness, and my arms tingled. I rammed my hands into my pockets, raking my nails over the wood of the amulet instead of my skin.

"Help me crush Puget and Eastgate. Make the three countries one again. Redefine yourself. Redefine alchemy if you'd like. I don't care. Call yourself whatever you'd like, but help me."

I swept the amulets from the table and spat upon them. "You are *killing people*, and you're using *my* bone oil to do it!" Every centimeter of my skin itched. Dozens, maybe hundreds of guilders broken apart, changed, having their sense of self stripped from their core. I had betrayed those guilders. I had failed them, and I could feel their pain—Watchara's pain as she cradled a violin she would never again play—in my chest. I could feel it under layers of cotton binding that reminded me with every step of the path I'd been meant to take.

"I will never make another solvent."

The queen's smile turned smug. "No? What if I offered you Magda?"

My hands had been in tight fists, rammed into my pockets to save the skin of my arms. Now my fingers went slack. My lips parted, and I felt blood rush to my face as I remembered how Magda had looked, sitting on the edge of the bed. The curve of her arms. The softness of her hair.

I would melt here, like dew on sorrel if the queen pressed about Magda, even if she was bartering her daughter against the souls of the guilds. So I forced myself to remember Magda's eyes when she had seen my breasts. I forced myself to relive the apprehension and anxiety that cut deeper than her words ever could. I used the emotions as a shield, for I had no other weapons.

I turned from my queen, and the forest of amulets, and walked away.

Twenty-Six: Congelation

"You aren't curious about the recipe?" the queen called as I reached the edge of the clearing. "When you storm back here with my daughter and her righteous anger, how will you reverse this for the guilders that still live?"

Damn it, and damn her. I stopped just before the ground transitioned back to snow.

"Explain the reversal." It sounded like a command Magda would give, and as I said it, I realized I could never bring her back here. What was to stop the queen from taking Magda's skill if she displeased her, or to force Magda's participation? Magda's life wasn't defined by the smithy, but she did love the fire and the hammers. And she could no more survive having that ripped from her than she could her sarcasm or her assertive presence.

"You can't see very well from there."

I turned on my heels, but I didn't walk back. Fear, or guilt, or shame, or some other emotion that didn't belong inside me held me in place. It seemed safer here, too, on the edge of the magic's influence, than standing in the middle near a table of amulets. "I can see well enough."

The queen clasped her hands in front of her body, lacing her delicate fingers together. "Well, I suppose for this demonstration, you are correct. Lovely. Amada!"

From the east side of the clearing, Mother and Walerian emerged, dragging a gagged, bound man between them. This time, there was no hesitation. I recognized his mop of black curls immediately.

"Sameer!" It was a whisper, born more from shock and fear than a need to stay quiet, I think. What in the name of the gods was he *doing* here? And if he was here, where was Magda? Not in this camp, surely. Not bound and gagged, at the mercy of some alchemical witch and an amulet, right? *Right*?

Sameer looked up and screamed at me through his gag. Mother dropped him at the queen's feet, and he stood, shakily, his face hot with rage. I forgot about the amulets, and alchemy, and the queen's promises. I ran to him and stripped the gag from his mouth, then pried at the rope on his wrists.

"Amada, just untie the man," the queen said, laughing. Walerian knelt and cut the length of rope tied around Sameer's ankles as I slid the rope from his wrists.

The instant his hands were free, Sameer pushed me back, hard enough that I stumbled onto my rear. "Run!" He grabbed the front of my tunic and bolted, half dragging me behind him.

"Sameer, wait!" I tried to pry his fingers away as I stumbled by his side, but Sameer didn't even look back.

"Debate later. Run now!"

"Sameer!"

"Now!"

I stopped clawing at his hand and focused on running. "Is Magda here too?" I asked as we left the clearing, and green sorrel once again covered the ground beneath us. "How did you get here?"

Sameer released me and sprinted ahead, leaping a small creek. I followed, although with considerably more difficulty. "I met a journey carpenter on the way out of town, who asked me to stay over and consult on some furniture. The town is filled with guilders, Sorin."

"More?" It was hard to speak and run, and I was falling more behind. "Are they all right?"

Sameer turned back briefly. "What do you think? The ones from Puget and Eastgate apparently received invitations to attend the treaty talks, but suddenly find themselves unable to measure, or blow glass, or weave, or whatever. And then I find out you went missing, Magda is out of her mind with worry, and when I set off to find you, Amada and a master of witchcraft accost me and haul me here. What the hell is going on, Sorin?"

"Just...just hold on, and I'll try to explain." I put on a burst of speed, thinking I would catch up, but in that same moment, Sameer fell back as if he'd run face first into a wall. He cursed and scrambled to his knees, his nose dripping blood.

"Keep running if you can," he yelled. "Don't stop."

"Leave you to witches? I think you're an ass, Sameer, but you don't deserve that." I slowed to a walk, my hands held out in front of me. I'd thought my growing warmth was from the heat of exertion, but now that I'd stopped, it was clear even the air around us was warm. The snow had begun to drip from boughs, the ground was turning soggy under my boots, and the edges of the forest seemed to blur.

My hands met firmness between two trees where nothing but air hung. "You don't have a sword, do you?" I asked. "Bow? Arrows? Dagger? Broken bobbin?"

Sameer pulled himself up on the trunk of a tamarack and blinked incredulously. "You want me to challenge our witch mother with a bobbin? You're the one with the magical-alchemical-whatever powders. You're also the one she is less likely to kill outright."

"I hadn't planned on killing anyone." Mother stepped from...from nowhere, from the other side of the wall we couldn't see. The queen appeared behind her, her steps gliding as if she were on polished marble, not damp leaves.

I'd thought to stand my ground, to face Mother and maybe, for once, not back down. But Sameer pulled me to him, to the comfort of the tamarack.

"I take back every moment of jealousy I had toward you," he whispered. "You can have all this creepiness."

The queen came toward us. Mother stepped ahead of her, refusing to look at me. I missed nothing about her—the wrinkles on her forehead, the way her lips pursed and slid along each other. It looked almost like she'd been storing emotions her entire life, and here they were, all coming forth *now*.

"Step away from Sameer, Sorin. I have work to do." She took two amulets from her pocket, one oval and of oak, the other circular maple. Her eyes flicked to mine, once, before her mouth set, and she stared at Sameer.

Sameer drew a thin knife from his belt.

I grabbed for the oval amulet, but Mother stepped back, and I batted at empty air. Still, she refused to meet my eyes. "Mother! He's your son! Our lives aren't a game, and we are not your toys! Mother, what are you *doing*?"

Damn it, Mother actually looked hurt. I didn't care. Not anymore.

"Why aren't you looking at me?!"

"Because Amada has known for a very long time what a skill like yours means to me, Sorin." The queen's voice lowered to a girlish whisper, and Mother turned away to stare into the forest.

"Leave Sorin, Maja. Sorin is a woodcutter by right of that tattoo. It was chosen."

I touched the scabbed flesh. The skin tingled with a dull throb of pain. I was no more woodcutter than alchemist, and Mother's insistence seemed out of place.

"I think not. Let us be done with that lie." Leaves circled the queen's feet, and from her pocket she pulled a cinched satchel that almost certainly contained alchemical powders. "Will you try to run from your place at my side, Sorin, as your mother always has? Will you fight me into futility? Or will you finally take what belongs to you? The guilds. The secrets. Magda."

In her other hand, she held a square amulet. "I'm asking because I believe you have a great deal left to discover. But I will take what you have now and leave it at that if I must. I can always start a new alchemist, with your knowledge as a base."

"My life belongs to no one but myself." I said the words back at her as my heart rammed in my chest. It was a challenge. The queen knew it.

Instead of looking away, the queen cupped my chin and tilted my head up. There was a smugness there, on her face, that sank my heart.

"Are you done with Magda, then?"

Sameer pushed from behind me and lunged with his knife.

It sliced through layers of fabric, but I couldn't tell if it hit flesh. The queen spun back, opened her satchel, and scattered a fistful of white powder into the air. The particulate hung above all of us—Sameer coiling for another lunge, Mother with her arms wrapped around herself, glaring at the trees—before the dust swelled into long, thin filaments that precipitated, or fell, or violated some other basic law, hit the strip of earth that separated Sameer and me from the queen and Mother, and absorbed into the ground.

"Both of you, come here!" Mother grabbed my arm just as a flurry of white stalagmites pushed from the earth in a circle around Sameer and me. A column sprouted centimeters from my face, and in it, I could see thousands, millions, of mycelial strands weaving around one another, congealing, into some woody fruiting form that would trap us in minutes.

Sameer's hand caught mine, and he pulled me back toward him. I tried to step, but another stalagmite burst up just under my right foot. I lost Sameer's hand and fell forward.

"Damn it, Sorin!" Sameer yelled as a column shot between us, widened into a fan, then began to shade brown and orange. It was red belt conk—some horrible, mutated, alchemist's version of a benign forest rot. No wonder Master Rahad had been so interested in my fungal pigments. I might have been the first to extract and make powders from pigmenting fungi, but I definitely wasn't the first to realize how a fungus's inherent properties could be extrapolated.

"Sorin!" Another tug from Mother and I was on my feet, tripping over the conk mounds as they split apart the dirt. Mother lost her grip as a mound came up fast between us and pushed her back. Again, I landed next to Sameer and, still, the pillars rose, meter by meter, penning us in.

"Maja, *stop!*"

"Sameer has no part in this!" I yelled in tandem with Mother, who could be impaled on a stalagmite for all I cared at the moment.

"Enough, both of you!" It was the first time I'd heard the queen raise her voice. Beneath the honey, I recognized Magda's strength and rigidness, and it raised the hair on my neck. I looked at her, over the rising mounds, and the queen met my eyes, unblinking.

I couldn't look away either. Her eyes stripped away my clothes and left me feeling nude despite layers upon layers of fabric. It was as if I had failed some grand test and was being dissected. But her plan was vile. She would rake the flesh of Sorpsi and boil the marrow of the bones into a cauldron of caustic bone oil distillate, poisoning anyone who crossed her.

"Sit on a sword hilt," I swore at her. "You're a poison to Sorpsi and a disgrace to Queen Iana."

A rigid calmness settled over the queen. Her face blanked, smoothing some of the wrinkles. "And you are a waste of talent, Sorin." Her eyes flicked to the mounds steadily growing around Sameer and me. "Encase."

The stalagmites pushed together and began to arch overhead, forming a golden-red dome speckled in torn roots and displaced insects. Sameer jabbed his knife into the woody forms and tried to slice, but they had already dried, and the blade caught. I ran at the mounds with my shoulder, but I merely bounced off. Sameer swore. I swore.

"Don't suppose you're secretly a witch?" I asked him as I again threw my shoulder at the wall.

Sameer looked up at the closing gap, and then at the spaces between the quickly shrinking conks. "No, I'm a weaver." He pulled a handful of loose roots from where they stuck out from the earth and, in five passes, braided a sort of bulging strut. He grabbed another set of roots and, in three quick twists of his hand, had a wide, round base to stick the strut into.

"And you wanted to be a woodcutter."

"Shut up, Sorin." He snorted, but his voice held humor. "I can shore the spaces, but I don't know for how long." He connected the strut to the base, then shoved it into one of the smaller gaps like a pillar. The stalagmite conk tried to push it in, but the woven roots held, sending soft bits of fruiting body and loose tree roots slopping to the ground. The air took on the musty smell of decay.

"You could help any time—unless you want this dome to be our coffin. I don't give a damn whether you are a woodcutter or not, but it'd be great right now if you could be an alchemist."

"I never meant for them to be weapons!" I yelled, though I wasn't angry at him, just at this looming, crushing, fungus cage. I pulled my belt off and unfastened the pouches, sorting them by weight. I had no yellow pigment left. The red had maybe a thimbleful. Maybe. The blue-green was full.

"Maja!" Mother's voice.

I looked up at Mother's voice to see parts of her through one of the windows Sameer had made. She looked...like some intangible thing inside her had snapped. Her eyes were wide and wild, her fists clenched in a rage she seldom showed.

"This isn't what we agreed, Maja!" she said. "For five years, we have had a deal. Five years I have studied magic for you, broken guild law for you. I have *killed* for you. Let them go! Keep your end of our bargain!"

"Damn it," Sameer muttered as the first of his columns was crushed. He had four more still in place, but there were no more openings in which to place new ones, and the arched "ceiling" was a lot closer than it had been moments ago.

"You broke guild law well enough on your own, with your choice of heirs," the queen said icily. Her hands went back to her pockets, and I could see them forming into fists beneath the cloth. "That is what began this in the first place. Do not forget. Besides, you're conveniently forgetting your own interventions in this, Amada. The tattoo Sorin has is illegal, both by my and guild standards. It doesn't count as a choice. The marks must be freely chosen."

A choice? I'd been meant to choose? I'd chosen *neither*.

"Sorin chose woodcutting!" Mother screamed. "You promised if woodcutting was chosen, you would leave Sorin be! That it wouldn't matter who Sorin was. It took five years, but my heir has made a choice." Mother looked gray, as if she were about to vomit.

A sick feeling crept into my stomach as well. I counted back the years. I counted back the years from my present age—seventeen. Five years ago, I'd found alchemy, and Master Rahad's workshop, but that couldn't have been the only catalyst. What else? Five years ago...

Five years ago, my body had begun a journey without my consent.

Five years ago, we'd halted our visits to the palace.

Five years ago, for the first time, we'd stopped pretending I was a girl, but I'd never stopped being Mother's heir. She should have fostered me out in that moment of declaration. I had no right to inheritance, not by guild law, and not by Queen Iana's law. Only daughters could inherit. Not sons, not...whatever I was. Mother had kept me, and no one had ever argued that decision. Not the Thujan villagers, not the woodcutting guild, not the queen.

The tattoo on my neck felt heavy, suddenly, like it might pull me down into the cracked earth. All the sheltering, all the hiding, the refusal to discuss alchemy, or to let me visit Magda, the cursed whispering on the glacier from Walerian, and this tainted tattoo—it was all because...because Mother had known what the queen was, what the queen wanted. She'd seen this future, and she'd wanted to keep me from it.

I fell to my knees. I stared at the sorrel and dirt beneath me.

I felt hollow. I was a chrysalis with a pupa that would never emerge. I was a sapling grown on a cliff that fell to the ravine before it could make a deep enough root system.

I wanted to cry, or maybe scream, but there was nothing left inside me.

"Sorin!" Sameer yelled. Another two columns collapsed. The ceiling had closed above us and was now creeping down. Severed roots swished above my head. One opening remained, and the root braid groaned under the pressure.

Sameer tossed his knife into the ground and sat. "I'm out of tricks. Don't suppose you have one of those amulets? Old or new, who cares? Maybe it has some magic in it? Maybe you can get a reaction? Sorin? Sorin!"

I tore my eyes from the sorrel to my brother, who clearly still wanted to live. He deserved to live, if only long enough to tell our mother what he thought of her.

I shook my head. "A reaction between the two could kill us just as easily as free us."

Sameer threw up his hands in exasperation. "We're going to die anyway! Be an alchemist! Be a witch, for all I care. Just use those damn things strapped to your belt."

Crashing noises came from outside our dome, and the temperature flared. The ceiling dropped again, which brought tree roots smacking against my head. I brushed them away and hunched closer to the ground, my mind spinning. I didn't know how to feel. Could you hate someone and love them at the same time? Did you have to make a choice about that too? Wasn't there a third option?

"Sorin!" Sameer yelled.

I tried to focus. Magic and alchemy were out there, fighting each other like they weren't just separated by semantics. I had both in here, with me, between my pigments and the amulet in my pocket. But it was old. Devoid of magic. All that was left was its structure, and the ethanol solvent it was still leaking from its pores. What else then? Reactions? Extractions? Alchemy without the magic part was...what?

It was solvents. It was chemicals.

That was what I'd been doing all along, wasn't it?

Chemistry.

It wasn't *between* magic and alchemy at all. It had parts of both, but it was a different field entirely. If magic and alchemy were either ends of a line, chemistry made that line a triangle.

It wasn't choosing between two ends; it was...it was an entirely different option. One that had always been there but...but that no one really cared about. It didn't break any rules; it was just used so little people forgot about it. It was a cult. A rumor. A bastardization. And it *fit*.

I pulled apart the pouch of elf's cup pigment, scooped the damp amulet from my pocket, and dumped it inside. *Chemistry*. Elf's cup was a poison, but it had to be carried in something. Dissolved in something that could penetrate human skin. I might not be able to break out of our prison, but I might be able to stop the person responsible.

The roof dropped again, bending the conks in half and forcing us onto our knees. I cinched the pouch closed and rubbed the leather between my hands, hoping, praying, that I might speed the movement of the ethanol into the pigment, and the pigment granules into the pores of the amulet.

The air inside our fungus grave had become heavy with respiration. My rubbing turned frantic. How long was long enough? With bone oil, it was near instantaneous, but ethanol was a poor solvent. A few seconds? A few minutes?

"Our agreement!" I heard Mother scream at the queen.

"As dead as your children."

"Sorin!"

At Sameer's plea, I took the amulet from the pouch. It sat heavier in my hand than when I'd put it in, and I could feel no blue-green residue in the lined leather. Thank the gods.

Chemistry.

I pulled off my pouch of red pigment and dropped the amulet inside just as twirling strands of fungal hyphae began to tickle my nose. I waited until the first popping of the red crystals and the telltale sound of ripping leather. I pushed myself against the wall of conk, stuck my hand through the opening, and threw the entire thing as hard as I could at the side of the queen's royal head.

Twenty-Seven: Chemistry

The queen didn't die. Not at first. Elf's cup was a subtle poison and had to work its way from the blood to the heart and brain before it could shut systems down. It also worked a lot faster if it was ingested than absorbed into the skin, but I hadn't had a lot of choices. She was *going* to die, and that was a comfort, even as the hyphae from the queen's magical fungus licked my cheeks and the smell of breakfast on Sameer's breath filled what little air we had left.

All we could do from our shrinking enclosure was watch. Just as the pouch hit the queen, jagged red crystals pierced the leather, then shredded it. The crystals cracked the amulet wide open, and the contents, a thin, blue-green liquid, slopped onto the queen's neck. Some ran down under her clothes, but most soaked into her hair and cape, and from there, I assumed, to her skin. Ethanol was great at penetrating skin. One drop was enough to kill a mouse, so an amulet the size of my hand was certainly enough for a human.

There was stillness then, for a few moments, as the queen clawed at her clothes and skin, desperate to be rid of the unknown damp compound. It was when the first bit of red crystal pierced the queen's hand that she jolted up and ran toward us, her eyes wide and angry, while bits of red crystal built and spun off of her.

"Down! Mother, the crystals!" I grabbed a fistful of Sameer's hair and pushed his face to the dirt. I didn't know if Mother could hear me through the thick walls of red and gold fungus, or if she had paid enough attention to my pigments to know what the red could do, but if she had, if she had truly done of all this to protect me, then she might be able to help.

I squeezed my eyes shut, remembering the explosion of Mother's house, and the bite of nails, knowing there wasn't enough of the red pigment to explode the mound, but there was plenty to rip into my flesh if any of those crystals got close enough.

I could hear the sounds of clothes tearing. The queen shrieking. Mother's grunt of surprise. The mound shook; the ground shook. Sameer reached out for my hand, and I held his, counting breaths, and heartbeats, and hoping, praying, that my pigments would be enough.

CRACKKK!

A fast exhale of breath, as if someone had been punched in the gut.

Another flare of heat magic.

A cry of pain from Mother.

How long had it been? A minute? Less? I opened my eyes and looked up, but our small opening had closed. Darkness surrounded us, the sounds of the outside muffled. I saw glints of light in a few places, perhaps where the earth had failed to come together properly, the legs of insects scratched my face, and hyphae tickled my arms.

"You'll be a great woodcutter someday, Sameer." It seemed right to say because I had no doubt he *would* make an excellent woodcutter. And because I hadn't really apologized, had I, for being an ass to him on the glacier.

Sameer snorted but squeezed my hand. "You're not a great alchemist, Sorin."

I wasn't certain if the comment was meant to sting or not, but I laughed anyway. "You're right. I'm a terrible alchemist. But I think I might be a decent bastard chemist."

"You won't be able to file the paperwork to change your title before we are crushed to death here."

There was a lightness in Sameer's words, and though the conks were now pressing on my chest, I felt light too. Maybe the borders of the three countries would fall apart, through loss of the guilds, industrial revolutions, or queen treachery. But I had a brother, and for the first time, maybe a mother, though there was some room for debate on that. I had chemistry, and it was something different, but not new. I hadn't had to make it up, just find it. Thinking about that seemed to loosen and cool my skin. The scars were still there on my arms, never forgotten, but they didn't itch, even with the hyphae curling around them.

The ripping sound began again. Except this time, it was louder and accompanied by screams and thunderous claps of dirt. Particulate rained down into my eyes and mouth, and I curled tighter against Sameer, coughing and gasping. Chunks of fungus slammed into my spine, my legs, my head. A bright light shone behind my eyelids, and the world spun. The screaming became louder. I brought my hands up to cover my ears and...and I could lift my arms all the way up.

I coughed again, then sucked in clean air. The screaming stopped as suddenly as it had begun. I heard Sameer sit up and try to clear his own airways.

"You okay?" I asked him.

"I'll live," he responded sourly.

I rubbed at my eyes, then opened them. All around Sameer and me were clumps of burnt conk, pierced by delicate, hook-ended crystals. The conks had turned brittle and were shiny in places. The air smelled of brick, and although the area was bathed in an apple-colored glow from the crystals, the ground was scorched black from magic. Another reaction, perhaps, between my crystals and Mother's magic.

"Do you see them?" I asked Sameer. Everywhere was just earth and smoke and fungus. He and I could have been the only living things in the entire forest.

Sameer stood, pivoted, then pointed. "Over there. Come on."

We walked only a few steps, and then I helped him lift an oblong slab of baked red belt fungus off of two intertwined bodies. The queen was curled in on herself like a bug. Mother wrapped around her, clasping the desiccated woman to her chest.

We tossed the conk and dropped to our knees. Both of them were still alive, but when I tried to unwind Mother's arms from the queen's shoulders, I saw they were speared together by tiny fragments of red crystal.

"Kept her against the mound," Mother wheezed. "Your pigments amplify the heat residue. Hope I didn't bake you." She didn't open her eyes, and I wanted, so badly, to look at her just then. To have her see me, and to really, truly, see her for the first time. I wanted to demand explanations, to vent the rage that still burned in my throat, but I held back. Again. "Thought...to get the crystals into the mound. Save you. So sorry, Sorin, the tattoo. Sameer. I'm sorry."

"You've destroyed Sorpsi." The queen's voice was barely more than a whisper as she struggled to draw in breath. Just like the mice in my experiments, she was calm and did not thrash. But in the last moments of life, her eyes flew wide open and she managed to glare at me. Her eyes stayed that way, too, as she choked, and hissed, and finally, exhaled.

I started to shake. "We have to get them separated. We need a solvent. Something to dissolve the crystals."

Sameer tried to pry at the conjoined areas of skin but pulled back sharply when Mother cried out in pain. "Do you have any more of the ethanol?"

"There are hundreds of old amulets at the camp. It will take hours, though, with the ethanol. We need bone oil. There are vats of it in the cauldrons."

"Treaty talks?" Mother's words were garbled now, and I had to lean in to hear her.

"I'm sure Magda has it under control, Mother." I stood. "Sameer, you stay here with her. I'll go back for the solvent. Hopefully—"

"Sorin."

"Damn it, Sameer, it's the only option we have. Just hold on. I'll be five minutes." Mother would be fine, I was certain. Mother was always fine.

"Sorin, Amada is dead."

Everything stopped, even the nuthatches. I looked down as tears collected in my eyes, at the queen's blank glare, and Mother's half-closed lids. They were both dead. As dead as my laboratory mice, as dead as the false guards. The queen was dead, leaving hundreds of guilder skills trapped within amulets. And Mother...with a reconciliation, perhaps a reckoning, that we'd never get to have.

Still, I didn't move. I searched for the next steps, for there had to be something proper to do when a queen died, or your mother died, but I could think of nothing. The ground around me was burned, my pouches empty. What was I supposed to do? Move? Maybe. It was cold without Mother's magic, and a thin layer of frost was forming over the bodies. Breathe? Yes, breathing helped clear my mental fog.

"Should we bury them?" I asked. I didn't know what else to say.

At the very end of my words, fungi began to poke through the ground in a halo around Mother and the queen. Sameer jumped back and yelled in surprise, and I, too, leapt away. Of the palest white, the mushrooms also glowed green despite the daylight, reflecting off the crystal fragments, the colors mingling together.

Now, with the crystals and the fungi and the frost, both women looked like they'd been purposefully placed in a glass coffin. In enchanted woods, they were a pair of fairy queens, and that seemed right, somehow, after all this. The ground might thaw and decay might take its course, but it might not, with the magic. Stories might grow, of magic and fairies and elves and foxfire, and of a queen and a woodcutter, and some powerful, unearthly force that had overwhelmed them.

"I think we should leave them."

"We can't just leave her here, Sameer. She's our *mother*."

"She was a terrible mother."

I wiped my hands over my face. She hadn't been terrible, not really. Or maybe really. Maybe it didn't matter anymore. I was still allowed to mourn, wasn't I? To dream of taking her back to Thuja and burying her next to her parents in the soft soil behind our longhouse? Maybe to erect a spirit house for her, as they did in Puget, so that her soul could come and watch over me as it always had when she was alive.

Thick, wet snow began to fall. The flakes coalesced quickly, and I watched, without blinking, as they coated Mother and the queen in downy white.

"We have no way to get them back, not stuck together as they are. You have to let her go, Sorin. Your life is yours now. No one else's."

I kept my eyes on the snow-covered bodies, the red glint of the crystals slowly drowning in silver. "My life was always my own. I just chose to put other people first."

Sameer snorted, but I didn't look back at him. Instead, I turned to the heap of amulets to my left, dropped by the queen and Mother, the ground haloed brown around them. I gathered all three and tucked them into my pockets.

"You really want to take those?" Sameer asked, surprised.

"You expect Magda to believe us without evidence? We could try to collect an alchemist or two, take them back to Celtis. But without the authority of the queen, I doubt we'd get out alive. We need Magda, and in order to get her, we need a few amulets."

And I want to leave. I have to leave. It hit me all at once. The absurdity that had kept me distant melted into reality. Mother was dead. The Queen of Sorpsi was dead. The guilds were dead, and if Sameer and I didn't get to Magda soon, Sorpsi would be dead as well. I rubbed at my arms, hard enough to peel the fresh scabs.

"We have to go. Now." My voice was dead of emotion, my sleeves damp and slowly turning crimson. Magda. Magda was who we needed. Magda would be the one who could straighten everything out. The royal daughter, Magda. *Queen* Magda.

"We're going to have to break into those treaty talks. It'd be easier if we rounded up the masters first. Even shaken, they'll make a strong statement."

Sameer seemed immune to any emotion. That should have made me angry, but it didn't. The wind that consistently blew strands of hair across my face should have chilled me, but it didn't. I turned away from Mother and began to walk south. If I lingered, I would come apart, and I couldn't do that yet. Not with so many guilders to rescue. Not with Magda waiting for us, and Sorpsi's autonomy hanging in the balance. I'd wanted to be free of Mother for so long, and now all I could think of was how little time we had truly spent together, and that she was dead, and that I was leaving her here, chained to her keeper until the spring thaw when fungi would consume their bodies.

"Let's get the masters first, as many as we can find," I said into the wind. "Then, we find Magda and see if there is any part of Sorpsi left to save."

Twenty-Eight: Mercury, Salt, and Sulfur

"You have to let us in! We have the guilders!" Again, I tried to rush past the guards who blocked the wooden door to the inner assembly hall of the Puget Palace. Again, they pushed me back and returned to their stiff poses.

"Let us in!" Sameer came up beside me and yelled. Behind him were some twenty masters and grandmasters, the most we had been able to find without wasting too much time in every little inn. Simple men and women in cottons, leathers, and silks, but they stood awkwardly, shifting on unsteady feet. Their hands rubbed over every surface, trying to make sense of materials they had once worked. They could talk, and understand, and had memories of their lives, but even with Sameer and I urging them on, urging them to action, they wandered. Watched. Mourned the part of themselves encased in transmuted wood, swinging from needled branches in the Puget forests.

"You may see Her Highness, the Royal Daughter of Sorpsi, at the conclusion of today's talks," the guard on the right said. "Until then, she cannot be disturbed."

I tugged at my hair in frustration. "But I have news about the Queen of Sorpsi! I have everyone's missing masters right here! Please!" When the guards neither moved nor spoke, I tried the only option left. If it ended with the entire palace coming out to gawk at me, so be it.

"Magda!" I screamed her name loud enough that I fell into a fit of coughing at the end. "*Magda!*"

No curious heads popped around corners, but it was enough to wake the guards from their rigid stances. They moved to either side of me, each taking an arm, and began to pull me into the east hall. Sameer ran forward and punched one of the guards, who fell back. I jerked against the hold of the other, dragging my feet as loudly as possible against the polished marble floor. "Magda!" I continued to yell. "It's Sorin! *Sorin!*"

The door burst open. The sound of it hitting the wall and rebounding back was loud enough that we all froze, Sameer in mid-punch and the guard on the floor ready to draw his sword.

"Sorin?" Magda's eyes were wide with confusion but heavy, too, with fatigue. Beyond her, thick furs of white and brown covered the floor, and stained glass and wood made up the walls. She held a hand up, and the guards fell back.

"I have news," I said, breathless. I pointed to the guilders.

"You...guilders? Masters?"

"And the queen," Sameer added smugly. "Though that will take some explaining."

"Royal Daughter?" A man's voice called to Magda from inside the room. "Is everything all right?"

The confusion on Magda's face gave way to a tight formality. "Come inside, both of you."

Sameer held up his hands and strode over to the guilders. "No way. I don't do politics. Besides, I don't want these ones wandering off, looking for lost looms and whatnot."

"You're sure?" I asked.

"Go talk to your girlfriend."

I rolled my eyes but let Magda lead me into a deep room of purples and reds, to a circle of chairs in upholstered leather, the backs of brown oak. Woven tapestries of sedges and bamboo covered the walls—a testament to the rangelands Puget was known for. A formal dining area was tucked into a far corner, the chairs there upholstered with hide and the table runner a stunning display of dark, handwoven silk.

We stopped in the center of the circle of chairs. In front of us sat two men, both with yellow hair and pale skin. They wore thin silk shirts and knee-high leather boots, and the sides of their pants were ruffled. The one on the left looked much older, with gray at his temples and a number of silver rings on his fingers. The chair to the right of the younger one was empty, and next to that sat a man, a woman, and a person of indeterminate gender. All had hair the same color as the brown oak chairs, but their facial features and skin tones ranged wildly.

Magda inclined her head to the people sitting, and I curtsied. "My apologies for the interruption. May I introduce King Rodolf of Eastgate and his son, Prince Teodor." We pivoted, and Magda again nodded. "The Triarchy of Puget—Lord Kamon, Lady Yiru, and Potentate Jun."

Magda stepped to my side and put her hand on my shoulder. It felt heavier than it should, and I shivered. "This is Sorin of Thuja, an..." She looked at me, then at my tattoo. Her eyes went wide, and she stuttered for words. "A..."

"A guilder," I finished for her. "My mother was a master woodcutter."

"Was?" King Rodolf raised a delicate blue teacup to his lips and sipped. Magda's hand tightened on my shoulder.

"Was," I responded, simply.

"And how might we address you?" Potentate Jun looked up and smiled. "Simply Sorin of Thuja?"

"I...yes. I don't know any other way."

Jun nodded. "As you like."

"Sorin? Why are you here? How did you find the masters?" Magda pushed me into the empty chair, then dragged another from a set with velvet covers over to the circle, and sat. Her words were as rigid as her back.

I swallowed a lump in my throat. With all that was going on, was she angry with me for running out? This was more important than an argument over body semantics, and yet... I took a moment to really look at her. Magda wore a long, formal gown made of chintz. I recognized the exotic cotton only from having been forced into it once when I had accompanied her to a formal tea at the palace. Her hair hung loose and well brushed, the tight curls falling about her shoulders and down her back. It was hard to clamp down on my surprise when I caught the glimmer of gold on the top of her head. Someone had given her a replacement crown to wear, and though her curls threatened to consume it, Magda looked, in that moment, like a near-exact replica of her mother. She looked like a queen.

"I..." The words died in my mouth. All that distance we'd crossed together was gone, replaced by an ocean of floral-print cotton and velvet-covered furniture. "Your Highness," I said instead, and bowed my head. "I apologize for the interruption."

Magda let her eyes close for a moment. "It's all right, Sorin. The guilders. Where were they? How did you find them?"

"They're...your mother...you're the queen." I snapped my mouth shut as soon as I realized what I'd said. Heat flushed my face. I hadn't meant the words to come out, and certainly not in a near-whisper. But there they were, hanging in the incensed air, and I couldn't take them back.

Magda blinked, then stared at me, her mouth slightly open and her eyes searching mine as if she could bore into my skull and take the answer from me. I wanted to speak, but my lips would not pull apart. There was too much to explain, and I couldn't do it to my queen. I needed Magda, not the defeated-looking woman in front of me stuffed into a childish floral-print dress that she clearly detested.

The other rulers shifted in their chairs, silent but impatient.

"The queen, my mother, is dead?" Magda asked finally.

I nodded.

"Your mother? You found her?"

"Dead as well."

"The masters?" Her voice this time was a whisper.

"I don't know if they can...be repaired." I shifted to my right hip and removed the amulets from my pocket. One of the triarchy gasped as I pushed the tea service to the edge of a gilded table and set the transmuted wood down. "It will take some time to explain. I'd like to confirm first, that the guilders across all three countries are missing? The census came back empty?"

The king sat forward in his chair. He didn't speak. He didn't need to.

"You told them about the factories?" I asked Magda.

"I did."

I pointed vaguely toward the hall. "Many are here, I think. In Celtis. And their skills—" I held up an amulet. "—are in these, and these are scattered about the northern forests. And there is no way to get the skills back out. At least not right now." I cupped my hands over my nose and mouth, then slid them down.

"You're saying the three countries have no guilds, that our collective repository of skilled knowledge is locked away, and Sorpsi is to blame?" Lady Yiru asked. "We're reliant on free traders to meet our export needs until—when? We find an alchemist or witch who can undo this work?"

I looked to Magda for help as I was unsure how to respond, but her head was in her hands as she stared intently at the floor. In that moment I'd have given anything to have her hand back on my shoulder, tense or no. I didn't belong with kings and queens and potentates. I didn't belong in Thuja, either, but I was well out of my depth here.

"Well?" Prince Teodor demanded. "How do you suggest we remedy this situation that you have dumped on us? Forget the treaty and the squabbling about boundary lines. We have no *economy* without the guilds. Trade-level skills are everywhere. On every continent. Guildware was the reason traders came to our shores. And even if we decided to completely forgo skill work for factories, Father and I could put those up tomorrow, but we'd have no one to staff them." He jabbed a spindly finger toward me. "Fix this."

"I don't know how!" I dug my nails into the upholstery of my chair. "If the mechanics stumped both of the unbound guilds, I don't know what I can offer. We could break the amulets, but I don't know what would happen to the insides. They might evaporate and be lost forever. They might drip out and bind into the ground, giving a tree some strange ability to forge horseshoes. The contents need to be extracted properly, but I'm certain the alchemists tried every solvent known. We'd need something new."

"Can you make it?" Magda finally looked up at me. Moisture glistened in the corners of her eyes, and beneath them, the skin was puffy. "Like your bone oil? Please tell me you would be willing to try. I can teach blacksmithing, and Sameer, textiles. Perhaps you could teach woodcutting. But aside from us, we have only free traders to rely on to restart our collective economies. We don't even have the infrastructure for factories right now. Thousands of people are going to go hungry, or die, while we try to build. We need guilders, Sorin. Even just a handful would help."

I couldn't bring myself to mention the factories on the glacier, and importing from those. Magda already looked like she was suffocating, between the velvet and the chintz, and her mother's betrayal.

"I could try." I looked from the rulers of Eastgate to those of Puget and smiled tentatively. "I don't think it will be fast, however, or easy, and I'd need as many amulets as you can recover. I'll end up destroying some in experimentation, I'm sure, but there are hundreds of amulets suspended amongst the trees. I suggest sending knights immediately to recover them from the witches and alchemists."

"Take whatever resources you need to begin your work. We will see to the amulets." The King of Eastgate stood and stretched. His son yawned, and the rest of the rulers, save Magda, rose from their chairs as well. "I want to talk to the guilders. Teodor, see if you can find someone in our country who can do timber-frame or concrete construction. Import if you have to. We'll prepare for the worst, and hope for the best."

Lady Yiru helped Lord Kamon to stand, then led him by the elbow toward the door. "Our knights will leave immediately. We have questions for the guilders as well. I suggest we reconvene tomorrow morning and work together, as one country. We can't afford to be separate now. Our economies are too fractured."

"Agreed," said the king. "Royal Daughter—Queen Magda, we will have a great deal to discuss with you tomorrow, especially about your mother."

Magda stood and bowed. "I understand, and I agree. Tomorrow morning."

The king pulled open the door, and the others followed, single file, into the hall. I could hear the guilders now, their chatting and Sameer's tired voice, begging them to sit and be patient. A guard reached in, grabbed the handle of the door, and shut it.

"The guilders' stories are all a little different as to how the queen found them. It will make for an interesting evening. Some left on their own and were intercepted. Some, the witches flat-out abducted. There are probably a hundred more still scattered across the inns. It will take time to round them all up. Also, I'm surprised the rest of the royalty took that so well. Do you think I should go out there in case they have more questions?"

Magda fell back into her chair and stared at a spot just above my head.

"Mag—Royal Daughter? My queen? Are you listening? Are you all right?"

"How did she die?"

"What?"

"How did it happen?"

Magda's voice was as lost as her eyes. I wanted to take her by the arm and haul her from the stuffy room, back to the inn where we could talk, away from china teacups and dramatic furniture. But this was the world she had grown up in. She was probably comfortable here, and she deserved comfort because we were going to have to go back to the woods to collect the amulets, and she was going to have to see her mother, speared to mine, encased and frozen on the forest floor.

I got up and knelt to face her. "She...she was killed." The next words felt like fire on my tongue. "I killed her. She's an alchemist. Mother is, was, a witch. They did this, all of it. Their bodies are in the forest, half a day's walk from here. I can take you to her, now or in the morning.

But we should bring others. There are too many witches and alchemists about."

"Killed," Magda repeated, her words as thick as syrup. "I don't...she wasn't that...I..." She squared her shoulders, sniffed, and made a show of not wiping the wetness from her eyes. "Now isn't the time." Magda gripped my hand unexpectedly, and while it was no lover's touch, neither was it painful.

"Magda, I'm so sorry. You might talk to the guilders, though, with the others. They're still alive, and they—"

"Damn the gods, Sorin, I don't care about the guilds!" The mask that painted Magda's face into a queen fell away, but it was still hard to find my childhood friend under the lines of worry.

"Your Highness?"

"Sorin." Magda said my name again, gentler this time. Her grip changed, and her thumb traced the top of my hand, almost tickling. She helped me stand, then leaned in as if to kiss my cheek in greeting, but her lips only brushed my skin before leaving haunting words in their wake.

"You left. Again."

My lips trembled, and I tried to pass it off as a cough. "I was angry. I hadn't meant to leave town. Mother found me, and everything spiraled from there."

Though she looked away, toward the door, tears welled in her eyes. "Are you still angry?" Magda tried to pull her hand away, but I held it and moved into her. She shuddered as she wrapped her arms around my waist and rested her forehead against my own. Her breath smelled of fruit tea. Her curls fell into my eyes, but I didn't brush them away.

"No. Yes. I know who I am, Magda. It's frustrating when other people can't see that, especially...especially people I care about."

Magda turned her head slightly and blinked back tears threatening to fall. When she looked back up, she paused, then tilted her head as she caught sight of my tattoo. "You're a woodcutter?"

I exhaled and rubbed at the sore skin. "No. I know it's misleading, perhaps as much so as my breasts. I'm just *me*. I like to wear leather pants with vests, and sometimes dresses with puffed sleeves. Short hair stays from my eyes, but long hair is fun to braid and pin. Our bodies match, yours and mine, but I am not a woman, and neither do I feel my body is incorrect. And woodcutter? Alchemist?" I slapped my empty pouches. "They're more words that don't fit me well."

I slid my hands to Magda's waist, then to her shoulders. I brought one hand up to brush a tangle of curls from her eyes before hovering near her cheek and tracking the lines of her tears with my fingers. "I don't have a home, and I don't have a guild, but I would very much like to have you, Magda, as a friend again." I brought my lips to her jaw, just below her left ear, and kissed her. "Friendship first. We have to find each other. Understand how we've changed. Then, maybe, we can try for more."

Magda exhaled, and the smell of fruit tea surrounded me. We stood there for years, or minutes, not moving our hands or our bodies, our cheeks brushing each other. Magda's breathing eventually evened out, and her grip on my hips turned lighter.

"Does that mean you'll stay near as we try to repair the damage our mothers have done?" Magda asked. "As my...friend?" she asked hesitantly.

A grin broke across my face. "Friend, yes, as well as...a chemist, I think. Your chemist if you prefer."

"I don't care what you call yourself, Sorin. I don't want to lose you again."

I took Magda's hand. Her fingers were warm, almost sweaty, and she wrapped them around mine as if she were pulling me from a sinking boat.

"Show me where the royal laboratory is?" I asked as gently as I could manage, for Magda still looked as though she could disintegrate to wood shavings with the slightest nudge. "Then perhaps we could share a bed again for the night. For sleeping." I squeezed her hand and smiled until the corners of her mouth began to turn up as well.

"You're sure?" Magda asked. She bit her lower lip, and mirth returned to her eyes. "I've been told I steal blankets."

"Are you afraid to sleep with me, my queen?"

Magda laughed, finally, and drew me into a hug. I buried my face in her shoulder and hair, and melted into her hands, and hips, and the faint smell of metal.

"No, no I'm not," Magda managed when she finally pulled back. "And I'm looking forward to learning about Sorin the Chemist, and how we can rebuild the three countries, together."

Acknowledgements

As with any book, thanks are due on multiple fronts. To the nonbinary sensitivity readers who helped with early versions, thank you so much for helping me expand Sorin's experience beyond just my own. To my critique group, thank you for sticking it out through countless rewrites and helping make Sorin's journey more generally accessible.

Thanks are also due to my agent, Sam, who believed in this book when no one else would, and to my editor, Elizabetta, who finally gave it a home. And to my Patreon supporters, *thank you* for your support, without which I wouldn't have nearly as much time to dedicate to writing.

About J.S. Fields

J.S. Fields is a scientist who has perhaps spent too much time around organic solvents. They enjoy roller derby, woodturning, making chain mail by hand, and cultivating fungi in the backs of minivans.

Email
chlorociboria@gmail.com

Twitter
@Galactoglucoman

Website
www.jsfieldsbooks.com

Patreon
www.patreon.com/jsfields

Other NineStar books by this author

Ardulum: First Don
Ardulum: Second Don
Ardulum: Third Don
Tales from Ardulum

Coming Soon from J.S. Fields

Queen

Mornings on Queen always looked like blood. Standing at the edge of the habitable zone of the tidally locked planetoid, Ember scanned the crimson-and-rust horizon all the way to the perpetual sunrise. Her wife's body was out here, somewhere, buried in the coarse red sand. Desiccated, mummified, likely stripped naked by the roaming packs of sand pirates Ember was out here to track.

Well... Track. Kill. The line was blurry when it involved a spouse, Ember mused, and it wasn't like the Presidium—the administrative body of Queen—really cared one way or the other. Ember had cared, once, but she was on day seventeen of perimeter duty, and her whole plan to deal with Taraniel's death by shooting grave robbers was starting to look a little thin.

A rabbit shot across her field of vision, registering in a halo of blue inside the face shield of her envirosuit. TOPA—the suit's AI—scrolled data across the screen, but Ember ignored it. Without thinking, she yanked out one of the wide, flat stones she carried in her exterior right thigh pocket (they were supposed to keep her calm, according to Nadia) and threw it at the flash of white, fluffy tail with precision honed from years of dealing with Queen's nuisance rabbit population.

The rabbit's hind legs skittered out from beneath it as it slipped on the sand. Ember wrapped her fingers around another stone, preparing to hit the head this time, when the damn thing started digging with its front feet, sand funneling around it, and Ember lost her clean shot.

She stepped forward, grinding her teeth with an adrenaline surge that would see no release if the little shit got away. She wiped sand from the front of her face shield with a gloved hand, smearing red across her vision.

The area where the rabbit had dug settled flat with a slight pock. Little fans on the outside of Ember's face shield blew the particulate from her vision.

The rabbit was gone and her stone along with it.

Ember cursed, the words bouncing around the inside of her rabbit-hide envirosuit, wasted on recycled air and a generic TOPA. Queen didn't have stones like that—perfect skipping stones for lakes that didn't exist on the barren planetoid—and those she carried in her pocket were some of her last reminders of Earth. And the rabbit... Ember knelt at the soft indent in the sand. Of course. It'd gone down into one of Queen's giant beetle galleries. Of course it had.

TOPA pinged as she reached a gloved hand into the depression. Ember debated the possibility of Queen's native beetles—approximately the height of a small school bus and twice the length—grabbing her wrist to pull her down in some pulp-era sci-fi fashion, and then dismissed the idea. If beetles hadn't accosted her yet at this site, it meant the gallery had been abandoned and being used by the feral European domestic rabbit population. They'd been brought over as food stock on the colony ships. Some had escaped. Big surprise.

Please read your notes, scrolled across the interior of Ember's face shield, in lettering so large it blocked most of the landscape from view.

"The rabbit got away. I was stupid for throwing a rock that can't be replaced. I wasted oxygen on the exertion. That about cover it?"

TOPA didn't respond directly, but it did fire up a series of reports. Landmass stability: within ten meters radius: moderate. Sand for at least three meters below the surface with scattered hollow tunnels reinforced with clay from the temperate zone. Sand transitioning to silt loam noted in geographic surveys, with increasing occurrence toward the colony dome. Silica content of the air: unbreathable. UV index: 10.5.

Ember snorted. That did explain the suit smell.

She balled her hands as tightly as she could in the double-layered leather of her gloves wishing, not for the first time that day, that Gore-Tex was still a thing. Leather didn't breathe, though both the buffer and electrical linings of the suit were supposed to. *Nothing* from Earth breathed outside the habitable zone, and as much as her suit filters tried, they couldn't cleanse the smell of human, slowly marinating in its own sweat.

A shitty day, even by Queen standards.

Awaiting input. Continue scan?

"Yeah. Sure. Why not?"

Ember stood, swallowing the dry air the suit pushed at her. The AI had a newly installed personality patch, but Ember would need to get a lot more bored before she turned it on. Instead, she pivoted on her right foot, keeping her eyes level with as much of the horizon as she could see, and let the suit feed data into the AI. Dunes and small valleys surrounded her, and TOPA disassembled each.

Silica = 100%

Silica = 97%, Chitin = 3%

Silica = 78%, Cellulose = 10%, Lignin = 10%, Chitin = 2%

Suggest moving 1.7 chains northeast for better visibility.

"Picturesque view?" Ember asked TOPA. *Maybe a body?* No point in asking that out loud. TOPA wouldn't have any clue what she was talking about, not the generic model anyway. At the very least, she should have keyed a new name into the system after she was assigned the suit and sentry duties. All the names she could come up with, however, were vindictive, so she'd left the default name in place. If she was going to be an ass to people who were only trying to help her, she'd get far more satisfaction doing it to their faces.

"Hey, Ember!"

The red dunes faded into a semitransparent image of her sister, Nadia, displayed on the interior of the face shield. Ember clicked her right canines together to increase volume. The fierce winds outside the colony dome hindered hearing much of anything without enhancement, even when the sound came from inside the suit. That wind was the same reason the damn rabbits tended to stay in the beetle galleries. Wind screwed with *everything* out here.

Nadia's transmission showed her just outside the dome, her image picked up by one of her suit's sleeve cameras. Sand licked her calves. Her goggles were up but her face shield down, and the redness of the landscape caked her envirosuit. The only part of her face that was visible were her lips—chapped but grinning as she tapped the front of her face shield, and instructions scrolled across the inside of Ember's own face shield. At the bottom of the message was a clear add-on from Nadia.

> *Your sentry duties now extend to Outpost Eight. Leave immediately.*
>
> *—Dr. Narkhirunkanok*
>
> *Hope you enjoy the sand. I'll make you dune-nuts when you get home. Extra sprinkles. Served on a tablecloth of rabbit hide since you love the little shits so much.*

Ember read the short message and scowled—a facial contortion Nadia would see in detail from the camera inside Ember's suit. Puns and throwaway comments about the excess rabbit population had no place on an official director request. Her willingness to deface government messages meant Nadia was worried, but she wasn't going to *say* she was worried because, historically, their ability to communicate had been right around "bug and speeding windshield."

"Leave for Outpost Eight? I'm supposed to be here for another three days." Ember cinched her mouth into a caricature of a frown. "TOPA will be heartbroken. It hasn't cataloged every dune within a one hundred-chain radius."

"There's been a change. Director Narkhirunkanok thinks the renegade mella are going to hit one of our storage units, the one where we keep sticking all the glassware we *probably* won't need again but can't get rid of. We need a sentry. You're the closest." The wind whipped her words away but the auditory sensors on Nadia's suit caught them anyway.

This time, Ember did frown. *Watching* for mella and daydreaming about shooting one so you could avenge your wife who didn't actually need avenging because she was about to die from cancer and had chosen to walk into a sand dune was one thing. *Chasing* mella, even if just to spy on them, so they could shoot *you* was something entirely different. She didn't have a death wish, just a need to see her wife's body and maybe punch someone.

Solitude had come as a bonus. You didn't get a lot of solitude living in a pimple of a dome on an all-woman planet, especially if your wife had just died. At the very least, out here she didn't have to unwind spools of hair from the shower drain and had half a moment to remember her wife the way *she* wanted to, not the way everyone else demanded.

"It's a two-day ride and a four-day walk," Ember said. "They'll get there before I do. They have beetles. I don't even have a flyer. The director turned down my requisition request."

"That's because, first, it's the presidium that approves those, not the director, and, second, because you suck at flying. You are *terrified* of flying. You are terrified of ships, even those that don't leave the atmosphere, which I get—yours almost didn't make it to Queen but still. This is a big group of mella. They're not moving fast, and they're still at Outpost Two. You'll make it. Move like a beetle. You kind of look like one in that suit when you have the antennae out."

Nadia leaned into her video feed until her eyes consumed the whole screen. Ember could see through her sister's goggles to the rich brown eyes that laughed behind them. Nadia always had a smile, even when you thought the dunes might as well sweep you to the cold side of the planet, where your bones would crack and your marrow freeze. Or to the hot side, where your skin would turn to leather in a day without the envirosuit, two days with it. Her sister smiled because she didn't remember Earth, not in color anyway. Not in sound, or smell, the way spring daisies gave way to buttercups in fields that wafted a perfume of silage. She'd never seen redwoods try to touch clouds, had never slipped on moss-covered stones in streams alive with nutria and frogs and ducks and migrating geese.

She'd been ten years Ember's junior at the Collapse, but they'd been put on different ships. She'd been too young to go into stasis, at eighteen, but she'd made it here, eventually. They'd been in transit nineteen years, Earth time. Their time here on Queen, only five years, felt like an eternity.

Now, the signs of aging showed in the silver of her hair and crinkles around her eyes, and in the way she kept rotating her wrist to ease some unspoken pressure. They had the same complexion though, a pale tan that flushed too easily. Nadia still smiled and joked as though Queen wasn't a desolate, isolated colony planet. As though Earth's memory didn't oppress them hundreds of light years away. She joked because she didn't want to leave. Queen was her home, even if they had no other family here and precious few friends.

For Ember, it was a way station. A bad aftertaste. A future gone horribly wrong.

"Botanists are not good with sand."

"Well, you know what they say about sand, Sis." Nadia smirked. *"Dune't* forget your—"

Ember shook her head but couldn't help smiling. "You've used up all the puns. Please don't invent more."

Nadia's eyes relaxed. The crinkles smoothed. A somberness took over, and it looked wholly alien on this sister she'd never gotten to see grow up. "We're just trying to give you what you want."

"If I wanted to look for Taraniel, I wouldn't have waited two months to do so."

The name burned Ember's mouth, and she sucked in her lips as an explosion of pain shattered her insides. Only sisters could make you hurt like this. Only sisters could dig up your most painful memories and talk about them as you would the weather at Sunday brunch.

"Doesn't matter. You have to go." There was no laughter in Nadia's voice now, no light in her eyes. "Maybe after, you'll finally want to come home. You're no good to yourself like this. You're a *botanist*. Finish your task so you can get back here and into the lab where you belong. Enough with your funk. The mella are done. There are two troupes left, and then it's just the outliers in their outpost, wherever that is. We've got a satellite reading that looks promising. We think it's the same group that raided the hospital last month. Find this group and send the coordinates to Dr. Narkhirunkanok. She'll send them to the presidium, and they will send out the flyers. One of these times, one of the mella will have a GPS on them, and our satellites will function correctly, and we can finally track them back to their main base."

"The plan sounds about as well cooked as most of the presidium's brains."

"Oh, for fuck sake's, Ember. Just take the job. We'll get the coordinates to their home; the presidium will take it out."

Ember, squatted, crossed her arms, and kicked the side of a dune. A smile flitted across her face. Poking the presidium would only get one of her minor research grants revoked, but poking Nadia got her some much-needed human interaction. "Yes, but then *I'd* be out of a job."

"*Lab.*" Nadia pointed back toward the dome. "Baby trees and whatever else you have growing in your greenhouse that won't survive two days once you plant it outside the dome. Science pays way better than this, and you've got tenure coming in, what, a year? Get a raise. You need a hell of a lot more money than you've got if you want to leave Queen. Leave us. I know what you and Taraniel talked about at night. Your voices carried through the walls."

Nadia's voice turned sour. "Aside from that, think about your future, Ember. Not this shit. Come *home.* Taraniel may be gone, but visit Dr. Sinha, at least. Call Taraniel's mother on Europa. Talk to her about her daughter."

"Stop talking about her, Nadia. Please."

"Why? Someone has to."

Ember wouldn't let the tears fall. She'd never be able to wipe them away. Instead, she kicked her boot into the dried red blood of the barren planet and watched the spray dissolve into oblivion.

"I'm going to record that as your verbal consent." Nadia sounded so smug. "You leave immediately. No one really cares about soil samples from a barren dune. Soil science is boring. Still, should just be you and the grit the whole way. Enjoy."

Nadia's image clicked off. Ember's viewscreen reverted to the red landscape, where a wall of sand rose with the wind. The world turned russet for several moments, and Ember's respirator whirred into high gear, filtering the air it brought in. It smelled of crisp nothing. It smelled of heat. It smelled of loss.

Ember stood at the base of the dune and waited for the small storm to subside. Nadia's words stripped her mind of every other thought, and she gasped mouthfuls of hot, processed air.

Taraniel. It had been two months now, give or take a few days, and Ember still expected to see her around every dune. Hoped for a mistake. Hoped the doctors had been wrong.

Cancer.

Earth's legacy, the one enduring gift that had come with the immigrants. Taraniel had preferred to meet death on her own terms. She'd taken no respirator, only clothes and things entwined with her memories, and left Ember with no body. No closure. No peace.

The wind died to a low rush. Ember turned and started the slow, plodding walk toward Outpost Seven, where she could recharge her envirosuit before going out again. Sand slicked under her feet. TOPA told her giant beetles scuttled along the parallel dunes, just out of sight, knowing better than to attack while she still moved. A sand funnel swirled. Her face shield registered the distance in the logging unit of chains, but the landscape remained fundamentally unchanged aside from the occasional dotting of twisted trees—Ember's work as part of the terraforming project. These trees were the farthest ones out from the dome. After here, nothing grew in the sand, not even small plants, no matter how many genes Ember edited and how much irrigation Nadia installed. They were two scientists with futile research, although their PhDs had gotten them quick acceptance onto Earth's newest outpost. Well, PhDs had helped, and their anatomy had sealed the deal. Vulvas got you onto Queen. Nothing could get you off. A pun worthy of Nadia.

Ember looked out at the patchwork desert forest she'd grown from Petri plates. She saw red and silver maples, mostly, but a few white aspens had taken the genetic modifications well too. Because of the winds, they couldn't grow upright, so they branched out more like bushes, staying low to the ground with fanning crowns to make the most of the perpetual morning. Mostly, they caught sand and died when their leaves became too covered for photosynthesis. But, well, that was job security if nothing else.

TOPA chirped. Another tooth click brought up a readout.

Wind dropped to 14 knots.

Funnel increasing in diameter by 0.35 meters per five seconds. Shape unstable and likely due to animal interaction.

Probability of human origin = 95%

"Well, yes, that would be the obvious conclusion noting the data, wouldn't it?" Ember muttered to herself.

The adrenaline hit like a punch anyway, snapping her body to attention. She stopped walking and watched the funnel continue to bloat across the horizon like some wave on a long-dead ocean. The wind wasn't strong enough to kick up that much sand, but giant beetles definitely were.

"TOPA, can you get a heat signature?"

The face shield blanked momentarily before a heat diagram splayed across it. Human signatures weren't discernable in the sand, but the five-legged beetles native to Queen ran colder than their surroundings due to some quirk of planetary genetics Ember didn't understand, likely because she'd managed to completely avoid entomology in her undergrad.

Beetles – two.

Her face shield blinked the words, and Ember pivoted. The beetles usually swarmed in the wild; they were seldom solitary or in pairs. Her suit's artificial intelligence quickly confirmed her suspicion.

No ID sent. Not of the colony. Strong possibility of mella attack. Retreat or find cover.

Two riders on beetleback exploded from the sand.

Shit.

Ember ran.

Also from NineStar Press

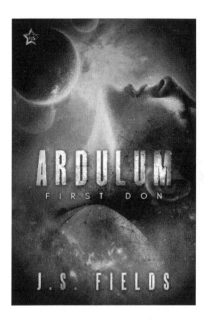

Ardulum: First Don by J.S. Fields

Ardulum. The planet that vanishes. The planet that sleeps.

Neek makes a living piloting the dilapidated tramp transport, *Mercy's Pledge*, and smuggling questionable goods across systems blessed with peace and prosperity. She gets by—but only just. In her dreams, she is still haunted by thoughts of Ardulum, the traveling planet that, long ago, visited her homeworld. The Ardulans brought with them agriculture, art, interstellar technology... and then disappeared without a trace, leaving Neek's people to worship them as gods.

Neek does not believe—and has paid dearly for it with an exile from her home for her heretical views.

Yet, when the crew stumbles into an armed confrontation between the sheriffs of the Charted Systems and an unknown species, fate deals Neek an unexpected hand in the form of a slave girl—a child whose ability to telepathically manipulate cellulose is reminiscent of that of an Ardulan god. Forced to reconcile her beliefs, Neek chooses to protect her, but is the child the key to her salvation, or will she lead them all to their deaths?

Give Me Grace by Bethany A. Perry

It's been six weeks since Halloween. Six weeks since Grace stumbled into the ER, almost dead and begging for help. Six weeks since she lost every single memory, including her own name.

Taken in by the mysterious Sisters of the Order of Saint Raphael the Healer, Grace's wounds are dressed and she is assured her memories will return—in time. But does Grace want her memories back? Maybe she's chosen to forget them, maybe there's a reason. The sisters hide things from her. They whisper things about her.

When a demon forces its way into the convent, it declares that Grace is a demon too. Grace demands answers. Answers that may reveal not only who she is, but that the sisters might not be who they say they are, either.

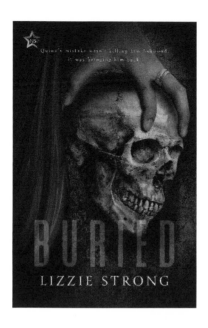

Buried by Lizzie Strong

Quinn's mistake wasn't killing Leo Ashwood; it was bringing him back. Now in a cat and mouse game with a monster she created, Quinn learns what her powers are truly capable of.

Brought together by a vision, Cecelia and Quinn are entangled in the chase for Leo Ashwood. Cecelia, a seer who is known for sticking her nose into other's business for their better good, is now sent into a world unknown to her with no defense against the monster, her own powers, and the budding feelings for Quinn. Maggie, however, was merely at the wrong place at the wrong time and left with no other choice but to join forces. An up and coming YouTube superstar struck down by sickness, her voice is both her magical survival and death wrapped in one.

These three young, untrained witches will have to lean on each other if they want to survive. Navigating the world of humans, the new reality of witches, and the horror of magic, they might just make it... if they can keep their secrets to themselves.

Connect with NineStar Press

www.ninestarpress.com

www.facebook.com/ninestarpress

www.facebook.com/groups/NineStarNiche

www.twitter.com/ninestarpress

www.instagram.com/ninestarpress

Made in the USA
Middletown, DE
24 September 2021